The Midwife:

The Pocket Watch Chronicles

By
Ceci Giltenan

Duncurra LLC

www.duncurra.com

Copyright 2015 by Ceci Giltenan

ISBN-13: 978-1-942623-28-1

Cover Art by Earthly Charms

Produced in the USA

Praise for Ceci Giltenan

"Few authors touch hearts so deeply."
- *Sue-Ellen Welfonder, USA Today Bestselling Author*

"Fine historical romance writing at its best."
- *Suzan Tisdale, Bestselling Author of Scottish Romance*

"Ceci Giltenan continues to leave me spellbound weaving her trail of exceptional books that are absolutely magnificent the ones that stay with you long after you have read it."
- *Barbara, Tartan Book Reviews*

"Ceci Giltenan tells beautiful stories with strong characters and an intriguing storylines"
- *Lily Baldwin, Bestselling Author of Scottish Romance*

Other Books by Ceci Giltenan

The Fated Heart Series

(Available as digital, paperback and audio books)

Highland Revenge, Book 1

Highland Echoes, Book 2

Highland Angels, Book 3

The Duncurra Series

(Available as digital, paperback and audio books)

Highland Solution, Book 1

Highland Courage, Book 2

Highland Intrigue Book 3

The Pocket Watch Chronicles

The Pocket Watch

The Midwife

Once Found

Dedication

To Dr. Edna Quinn PhD—midwife, professor,
and dear friend—thank you.
Your friendship and support throughout my life
is precious to me.

To my friend and colleague, Dr. Susan Wilson
DVM, PhD, who helps make sure my characters
know there is more to riding a horse than "climbing
up and holding on." Thank you for everything.

And, as ever to my dearest, Eamon, I adore you.

Glossary

Bairn	(BAIRn) A baby
Brathanead	(BRA huh need) the name of the fictional MacLennan stronghold
Canonical hours	The medieval day was ordered by these times, rather than clock times Vigil, Matins, Lauds, Prime, Terce, Sext, None, Vespers, Compline
Carraigile	(Kah rah GEEL) the name of the fictional MacKenzie stronghold
cods	testicles
compline	(COMP lin) Night prayer, after sunset, before bedtime
eejit	A slang term meaning idiot
gob	A slang term meaning mouth
kertch	Also called a *brèid* (BREEdt): a square of pure white linen folded in half and worn by married women to cover their hair. It is a symbol of the Holy Trinity, under whose guidance the married woman walks.
lauds	(LAWDS) Sunrise
léine	(LAY in ah) A full tunic-like garment. A woman's *léine* is a full-length dress with full sleeves that is worn belted at the waist. A man's *léine* would only come to his knees, similar to a long shirt. Both men and women generally wore another garment and/or a plaid over.
matins	Just before sunrise
none	(rhymes with bone) Literally the ninth hour, about 3 in the afternoon
prime	After the first hour of daylight, about 6 in the morning
sext	Literally the sixth hour, noon
skelping	A beating
sweetling	An endearment
terce	Literally the third hour of daylight, about nine in the morning
wheesht	Shh, hush
vespers	Evening prayer, sunset
vigil	The night office, the period from compline to matins (just before dawn)

"Every man has his own destiny: the only imperative is to follow it, to accept it, no matter where it leads him."
~ Henry Miller

Chapter 1

Angus MacKenzie's wife had been unusually quiet and tense for several weeks. He knew something was bothering her. He had asked several times, and she had made one excuse or another. He hated to push her, but seeing her upset always caused his heart to ache. When they retired to their chamber that evening, he tried one more time. "Wynda, my love, ye've seemed out of sorts for quite a while now, and it's only getting worse. Please tell me what's upsetting ye."

She trembled and burst into tears, his words appearing to shatter whatever fragile hold she'd had on her emotions. He gathered her in his arms, "Wheest, darling. Please don't cry. Tell me what has ye so distressed."

She regained enough control to say, "I-I-I'm pregnant," before breaking into sobs again.

His heart fell. He lifted her into his arms and carried her to a chair near the hearth where he sat, holding her as she cried. It wasn't that they didn't want a child—he wanted nothing more. But in the thirteen years since they had been wed, Wynda had been pregnant four times; each time the bairn came too early. Only the very first one—a tiny lad, born in the seventh month—ever drew breath. Their wee precious child, lived but a few hours.

Their hopes rose with every pregnancy, only to be dashed each time a babe was lost. He knew she loved and wanted this one every bit as much as she had the others, but the fear of facing that crushing loss again overwhelmed her.

When her tears subsided, he brushed the moisture from her cheeks. "I know ye're afraid. I am too. But, my darling, we must maintain hope. A battle is lost that is never entered."

"I don't think I can live through losing another one." Her voice was barely above a whisper.

He wasn't sure he could live through it either, but he said, "Ye certainly can. Ye're braver and stronger than any woman I've ever known. We'll pray fervently that this time will be different."

Angus vowed silently to do anything in his power to make certain that it was.

~ * ~

The next afternoon Angus sat in his solar considering his options. His thoughts were interrupted by a knock at the door.

"In," he called.

Cade, his son by his first wife and his only living child, entered. Cade was an accomplished warrior and a strong, well-respected leader. His ability to read and control any situation was remarkable. However he enjoyed women, drinking and sword-fighting—in that order—and occasionally he was a bit too arrogant for his own good. "Ye sent for me, Da?"

"Aye, come in and sit down."

"Come in and sit down? What have I done now?"

"For once, nothing. I need ye to do something for me."

"Ah…well then, set me my quest," Cade said as he sprawled in a chair across from his father.

"Wynda is expecting again."

Cade sobered, sitting up straighter. "Really? How is she?"

"Physically she's well, but she's also terrified, as ye might imagine."

"I have no doubt. I'm sorry, Da. I hope this one…well I hope everything turns out well."

Angus acknowledged his son's heartfelt concern with a nod. "I do too and I want to do everything I possibly can to see that it does. I've recently heard tell of a particularly skilled midwife. There is a chance she might know something that will help."

Cade leaned forward. "Really? That's wonderful. Where is she?"

"Well, that's the problem—she's a Macrae."

His son frowned. "I guess it could be worse. We aren't openly feuding with them."

"Nay but there has always been tension between our clans."

"So, ye want me to go to Laird Macrae and ask him to send ye this lauded midwife?"

"Nay, I want you to mind things here. I intend to ask myself."

Cade shook his head. "Da ye can't do that. Ye can't just ride up to the gates of Castle Macrae uninvited. They might kill ye before ye can tell them why ye've come."

"This is too important to send a messenger and it would be too easy for Laird Macrae to refuse someone of no consequence."

"And what if he looks *ye* in the eye and refuses ye?"

Angus stared at his son. He hadn't considered that. "I would be…disappointed."

"Da, ye'd be furious. Ye'd have but two choices: call him out—and likely be killed—or hang yer head and leave."

"What man, with compassion, would deny this to a man who has lost four bairns?"

"I don't think most men would, but the Macrae has a reputation for cruelty. He might tell ye nay, just to see ye beaten. Ye cannot do this. It's a fool's errand."

"I have to try. If I don't at least attempt it, and we lose one more child, I'll never forgive myself."

"Then let me go."

"Why would it be different for ye?"

"I'm not Laird MacKenzie."

"But if Macrae turns ye away, ye'd have the same choices I'd have. Son, ye're not known for yer forbearance. Ye're more likely to get yerself killed than I am. And it would be no easier for ye to walk away."

"Perhaps not, but it would hurt the clan less if I were the one forced to do it."

"And ye'd do it? Ye'd go into a situation knowing ye might be humiliated?"

Cade looked his father directly in the eye. "I would for this. I would for ye and Wynda."

Angus considered his son for a moment. "Ye'll be laird someday. Why do ye think it would damage the clan less for ye to be defeated than it would for me?"

Cade gave him a devilish grin. "Because I will not be defeated."

Angus shook his head. "Ye're an excellent swordsman, but short of taking a force large enough to lay siege, ye'll not be able to force the Macrae into this."

"I have no intention of forcing the Macrae. If he says nay, I'll simply take the midwife. It isn't as if she's a member of his family who will be guarded day and night."

It was a measure of how desperate Angus was that he agreed to this.

~ * ~

Castle Macrae
Saturday, February 11, 1279

Alban Macrae observed the four MacKenzie warriors entering his hall. He recognized Laird MacKenzie's son, Cade, and could not imagine what business brought him here. He didn't have to wait long to find out.

Cade inclined his head. "Good afternoon, Laird Macrae. Thank ye for receiving us. I am Cade MacKenzie, Laird MacKenzie's heir."

"Good afternoon Sir Cade. I must say, I was surprised to hear that a party of MacKenzies approached and I'm curious about what's brought ye here."

"Then I'll get straight to the point. My father sent me with a humble request."

Alban wanted to ask what the mighty Laird MacKenzie could possibly want from him, but it would be so much more entertaining to hold his derision until after Cade groveled a bit. "I see. And what is it?"

"He has been married for fourteen years and in that time, his wife, Lady Wynda, has been pregnant four times. Each bairn came much too soon."

"I'm very sorry for their losses." Alban was beginning to see where this was going.

"Thank ye, Laird. As it happens, Lady Wynda is with child again and my father would like to do everything possible to ensure that this babe lives."

"I can well imagine, but I fail to see what service I can be."

"We have heard clan Macrae has a very skilled midwife. My father hopes that perhaps ye would be willing to allow her to come to Carraigile and attend Lady Wynda."

Alban nodded with what he hoped was a concerned expression. "I see." *I will appear to contemplate this ridiculous request for a moment.* Just as he was about to laugh them out of his hall, Drummond, one of his most trusted and ruthless guardsmen, caught his eye. The man shook his head ever so slightly before glancing towards the tower stairs.

His message was clear: *don't do anything yet.*

Alban stroked his beard a moment more before saying, "Gentlemen, I would like to help. Truly I would. As the father of three healthy children, I understand Laird MacKenzie's loss. But, I need to consider this a bit. I must check with the woman herself and ensure that none of my clanswomen will suffer in her absence. Surely ye understand that?"

"Of course, Laird Macrae." Cade's expression was inscrutable.

"Well then, please excuse me while I attend this matter. Ye may wait here in my hall. I'll see ye're given some refreshment." He motioned to a serving maid who curtsied and hurried to do his bidding. He also signaled for Drummond to follow him.

Once they reached the privacy of his solar, he said, "I am assuming ye have a good reason for this. I was ready to serve that arrogant MacKenzie pup his pride instead of a tankard of ale."

"Aye, Laird, I have a very good reason. The MacKenzies are a powerful clan and ye're poised to make either a strong ally or a dangerous enemy."

"Surely ye don't mean for me to send Dolina to Laird MacKenzie?"

"Of course I don't. But consider this. MacKenzie doesn't know who the midwife is. Ye can send anyone and he'll be grateful."

"But I doubt Dolina can be of any help—much less some other midwife."

"I agree, Laird. In fact I'm fairly certain no one can help. Some women just can't carry a bairn and MacKenzie must know he's grasping at straws. All he seeks is peace of mind that he's done what he can. If ye send him someone who pretends to care for Lady MacKenzie—at least until the inevitable happens—the outcome won't matter. He'll be forever in yer debt for the kindness ye showed. Ye'll have gained a powerful ally, without having done anything."

"Drummond, that's brilliant. I could send any midwife."

"Laird, ye don't even have to send a real midwife. Dolina's niece, Elsie, has helped her over the last few years. She'll know enough to be able to fake it for a few months."

"Elsie is one and twenty and has never had children. No one will believe she's a skilled midwife."

"Ye'll tell Elsie exactly what she must do to make people believe, as well as what will happen to her if anyone finds out the truth. The threat of a severe whipping should be a powerful motivator."

Aye, Drummond was ruthless. "Bring her to me."

~ * ~

Elsie had just finished sweeping Aunt Dolina's cottage. Drummond's sudden appearance at the door startled her and she took an involuntary step backwards. She was a little afraid of the huge guardsman. In truth, she was more than a *little* afraid. He had a reputation for cruelty and she was happy enough to stay out of his way.

While he filled the doorway it was impossible to avoid him. Not wishing to make eye contact, she glanced down. "Good afternoon, Sir Drummond."

"The laird has need of ye. Gather yer things."

"Why do I need to gather my things?"

"Because I told ye to, ye insolent chit. The laird is sending ye on an errand. If ye waste any more of my time with questions, ye'll go with nothing but the clothes on yer back."

An errand? Where? To do what? Nay, she didn't dare ask. This could not lead to anything good, but she figured it was best to just do his bidding. She only had a few garments. Laying them on a linen sheet with her comb and a silver brooch that had been her mother's, she folded the sheet inwards over the clothes and rolled them up, tying the bundle with a ribbon. She folded a blanket in half and rolled it around the bundle, securing it with a belt. She had barely wrapped her mantle around her shoulders when Drummond grabbed her arm, practically dragging her from the little cottage and up the lane through the village.

Elsie didn't complain. It would do no good and likely result in worse treatment. All she could do was try her best to keep up. They were halfway to the keep when a horrific screeching sound assaulted her ears just before a searing pain tore through her skull. Gripping her head, she fell to her knees, dropping her bundle.

Chapter 2

Elizabeth Quinn had spent the entire flight with her laptop open, working on finalizing her presentation. She still wasn't quite through when the flight attendant announced that all portable electronic devices needed to be turned off and stowed. She sighed, saved her work and shut it down. It hadn't been a good day. On-call the night before, she'd ended up working non-stop and was exhausted by morning. She wanted nothing more than to take a shower and go to bed for a few hours. Unfortunately, she had promised to meet her boyfriend for brunch and, having cancelled their last three dates due to work, she couldn't do it again. So she settled for just the shower, and picked him on the way to the restaurant.

In hindsight, she wished she had cancelled the date. Although brunch was pleasant enough, David had seemed preoccupied by something. When she finally pushed him to tell her what it was, they had argued and he broke up with her.

During the whole ridiculous argument, David had told her he loved her.

Twice.

She didn't know if she had loved him or not. She liked him and enjoyed going out with him. Perhaps it would have developed into something more with time, but that was the problem. She never had time.

She frowned, remembering his parting words.

"I will miss you, my beautiful girl. And someday, I hope you work your way free of expectations and you allow joy to enter your life."

Her thoughts were interrupted by the pilot announcing that, due to weather conditions and air-traffic over New York, they would be flying a holding pattern for at least thirty more minutes. That, added to the more than ninety-minute delay leaving Cincinnati, meant they were arriving over two hours late.

"Well that's just effing brilliant," she muttered. "Nothing has gone right today."

"What's that dear?" asked the elderly lady sitting beside her.

Elizabeth sighed. She had managed to avoid any interaction for most of the flight. The first rule of travel—if you wanted to be left alone—was to always appear engrossed in something, and never, ever, speak. Too late. The absolute last thing she needed right now was a conversation with a chatty senior citizen. "I'm sorry. I'm a little frustrated with all the delays. I still have work to do and I can't use my laptop. I just don't have time to sit and do nothing."

"No time to waste, eh? Rush, rush, rush, is it?" The older woman had a light Scottish accent.

"Does anyone enjoy wasting time?"

The woman chuckled. "I've got nothing but time, so I guess there's no harm in wasting a bit of it now and then."

"Well, I never seem to have enough time."

"Do ye not? That is a shame. Perhaps these delays are the powers that be stepping in to slow ye down a bit."

It took great control for Elizabeth not to roll her eyes. "Well, I wish the *powers that be* would pick a slightly more opportune occasion."

"Tell me, lass, what work is this wee delay keeping ye from?"

"I am presenting a paper at a professional meeting on Monday. I need to finalize my slides and speaker's notes."

"There's always tomorrow."

"I suppose but I had other plans." The truth was, she'd planned to fly in tomorrow. But a winter storm was bearing down on the northeast and she'd feared her flight would be cancelled. For once in her life, she actually had a whole day with nothing planned.

The old woman gave her an understanding smile. "I see. Well perhaps you could tell me what ye intend to present—without yer slides or notes. I've always found speaking extemporaneously on a topic helps organize my thoughts."

Elizabeth wondered just how many presentations the old woman had ever given. "You wouldn't find it interesting."

"Ye might be surprised. I have a rather wide range of interests."

Right. Knitting patterns? The health benefits of shuffleboard?

The woman cocked her head, looking amused. "Now, lass, ye mustn't judge a book by its cover. I don't know the first thing about knitting, but I never miss the opportunity to learn about advances in medical science."

Elizabeth frowned. "I'm sorry. You're right; I made an unfair assumption. But how did you know—"

"—that ye're a doctor? Lucky guess."

Elizabeth was more interested in the knitting comment, but she let it go.

"So Doctor..."

"Quinn. Elizabeth Quinn." Elizabeth offered her hand.

Shaking Elizabeth's hand the woman said, "I'm Gertrude. It's lovely to meet ye Doctor Quinn. Tell me, do ye ever get teased?"

Elizabeth laughed. "About Doctor Quinn, Medicine Woman? All the time."

The old woman smiled. "Then I shall refrain. So, Doctor—"

"Please, call me Elizabeth."

"All right, Elizabeth, tell me what ye're presenting tomorrow."

"I am discussing some new developments in pain management after caesarian section."

"So ye practice obstetrics. How nice. It seems more and more doctors are leaving that specialty."

"Sadly they are. Some doctors want more controllable hours, but part of the decline can be blamed on the risk of malpractice suits. It's disheartening."

"Aye, I'm sure it is."

"I'll be honest, I'm considering pursuing something else myself. Obstetrics isn't what I thought it would be."

"Ye don't like bringing new lives into the world?"

Elizabeth laughed. "When you put it like that, it is hard to say I don't. But truthfully, sometimes it feels like I deliver one baby, then move onto the next almost before the umbilical cord is cut. I have no time to connect with patients or their families. No time to rejoice in—how did you describe it? Bringing new life into the world? That's what I thought it would be…but it isn't. It's ever on to the next baby."

"Pardon me if I'm the one guilty now of judging a book by its cover, but ye look awfully young to be so disenchanted. Ye can't have been at it long. Are ye even out of yer residency?"

"I have been out of residency for a year, but I am young. I have always been…bright and driven." She smiled apologetically. "I have pushed myself my whole life. I graduated from high school and college early." She gave a little laugh. "I was two years into medical school before I could legally buy a beer."

"So that makes ye twenty-seven?"

"I just turned twenty-eight."

"And if ye left obstetrics, what would ye do?"

"I'm not sure. Pediatrics or family medicine maybe. Of course if I did pediatrics and didn't care for it, it would be rather easy to switch to family medicine."

"Are ye a chess player, Elizabeth?"

The sudden change in topic surprised her. "I learned how when I was young. I don't take much time to play games. Why do ye ask?"

"Because chess players—good chess players— always plan at least three moves ahead. Ye seem to be racing through life, always looking well beyond the next steps."

"I guess so. But that's a good thing."

"It can be, but the thing ye don't like about obstetrics is the constant demand to move on to the next patient. It sounds as if ye're looking for an opportunity to stop and experience the joy around ye."

"I suppose I may be, but there isn't really a way to do that and practice medicine these days."

"What if I could give ye a way?"

"I don't understand."

"There was a time when doctors, healers and midwives experienced exactly what ye say ye want. They knew their patients and spent time with them. When they brought a new babe into the world they could rejoice with the family. When a life was tragically lost, they could mourn. They experienced the full spectrum of human emotion and existence, and helped their neighbors through it."

"That time is long gone."

"Aye, perhaps it is. But what if I could show ye what it was like, just give ye a taste of a different time?"

"No one can do that."

"Set yer disbelief aside for a moment. If ye could go back in time, for a little while, and experience life as a doctor or midwife in a different era, would ye want to?"

"Who wouldn't want to at least see what it was like?"

"That's a very good answer. So keep yer disbelief to one side a moment longer while I explain."

This is what I get for allowing myself to be pulled into a conversation, Elizabeth thought wryly.

The old woman gave her a knowing look. "At least I have more to discuss than knitting patterns and, as entertainment value goes, the possibility of time-travel beats looking out a dark airplane window."

Elizabeth frowned. "How do you do that?"

The old woman smiled. "It's a gift. Now, will ye suspend disbelief for a few minutes?"

Elizabeth truly had nothing else to do. She may as well kill the time listening to Gertrude's delusion about time-travel. It did have to be more interesting than staring out the window. "Okay."

"Good." The woman smiled broadly, reached into the pocket of her jacket and pulled out a pocket watch on a long chain. "This unassuming little device is a conduit for time-travel."

Elizabeth arched an eyebrow at her.

"Och, lass, ye promised to suspend disbelief."

"You're right. Go on. How does it work?"

"Very simply, ye put it 'round yer neck, or even in yer pocket before ye go to sleep, and ye'll wake up somewhere else."

Elizabeth smiled. "Don't you mean sometime else?"

The woman chuckled. "That too." She opened the cover to the watch.

"It only has one hand."

"It only needs one hand. When it takes ye back in time, the hand will move forward one second for every day ye're in the past."

"And when it reaches midnight—sixty days later—I return?"

"Not exactly. Before ye go to sleep, ye must tell it a word. Something ye aren't likely to say by accident. When ye're ready to come home, as long as the hand hasn't reached midnight yet, ye say the word, and the watch will return ye instantly. Ye don't even have to have it on yer person. If it's in the same time with ye, it will work from wherever it is."

"Well, that's certainly handy." Elizabeth had trouble keeping the sarcastic note out of her voice. "And if I don't say the word before midnight?"

"Ye stay there forever."

"So, I tell it my safe-word, go to sleep and wake up somewhere in the past in my jammies? Won't that be a little hard to explain?"

The woman chuckled again. "Aye, I suppose it would be, but that isn't what happens. Only yer soul travels through time. It's called *soul exchange*. Yer body stays here."

"Excuse me?"

"Ye heard me correctly. Yer soul travels backwards and enters the body of someone who is about to die, or at least has set an inevitable course towards their own death. Ye will do something as soon as ye arrive to change that."

"I'll save that person's life?"

"Not precisely. Ye will enter her body and she will enter yers."

"So someone from God knows when will be running around the twenty-first century in my body?"

"Nay, because while the hand on the watch advances one second for every day ye're in the past, time in both places is not equal. Only a second will pass here. If ye come back within the sixty days, the other soul will have resided in yer body for a minute or less."

"So then she'll wake up sixty days later with no memory of what I did? That doesn't sound fun."

"Elizabeth, she will not wake up. Her life was essentially over the instant ye entered her body. So her body in the past will die and her soul will move onward, as it should have."

"I don't know if I like the sound of that."

The woman gave her a sad smile. "I know it's hard to accept. But the life into which yer soul will jump was over. By entering that person's body, ye are given a chance to learn about another life and perhaps do a bit of good."

"But how do I explain not remembering anything about being that person—or what if I don't speak the local language?"

"While yer soul and memories go with ye, ye will be in her body, with her brain and memories. Ye'll experience some of her memories immediately. Language is so ingrained, ye'll know and understand whatever language she speaks. It will feel as if ye're speaking English. It is possible that other memories will emerge with time."

"But I won't remember everything. How do I handle that?"

"When an excuse is needed, some time-travelers claim amnesia. But sometimes, they have a few of the other person's memories, and they can pick up on enough context clues that they don't have to. This is especially true if they don't stay long."

Gertrude seemed so convinced that time-travel was real, Elizabeth was beginning to wonder about her sanity. "Do ye really believe this?"

"Ah, Dr. Quinn, I do believe it and I am perfectly sane."

"Well that's quite a story."

"So, while yer disbelief is still suspended—and I do hope it still is—if everything that I've told ye were true, would ye try it?"

"If I continue to suppress my innate skepticism, yes. Like I said before, who wouldn't take a glimpse of the past if it were offered?"

"Well then, I am offering it to ye. Take the watch. Try it. If it works, the watch will find me after ye return home. If it doesn't, ye have a pretty—if useless—bit of jewelry."

"It sounds intriguing." Elizabeth allowed herself a moment to imagine the possibilities before shaking her head. "Still I'll have to say no. But thank you."

"Ye have nothing to lose and everything to gain. Moreover, Elizabeth, what I am about to tell ye is profoundly true. If ye do not do this, if ye do not try, simply to prove to yerself it isn't possible, ye will wonder about it, and what's worse, regret it, until yer dying day."

Bewildered, Elizabeth simply stared at Gertrude. The old woman might be a little eccentric, but she was harmless.

And, she was dead-on.

Even believing that it would be absolutely impossible to trade souls with someone, Elizabeth knew she would regret not trying it. Just in case…

"Ye know I'm right, lass."

Elizabeth nodded. "Yes, you are. This might be the craziest thing I have ever done, but I'll try it."

At that moment, the pilot announced that they had been cleared for landing.

Gertrude smiled and placed the watch in Elizabeth's hand. "Perfect timing."

Elizabeth looked at the watch more closely. It appeared to be very old and valuable. She frowned. "This looks like an heirloom. At least give me your address, so I can mail it to you."

Gertrude laughed merrily. "Oh, lass, I am a citizen of the universe. The watch will find me itself, much faster than any mail carrier could."

"I'm sorry, Gertrude, I can't accept this with no way to return it to you."

"Yer disbelief is rearing its ugly head again, Dr. Quinn, but how about this. Ye take the watch and give me yer business card. I'll call ye tomorrow evening and ye can tell me all about yer adventure. Then if the watch hasn't found me, we'll sort that out too."

Elizabeth considered it a moment more. "Okay." She put the watch in her pocket and pulled out a card. "You promise you'll contact me."

"Aye, I promise. Now, since we have a few minutes before we get to the gate, tell me about what ye're presenting on Monday."

Elizabeth smiled and gave Gertrude the high-level summary, finishing when they were about to deplane. As they walked into the terminal together, Elizabeth asked, "Where are you going? Will someone be meeting you? If you're going into Manhattan, you're welcome to share my cab."

"Oh, nay, lass. Thank ye, but I'm not staying in New York. I have another connection to make."

"Are you sure you haven't missed it? We're so late getting in."

"Ye needn't worry about me. Go on now. Ye were up all night; ye're tired and still have a bit to do on that presentation before ye sleep. I suspect ye'll have a fascinating tale to tell me tomorrow."

Elizabeth smiled and shook her head. "I think you're having one over on the young doctor, but I look forward to hearing from you."

As Elizabeth walked towards the front of the terminal, it occurred to her she hadn't told Gertrude she had worked all night. Elizabeth turned around to ask her how she knew that, but the old woman had disappeared into the crowd. It would have to wait until Gertrude called tomorrow.

Elizabeth only had a carry-on so she went straight to ground transportation and got in line for a taxi. It was bitter cold and heavy snow was just beginning to whiten the ground. When she finally reached the front of the line she was chilled to the bone. Thankfully the taxi was toasty warm.

As soon as she was inside, she reached for her laptop. She could have the last bit done in the time it would take to get to her hotel. But she stopped herself. The falling snow was beautiful. It occurred to her that if her plane hadn't been delayed, she would be inside a hotel room, curtains drawn, either working or sleeping, and would have missed seeing it. What had Gertrude said? *Perhaps these delays are the powers that be stepping in to slow ye down a bit.*

Elizabeth smiled. For once, she would set work aside and just enjoy the peace of a snowy evening. It had been a crazy day. Speaking of crazy—she pulled out the pocket watch and popped it open to take a closer look.

"Are you in town for business or pleasure?"

No, not a chatty cabby. "Business."

"What kind of business?"

"Healthcare." Maybe the one-word answers would encourage him to stop talking.

"That's a big business. Do you work for a drug company or something?"

"I'm a doctor."

"You ain't no doctor. You're nothin' but a little girl."

"Whatever."

"Are you really a doctor?"

Elizabeth sighed. "Yes."

"What kind of doctor?"

This will shut him up. Men hate this answer. "An OB-GYN."

"No foolin'? You deliver babies and stuff?"

"Mm hmm."

"My wife and I had a baby in July. That baby took forever to get here. Finally they had to…you know, what is the stuff they give to start labor?"

"Pitocin?"

"Yeah they gave her that. But there was something else they gave her the night before."

"Prostaglandin gel?"

"Yeah that was it. You ever have to do that? Give a lady that gel stuff?"

She smiled. "Once in a while."

"You ever deliver twins?"

"Yes."

"Triplets?"

"Once."

"Were they identical?"

"Fraternal."

"What does that mean?"

"It means they weren't identical."

"My sister had twins. She had to have a C-section. Hey, what does the 'C' stand for?"

"Caesarian."

Perhaps he had heard the irritation in her voice, because he stopped asking questions for a minute. She turned her attention back to the pocket watch. There was some engraving on the cover, but in the dim light of the cab she couldn't quite make out what it was.

"Hey, Doc, mind if I turn on some music?"

"Not at all." Maybe that would stop the rapid-fire questions.

"What kind of music do you want?"

No such luck. "Anything is fine."

"Nah, what's your favorite kind of music?"

"I like country-western."

"Eh…you mind if we don't listen to that?"

"Anything is fine."

"Is there anything you don't like?"

"I don't think so."

"Christian Rock?"

"That's fine."

"Salsa?"

"Whatever."

"Gangsta rap?"

"I guess I don't really care for gangsta rap."

"How about Nintendocore?"

"*Nintendocore?*" What on earth was that? It sounded like it had something to do with video games.

Before she could ask, she saw a car way ahead of them begin to slide into the next lane. A driver in that lane slammed on his breaks but hit the skidding car sending them both into a spin, crashing into other cars. The sound of screeching metal on metal filled the air as more cars slid into the first ones. To his credit, Elizabeth's driver was able to slow the cab down and stop before reaching the pile-up. Unfortunately, the driver of the car behind them wasn't as skilled and hit the right rear bumper of the cab, shoving it sideways into the wreckage.

Elizabeth turned her head to look at the road behind them just as another car plowed into the rear driver's side of the cab. The force sent her head slamming into her door window. A searing pain tore through her skull and everything went black.

Chapter 3

Elizabeth woke instantly. The blinding pain in her head was disorienting for a moment, but then suddenly it was gone. How had she gotten out of the cab? She blinked her eyes and gave her head a shake, trying to clear the confusion and process her surroundings as quickly as possible. It was daylight and she was on her hands and knees on a dirt lane. *No, it can't be.*

"Get up!" a low coarse voice demanded.

She glanced around, scarcely able to believe her eyes. She appeared to be in a medieval village.

"I said, get up," the man growled before grabbing her elbow and jerking her to her feet.

OhGod ohGod ohGod ohGod ohGod.

"And pick up yer bundle. I swear, lass, I'll give ye a skelping if ye keep dragging yer feet."

Okay, focus, Elizabeth. Just do what he says until you can figure out what's going on here. Something that looked like a bedroll, bound with a belt, lay at her feet. No sooner had she picked it up than he jerked her forward, practically dragging her down the lane beside him, towards a walled castle.

A castle? Think, Elizabeth. You were going to New York. The plane was late leaving and then couldn't land.

Her head cleared a little. She remembered talking to the old lady next to her. Elegant. Scottish accent. *Gertrude.* That was it. Gertrude had asked her, "If ye could go back in time, for a little while, and experience life as a doctor or midwife, would ye want to?"

Dear, God, she had said yes. But how had Gertrude done it? The image of a beautiful gold pocket watch flashed through her mind. The watch with one hand. Soul exchange. *Yer soul travels backwards and enters the body of someone who is about to die, or at least who has set an inevitable course towards their own death.*

She glanced down and for the first time realized she wasn't in her own body. Elizabeth wasn't very tall, only about five foot three and while she wasn't exactly heavy, she'd had generous curves. The body she was in now seemed taller by an inch or so, and much leaner. She had always wanted to be svelte. Now she was, and there wasn't a pair of cute jeans in sight. Instead she wore several layers of dresses. She thought the bottom layers, next to her skin were linen, but the outer layers were heavy wool with a blanket like cloak over everything. She also wore some sort of heavy stockings and leather shoes.

She stumbled, nearly falling, only to be yanked upright again. There didn't seem to be anyone around to stop mister tall, dark and brutal from nearly yanking her shoulder out of the socket. She would have to worry about how she ended up here later. For now she needed to focus on her current predicament.

When they reached the gate in the wall, the men standing guard nodded them through. He must be someone important. The huge man with her dragged her around to the back of the keep where they met one young man.

"I was just coming to see—wait, what are ye doing to her?"

"Ye'll mind yer own business, if ye know what's good for ye," growled her captor before shoving her through an entrance and then up a set of steep, curving stairs. When they reached the second level he walked her down a hall, stopping before a door and knocking.

"Come in," was the response from within the room.

He pulled her inside. The room looked like the medieval version of an office or study, and a man sat at a table. "Laird, here is Dolina's niece, as ye requested."

Laird? Something compelled her to curtsy. "Good

afternoon…uh…Laird."

"Thank ye, Drummond. Elsie, I have a very important task for ye."

Her name was Elsie. Good to know, but how odd—her mother had called her Elsie when she was little. "Aye, Laird, what is it ye wish?" Again—where did that come from? Not, *what do you have in mind*? Or *I'll do what I can*. Obedience seemed to be a foregone conclusion.

"Yer Aunt is an extremely skilled midwife. So much so that her reputation has spread to other clans. Laird MacKenzie's wife has lost four pregnancies. She's pregnant again and he is desperate. He sent his son to ask if yer aunt could come and attend Lady MacKenzie. But ye and I both know there are just some women who can't carry a bairn to term."

Elizabeth frowned but decided it probably wasn't a good idea to argue.

"I can't possibly send yer aunt on such a fool's errand. If she were needed here by one of the women of the clan, and I had sent her away, I would never forgive myself. Ye aren't without skills—ye have begun training with Dolina. Other than Dolina, ye have no family. Nothing holds ye here. I've decided ye'll go instead, but I intend to tell Laird MacKenzie that ye're the renowned Macrae midwife. It will improve my relationship with him to do so, and there is no harm in it, since nothing can be done to help his wife anyway. When she loses the bairn, he'll send ye back but be forever in my debt because I tried to help."

Elizabeth was incredulous. "Ye're asking me to go with them, lie about who I am, and attend a woman who is desperate to carry a child to term?"

"You impertinent wench, I'm not *asking* ye to do this—I'm ordering ye to. I need MacKenzie as an ally."

Elizabeth seethed inwardly but again held her tongue. Capitalizing on a couple's fear was just plain cruel.

As if he sensed her anger, he added, "And let me make

this clear—if ye refuse this order, I will have ye whipped for disobedience. The same is true if ye tell anyone about this little ruse. And believe me, I'll find out if ye do. Make no mistake, if ye fail in any way, ye will be severely punished. Do ye understand me?"

What an awful man. Elizabeth would have gone just to get away from him. She almost found it amusing that she was likely to have more knowledge than a medieval midwife about what might be wrong with Lady MacKenzie, and could possibly provide real assistance. She inclined her head. "Aye, Laird, I understand."

"Good. Come with me. The faster they leave with ye, the less likely they are to find out ye aren't actually the midwife they seek."

Elizabeth followed him out of the room, down the stairs and into what must be the castle's great hall. Four very large men waited there.

They were all striking but her eye was instantly drawn to one man. Tall, broad-shouldered, with sandy blonde hair and grey eyes, he was easily one of the most attractive men she had ever seen. But more than that, he had a presence that instantly commanded respect. She had no doubt that this was Laird MacKenzie's son.

She had almost forgotten Laird Macrae's presence until he said. "Sir Cade, I have considered the matter and discussed it with my advisors. Elsie here assures me that no Macrae woman will be at risk if she accompanies ye. So, I've given her leave to go."

"This...this lass is yer renowned midwife?" Cade asked in disbelief. "She's little more than a child herself."

Elizabeth almost smiled. Even in the—whatever century she was in—she was being judged by her age.

"She is one and twenty—"

"*One and twenty?* Do ye expect me to believe that yer *renowned* midwife is only one and twenty?"

Laird Macrae had the nerve to look affronted. "I assure

ye, Sir Cade, she comes from a long line of midwives. She has been learning the art from childhood. Her instincts are remarkable. If anyone can help, she can."

That was a safe thing to say if ye believed that no one could help. The fact that Elizabeth could likely be of some benefit brought a confident smile to her face.

Sir Cade turned on her. "Is this the truth? By God's bones, lass, if I find out ye and yer laird have tried to fool us, ye'll both be sorry."

In all sureness, Elizabeth said, "Sir, I swear to ye, what Laird Macrae has told ye about my ability is true. There is no one better able to assist Lady MacKenzie than I."

She wasn't completely sure how she had landed in this time and place, but the opportunity to help the poor woman filled Elizabeth with purpose. It suddenly became very important to her to convince Sir Cade to take her with them. "Ye have nothing to lose, and everything to gain."

Sir Cade seemed taken aback. Elizabeth cast the slightest glance towards Laird Macrae and was pleased to see that even he was shocked by her confident statement.

Recovering quickly Cade said, "For yer sake, I hope so." He turned his attention to Laird Macrae. "How soon can she be ready to leave?"

"She's ready now. I suggest ye leave immediately if ye don't want to spend three nights on the road in order to reach Carraigile."

"Ye're sending her by herself? Laird Macrae, we assumed...well, we weren't expecting to travel with such a young woman...alone. We have no other woman with us."

Elizabeth, tilted her head to one side. "Do ye intend to despoil me, Sir Cade?"

"Nay, of course not. I've no need to take an unwilling lass."

"That's good to know. So, do ye intend to let anyone else?"

He frowned darkly at her. "Ye'll be in my care. What

do ye take me for?"

"I don't know. I'm trying to figure why ye would think I shouldn't travel alone with ye. But if ye don't intend to molest me, or allow anyone else to, then ye must be worried about yer own virtue."

"*My virtue?*" He barked a laugh, casting a sideways glance at the other warriors, all of whom looked exceedingly amused.

Elizabeth adopted a bland expression. "Well, sir, while ye're undeniably attractive, ye needn't worry. I think I can restrain myself." Although a tiny part of her wondered why she would want to.

Sir Cade looked momentarily shocked, but recovering quickly, winked and said, "Ah, my bonny lass, ye'll be the first."

This statement, coming from any other man, would probably have sounded like the height of conceit, but from this magnetic warrior she suspected it was simply the truth.

The other men laughed heartily.

To Laird Macrae, Cade said, "Since neither ye, nor the lass feel the need for a chaperone, we'll take our leave. Thank ye again, Laird. We are in yer debt." He made a small bow, as did the other men with him.

Laird Macrae gave an obsequious nod. "It's the least I can do."

Elizabeth couldn't suppress a wry smile. Considering the man thought he was sending an apprentice with no special skills—that that was absolutely true.

"Tell Laird MacKenzie that his lady will be in our prayers. I wish ye a safe journey," said Laird Macrae.

It was all Elizabeth could do not to roll her eyes.

As the MacKenzie warriors walked towards the front doors, Laird Macrae grabbed Elizabeth's elbow and hissed in her ear, "Remember, not a word to anyone."

"Aye, Laird." She could not stop herself from bobbing a curtsy before hurrying to follow the MacKenzies.

Chapter 4

Cade and his men saddled the horses while the Macrae midwife waited outside the stable. He didn't know what to think of this turn of events. He had never heard of so young a midwife but she exuded self-assurance. Cade was considered a good judge of character and generally knew when someone was dealing falsely. He was nearly certain that Laird Macrae was not telling the truth. On the other hand, he was absolutely sure the lass was.

As if reading his thought, Eric said, "She's certainly a surprise."

"Aye, cheeky little bit, isn't she?" added Stephan.

Cade grinned. "That she is. And bonny too."

Sully, a much older guardsman, frowned. "Aye, but I fear that pretty face and bold manner may be turning yer heads. Cade, I do not believe she's the midwife we came for. I don't trust Macrae."

"Make no mistake Sully, I don't trust him either. He's lying about something."

"Then why are we heading back to Carraigile with an imposter?"

"Because I don't think she is an imposter. She seems supremely confident in her abilities, and I am dead certain she's telling the truth. I can't believe so young a woman could dissemble so well."

Sully frowned. "They both tell us the same thing? How can Laird Macrae be lying while the lass is telling the truth?"

Cade considered Sully's question. He had relied on instinct but how could it be possible? His thoughts went back to the young woman's demeanor and the answer hit him. "That's a fair question, Sully, and I can only see one answer. I firmly believe she has been honest with us. So the only explanation I can think of is that she knows much more than her laird believes she does. Given we have no other choice now, I'm inclined to take her to Carraigile and see what Morag makes of her."

"Aye, Morag's a fine midwife, she'll be able to tell," Sully agreed. "But what will ye do if Morag calls her out as a fraud?"

Cade's expression darkened. "If she's a fraud, Macrae will rue this day…and that lass will pay for her role in the deception too."

They led their horses out of the stable. They had brought an extra mount, confident that one way or another they were going to leave with the midwife. Cade had believed the odds were good that they would have been forced to steal her, and he hadn't wanted anything to slow their return.

He led the sturdy brown mare to Elsie. "Ye'll ride Edda, here."

~ * ~

Elizabeth furrowed her brow and stared at him. She hadn't actually given any thought as to *how* they would travel until the men had entered the stable. Of course they would be going on horseback. The problem was, she had never ridden a horse. As she had waited for them, she tried to convince herself that this wasn't actually a problem. How hard can it be? *Climb up—hold on.*

She almost believed it until he stopped in front of her with Edda.

Edda was really big. Granted the other horses were bigger yet, but the distance from Edda's back to the ground was much farther than Elizabeth wanted to fall.

"Is something wrong, lass?"

"Uh…nay."

"Give me yer bundle and I'll tie it to the saddle."

She did, and when he was done, he turned back to her. "Here, I'll give ye a leg up." He moved to stand with his left shoulder against Edda's chest, his hands out, clearly expecting Elizabeth to do something.

"What am I supposed to do?"

"Do ye not know how to mount a horse, lass?"

"I don't really ride much." *I don't really ride at all.*

Incredulous, he asked, "How do ye get from place to place?"

"I walk." Even as she said it, the memory of getting into a cab on a snowy night, flitted through her mind.

"Well we can't walk to Carraigile. Come here. I'll lift ye up."

She stepped cautiously towards him. He put his hands on her waist and lifted her onto Edda's back. He continued to steady her as he said, "Bring yer right leg over. And be careful, she won't like it if ye kick her neck as ye do it."

Elizabeth did as he said.

"Good. Now, put yer feet in the stirrups. I'll adjust the length if necessary."

Again she followed his order.

"Don't put them so far in. Ye want the stirrup under the ball of yer foot."

The other men were already on their horses, watching with amusement. Cade adjusted the length of her stirrups and handed her the reins before mounting his horse.

They left the bailey and rode through the village at a walk. Edda followed the other horses without Elizabeth having to do anything. This was easy enough.

The few people they passed as they went cast quizzical looks towards her, but no one said anything until they met one elderly woman when they were nearly to the edge of the village.

The woman called, "Elsie, lass, where are ye going?"

Before she could answer, Sir Cade said, "She's going with us to Carraigile."

The old woman frowned, looking worried.

Elizabeth wanted to reassure her, without risking any questions that might reveal too much. She settled on, "The MacKenzies have asked for my help."

The old woman looked even more concerned but didn't ask another question.

When she and the MacKenzies had left the village, the men urged their horses into a trot. Again, Edda followed suit. Riding at this pace was not quite as easy. Elizabeth bumped up and down in the saddle. Not only was it was uncomfortable; she felt unstable—as if she were going to be bounced off altogether. She leaned forward, gripping the edge of the saddle. This seemed to make Edda trot faster, so Elizabeth pulled back on the reins to slow her down. Edda didn't seem to like having her reins pulled, and tossed her head, but she did slow down.

The cycle repeated itself over and over.

Edda trotted.

Elizabeth leaned forward to hang on.

Edda went faster.

Elizabeth reined in.

Edda tossed her head, seeming to grow more irritated each time.

Finally, after about three quarters of an hour of this, Edda simply stopped.

Not that Elizabeth blamed her—this was exhausting—but she had no idea how to make the horse go again.

"Giddy up?" That worked in cowboy movies didn't it?

Nothing.

Come on, sweetie, don't do this to me.

Elizabeth tried bouncing a little in the saddle and nudging Edda's sides with her feet.

Edda started trotting again and the frustrating cycle restarted. Only this time, when Elizabeth reined in, Edda tossed her head and danced, scaring Elizabeth even more. She didn't think she could stand ten more minutes of this, much less several days. She glanced up the road. The MacKenzie men had stopped and were looking back at her.

Cade shook his head. "God's teeth lass, ye're bouncing in that saddle like a drunkard and if ye keep yanking on her reins, she'll throw ye. Do ye not know anything?"

"I told ye I don't ride much."

"I'll warrant that's an understatement. Never mind. Ye'll ride with me so we have a hope of getting ye there in one piece."

He rode towards her, dismounted and took Edda's reins. He crooned to the horse, "There now, lass, I'll save ye from the ignorant beastie on yer back."

Elizabeth frowned, but she couldn't really argue the point. She was completely ignorant of how to ride a horse. Clearly climbing up and holding on wasn't sufficient.

When the horse had quieted, he lifted Elizabeth off.

"I'll take the *four-legged* beastie," said a very handsome dark-haired man, grinning broadly. He rode towards them, taking Edda's reins.

"Thank ye, Eric."

So his name is Eric. Cade and Eric—just two more to figure out.

Cade led Elizabeth to his horse. She groaned with her first few steps. After less than an hour in the saddle, her thighs and bottom ached.

He arched a brow at her. "Is that soft, round backside hurting?"

She glowered at him but he only chuckled. "That's what bouncing around in a saddle will do to ye. Ye'll learn to ride properly before we bring ye back."

He lifted her onto his horse. She started to put her right leg over, as she had before, but he stopped her. "Nay, lass, stay as ye are." He mounted behind her, pulling her close to him and adjusting her right knee over the pommel. She was effectively sitting in his lap.

Oh. My. God. Forget Superman; *this* was the man of steel. His thighs, under her "soft, round, backside" were rock-hard. The arm wrapped around her waist felt like a band of iron. She could feel the rippling muscles of his chest against her back. No, that was an exaggeration—she had on too many layers of clothing. But she was certain that they rippled nonetheless. *Good Lord, Elizabeth, you're a grown woman. Stop reacting like a teenager.*

That thought had no sooner crossed her mind, when he leaned close to her ear. His voice was soft and his warm breath tickled her neck. "Ye feel rather good in my arms. I may have to rethink teaching ye to ride."

She nearly lost her composure again. Elizabeth suddenly became much less confident about her earlier assurance that she could restrain herself. Where this insanely desirable man was concerned, she wasn't sure of anything at the moment. The heat rose in her face, at her wayward thoughts and—discretion being the better part of valor—she said nothing.

He chuckled richly, the sound enveloping her in a cocoon of warmth, if anything, only deepening her blush.

They rode on in silence.

She had to steer her mind away from carnal thoughts about the medieval warrior on whose lap she sat.

Medieval.

Right. She needed to remember how she had gotten here. Perhaps sorting out her jumbled memories of the events of the day, would rein in her libido.

She reviewed what she had remembered so far. She met the old woman, Gertrude, on the plane. Gertrude had given her the pocket watch and explained soul exchange...*ye will be in her body, with her memories. Some of them you will experience immediately.* She supposed that explained the compulsion she felt to accept orders from Laird Macrae and to curtsy. She had never curtsied in her life. For a moment she wished riding skills had been among Elsie's residual memories.

Wait. No I don't. I quite like riding on Cade's lap.

What Gertrude had said about language was true. She felt as if she were speaking English, but based on the names Macrae and MacKenzie, she had to be in Scotland. The absence of kilts meant it was likely more than five hundred years in the past—so they must be speaking Gaelic.

But Elizabeth was certain Gertrude had said she would have all of her own memories. This didn't seem to be the case. *Think back Elizabeth, walk through what you do remember.*

She thought about the watch. It had one hand. That was significant. *When it takes ye back in time, the hand will move forward one second for every day ye're in the past.* That's right. She had up to sixty days—but she could return home sooner. She also remembered that the watch was supposed to have come with her. She touched her neck but found no chain. It must be in a pocket but she couldn't very well check now. She would find it when she had a private moment.

Her conversation with Gertrude was becoming clearer. She concentrated on what else the old woman had said.

Before ye go to sleep, ye must tell it a word. Something ye aren't likely to say by accident.

Oh no.

She was supposed to have given the watch a "safe-word" before she went to sleep. But she couldn't remember going to sleep and had no idea what the word was. Dear God, she was going to be stuck here forever.

Elizabeth tamped down her panic. *Relax. You'll remember.* She just needed to take a step back and think about where she had been going.

The conference. She was presenting at a conference and had reservations at a hotel in Manhattan. She closed her eyes, trying to visualize the lobby, and while she could remember what it looked like from previous stays, she couldn't remember checking in today.

Okay, take another step back. What happened after you got the watch?

She walked off the plane with Gertrude and…nothing.

Damn.

"Ye're a quiet one, lass."

Cade's voice jarred her out of her contemplation. "No quieter than ye lot."

"Well that's a fair point," said Eric.

"Tell us a bit about yerself, then," said the oldest of the four men.

"What would ye like to know…uh, I'm sorry, what's yer name?"

"Forgive me. I should have introduced ye," said Cade. "That's Sir Sully." He gestured to the older man. "He's the captain of my father's guard. That hulking warrior there, with the shocking red hair is Sir Stephan, one of my father's guardsmen. And Sir Eric here, is another guardsman as well as my cousin."

"Very nice to meet ye," said Elizabeth.

Sully frowned. "So, Elsie, now ye know who we are, but all we know about ye is that ye're exceedingly young. And yet, we're meant to believe ye're the best midwife Macrae has." His tone was slightly mocking.

Elizabeth sighed. She was uncomfortable lying but if she were careful, she wouldn't have to. "I am very skilled at tending women who are carrying."

Sully shook his head. "Now ye see, I just don't believe that from someone yer age."

"Sully, we've been through this," said Cade.

"Nay, it's all right. I understand and am used to it but, Sir Sully, I have been learning about pregnancy and how to deliver babies for over eight years now."

"That would have made ye twelve when ye started training," said Cade.

"That's not possible," said Sully.

Dammit. I'm twenty-one not twenty-eight. Go with the truth. "I was very young when I started training—much younger than most—but no one starts out just delivering babies. There are other things to learn first. Then ye watch someone with experience, and help them as ye can. Eventually they watch ye to make certain ye know what ye're doing. All of this happens before ye do anything on ye're own." Essentially this was the way healthcare professionals had been trained for centuries.

"Laird Macrae said ye come from a long line of midwives," said Eric.

This was trickier. She was unaware of any midwives in her family tree. But still she could make a true statement. "Aye, I followed in my family's vocation." Her mother's side of the family were all lawyers in her grandfather's firm. Elizabeth was a bit of a disappointment to them. However, her father was a surgeon, as was his father. While they were not happy with her choice of specialty, at least she had become a doctor.

Sully rode up beside Cade and turned to look her directly in the eye. "I refuse to believe ye're the midwife we came for. If ye were trained by others and are still so young, they have to be more experienced than ye."

Elizabeth met his gaze without flinching. "I will say this one more time, and then this conversation is over. I am absolutely, without a doubt, the person best able to help yer laird's wife."

Her pronouncement was met with stunned silence. After a moment, Sully inclined his head and fell back. She still wasn't confident that she had convinced him, but at least he had let it drop.

Cade leaned down to whisper in her ear again. "If I'm not much mistaken, ye just told a man—a warrior who is more than twice yer age and size, no less—to shut his gob."

She bristled. "I did no such thing."

"Nay? And what exactly does, 'this conversation is over' mean, if not 'shut yer gob'?"

He might be attractive but he was also irritating. "It means," she hissed, "I have given everyone my assurances already and I have no other proof. If he didn't believe me the first three times, asking me again will do no good."

His chuckle vibrated through her. "Ye're too bold by half, little midwife. Does Laird Macrae tolerate this?"

"I have seldom been in Laird Macrae's company for more than a few minutes, and I have never had to convince him of my skills." Another absolutely true statement.

"I'm thinking *I* need to spend a bit more time in yer company. Perhaps I can teach ye a few skills we'll both enjoy." His suggestive tone left no doubt as to which skills he meant.

Elsie shook her head in exasperation, but she couldn't suppress a smile. Were men in any century different? "Based on yer earlier assertions, Sir Cade, ye have more than enough willing apprentices. Ye probably shouldn't waste yer precious time on me." Although a little wicked voice within her suggested that she might quite enjoy his tutelage.

He threw his head back and laughed.

Cade found the Macrae midwife beyond enticing. She was a little taller than the average woman. Seated, the top of her head came up to his chin. She had silvery gray eyes that sparkled when she was cheeky. She also had an air of confidence that seemed wholly out of place in one so young. As to her other assets—the feel of her soft round backside, nestled against his groin all afternoon was pure torture. He had managed to reposition the arm he held around her waist several times, until it rested just under her bosom. She was well enough curved to please a man and it took sheer force of will to refrain from cupping his hand around one tempting breast.

He had promised he wouldn't *despoil* her. Still, he had said nothing about enticing her willingly into his bed. That was something he would make every effort to do.

As evening began to fall, the wind picked up, turning colder, and Elsie began to shiver. "Are ye cold, lass?"

"Aye, 'tis a penetrating wind."

He pulled her snuggly against him, wrapping his plaid around them both. "Does that help?"

"Aye, it does. Thank ye." She sounded slightly breathless. He smiled to himself, glad she wasn't completely unaffected by his nearness.

"Cade, with the weather turning foul, we should consider trying to reach Brathanead Castle instead of continuing on and making camp," said Sully.

"Aye, ye're right. Tis an awful night to be sleeping on the ground. And alas, we have no willing lass to warm us."

She huffed with disdain, causing him to chuckle.

"If we turn to the east now, we should reach MacLennan land in about an hour and the castle not long afterwards."

The snow started to fall just before they arrived at Brathanead. The MacLennans and the MacKenzies were allies, albeit not extremely close ones.

The watch had announced them and Laird Revelin met them in the bailey.

"To what do I owe a visit from the MacKenzie heir?"

"Laird MacLennan, I am escorting a Macrae midwife to Carraigile so she may tend Lady Wynda."

Sadness crossed the laird's features. "Ah, Lady Wynda is expecting again. I understand. Lady MacLennan has never had trouble bearing children, but we have lost three in infancy. Even now, our four-year-old son, Kelvin is gravely ill with a lung ailment. Ye are welcome to stay as long as necessary."

"Thank ye, Laird. I am sorry to hear of yer trouble."

Cade dismounted, as did his men.

Before he could lift Elsie off his horse, she said, "Pardon me, Laird, I have other healing skills. Perhaps there is something I can do to help."

Revelin's expression was skeptical. "Ye're very young to be a healer or a midwife."

"I am young, but I am well trained. I may be able to provide some assistance."

Revelin addressed Cade as he lifted Elsie off the horse. "Is what she says true?"

Cade was momentarily amused by the irritation on Elsie's face. He considered her for a moment before answering. "Laird MacLennan, I don't know for certain. However, she has a very good reputation as a midwife and Laird Macrae vouched for her. She may be able to aid ye and I believe she would do no harm."

Revelin nodded. "I cannot bear to lose my son. Aye, lass, if ye think there's anything ye can do, follow me." To Cade he said, "Once ye've seen to yer mounts, there will be food and drink waiting for ye in the great hall." He turned towards the keep.

Elsie started to follow but Cade grabbed her arm and leaned close to her ear. "Mind yer tongue, lass. Ye may be a fine healer, but if yer audacious manner offends, I will not be happy. Do ye understand?"

Her eyes flashed with annoyance but she hissed, "Aye. I understand."

He let her go, watching her stride angrily towards the keep.

Eric, who had been standing close enough to hear, grinned. "Do ye think it was a good idea to set her off just before letting her go with Laird MacLennan?"

"Do ye think Laird or Lady MacLennan would have tolerated her boldness?"

"Fair point. But I suspect they will be less likely to goad her than ye."

Cade chuckled. "I've never encountered a lass quite this much fun to needle."

"Because they usually fall willingly into yer arms. That one will lead ye a merry chase."

Chapter 5

Elizabeth followed Laird MacLennan into the keep. He called orders to servants to see to the MacKenzie visitors, then led Elizabeth upstairs to the chamber where his son was being cared for. A haze of pungent smoke from burning herbs hovered in the room. She remembered reading once that in the dark ages, incense or rosemary was often burned to ward off bad humors. It couldn't possibly be worse for someone with a lung ailment. Although she wanted to toss the offending herbs in the hearth immediately, she stopped herself. She would see it done, but she needed to be careful.

An older woman stood to one side and a small woman with dark hair sat next to the bed holding the boy's hand. She turned towards them. The dark circles under her despair-filled eyes suggested she'd had very little rest recently.

Laird MacLennan crossed the room, resting his hand on one of her thin shoulders. "Maeve, my darling, how is he?"

"His fever continues to burn. Revelin, I cannot bear losing him."

"Let's not borrow trouble. Cade MacKenzie just arrived, seeking shelter from the storm. He and several of his men are on their way back to Carraigile with this Macrae healer. She believes she may be able to help."

"Can, ye? Can ye truly?" The hope in Lady MacLennan's expression caused a deep ache in Elsie's heart.

"There may be something I can do. Will ye allow me

to examine him?"

"Aye, of course. What's yer name, lass?"

Doctor Quinn was on the tip of her tongue. "Elsie, my lady."

Maeve caressed the lad's cheek. "Kelvin, my little one, Elsie is going to try to help ye get better." She stepped away from the bed.

The child was pale but for the unnatural flush of fever in his cheeks. He looked as if he were barely breathing. She laid a hand on his cheek. His skin was hot and dry to the touch. "Kelvin, can ye open yer eyes for me?" His eyes fluttered open. She breathed a small sigh of relief—at least he could be roused. She pulled one of his lower eyelids down gently looking for jaundice, pleased again not to find any. "Do ye suppose ye could sit up if I helped ye?"

He nodded.

She put an arm under his shoulders, raising him to a sitting position. Lifting his nightshirt, she put an ear to his back, listening as best she could to his lungs. He definitely had some congestion in his lower lobes but there was some air moving. She percussed his back. There was resonance in his upper lobes—as there should be—but it was decreased in the lower lobes. The only other abnormal finding she discovered on her assessment was that he seemed very dehydrated. He likely had pneumonia and in the twenty-first century this would be an easy fix. Intravenous fluids, antibiotics and respiratory therapy. She didn't think his fever was dangerously high. As long as it wasn't, she would do nothing to bring it down; it was one of the body's defenses against infection. But there were things she could do to help him.

She looked at Laird and Lady MacLennan with as reassuring an expression as she could muster. "I believe I know a few things that could help."

"Tell us, we'll do whatever we need to," said Lady MacLennan.

"Well first, we'll need to remove the burning rosemary."

"But it is to keep the evil humors away," said the older woman who had been silent until now.

"I understand, but I've found that the smoke makes it harder for someone with a lung ailment to breathe. Instead, I put a tiny bit of rosemary into water and have the person breathe the steam. It seems to drive the evil humors away faster."

"Does it?" asked the woman.

Yes, converting what they believed about illness to what she knew to be true might actually work. "Aye it does. In fact, if we concentrate the steam the lad breathes, he will soon start coughing up all of the evil phlegm. It is most important to get him coughing effectively."

"How do we concentrate the steam," asked the woman, truly interested.

"Well—I'm sorry, what is yer name?"

"Barabal."

"Barabal is our healer," explained Laird MacLennan.

"I'll show ye. We need a kettle of hot water, a bit of rosemary, a large bowl and toweling. We also need to get him to drink as much as we can. An infusion of peppermint and honey will work well. We can add a sprig of rosemary too so it works from the inside out."

"Really?" Thankfully, Barabal seemed fascinated instead of threatened.

"Do ye believe this can work, Barabal?" asked Laird MacLennan.

"Laird, nothing else has worked. I cannot see that it will do any harm at all."

"Then please, see that Elsie has what she needs."

"Aye, Laird. Excuse me for a moment while I send someone to fetch everything." She bobbed a curtsy and left the room.

Laird MacLennan turned his attention to his wife.

"Now, Maeve, please come with me. Ye need to rest or ye'll fall ill yerself."

"I will not leave my child! I have told ye that over and over," she snapped at her husband.

It was clear to Elizabeth that Maeve did need rest but she also knew the worried mother couldn't be forced to leave.

"Pardon me, my lady, Laird, perhaps I could offer a suggestion. My lady, I agree that ye look exhausted and could fall ill yerself. But I also know ye can't leave yer child, and I think he would want ye here. Perhaps ye could just lie on the other side of the bed and rest a bit. I will be right here and I'll wake ye for the smallest thing."

"Ye swear?" Maeve asked.

"I swear, my lady."

"Ye'll stay, Revelin? While I rest?"

"Of course, my darling."

Maeve nodded, a tear slipping down her cheek. "All right. I'll rest a little while."

Laird MacLennan gave a sigh of profound relief. He walked with Maeve to the other side of the bed and sat in a chair next to her as she closed her eyes.

Elizabeth dumped all of the burning herbs into the hearth. If the weather wasn't so awful, she would have opened the shuttered windows. But the room was drafty enough that the smoke cleared fairly quickly anyway.

When Barabal returned, Elizabeth filled the bowl with steaming water and a sprig of rosemary. As far as Elizabeth knew, the rosemary had no therapeutic value—but it didn't hurt and it satisfied their medieval sensibilities.

Elizabeth lifted Kelvin from the bed and, holding him on her lap, draped the towel over the bowl and both their heads.

"Oh, I see," said Barabal. "The towel holds the steam in a bit."

"Aye, but we have to keep replacing the hot water to

keep it steaming."

"It smells good," said Kelvin.

Elizabeth smiled. "Well, little man, if ye think this smells good, ye need to taste the lovely drink we've made for ye."

She spent the next few hours doing everything she could do—with what she had to hand—to loosen the congestion and help Kelvin start coughing it up. Both Barabal and Laird MacLennan assisted, doing whatever Elizabeth asked. Finally Kelvin was able to take deep breaths and give a nice strong cough, bringing up phlegm. While it was a greenish yellow color, Elizabeth was thrilled that it wasn't rusty or tinged with blood.

Barabal was amazed that it had worked. "I've never seen anything like this."

"He needs to rest for a while, but we can keep the bowl of steaming water near the head of his bed. It will still help."

"Elsie, I don't know how to thank ye," said Laird MacLennan.

"Laird, he isn't out of the woods yet. But if we keep doing what we've been doing, I think we will be able to bring him through this. Now, both of ye need to rest a bit, while Kelvin does. I'll stay awake with him and wake ye if anything changes."

It was a mark of how tired they both were that they agreed. Laird MacLennan, gently moved Maeve towards the middle of the bed and laid next to her. Barabal made a pallet of blankets and laid on the floor not far from the hearth.

Elizabeth sat in a chair next to Kelvin. She had been so focused on her little patient and his parents, that this was the first opportunity she'd had to think about her predicament since she had ridden through the gates with Cade.

Gertrude's words floated to her: *There was a time*

when doctors, healers and midwives experienced exactly what ye say ye want. They knew their patients and spent time with them.

Elizabeth smiled to herself. She had told Gertrude she wanted this and she couldn't deny that it was fulfilling.

Gertrude.

Elizabeth tried again to remember what had happened after the airplane. *I had to get into the city. I must have taken a cab.* That was it! She remembered standing in line for a cab at the airport…it was freezing cold…and snowing. The cab had been toasty warm. Elizabeth tried to picture getting out of the cab at the hotel, but she simply couldn't.

Go back to something you do remember. She walked herself through the previous night on duty. It was a bit of a blur but nights on call were seldom memorable. On the other hand, every moment of the unpleasant brunch she'd had with David was crystal clear. Even the details of her slide presentation were sharp, but all she remembered after the airport was getting into the warm cab and looking at the pocket watch.

The pocket watch. It was supposed to be with her. She felt for pockets in her clothing and found none. She checked her mantle, which hung over the back of her chair, but it didn't have pockets either. Perhaps it was in the bundle of Elsie's belongings Cade had tied to Edda's saddle, but at the moment she didn't know where that was. Finding the watch would have to wait a little longer.

Kelvin stirred in his sleep, drawing Elizabeth's attention back to her patient. He woke needing to use the chamber pot. That at least meant he was beginning to rehydrate. She had him drink more of the mint tisane, then sat with him under the makeshift steam tent.

Elizabeth heard movement behind her. Lady MacLennan had awakened. While she didn't look fully refreshed, the rest had clearly done wonders. "How is he?"

she asked tentatively.

"The congestion is clearing."

"And the fever?"

"He still has a fever, but he isn't terribly hot. As long as the fever isn't too high and he drinks a lot, it...well," how was she going to say this? "...I've heard it helps burn off the bad humors. It's only a problem if it burns very hot."

"Mama, this smells nice," Kelvin said from under the towel.

"Does it, sweetling?" Lady MacLennan smiled at Elsie. "Would ye like for me to hold him for a while?"

Elizabeth nodded. "That's a very good idea." She put Kelvin on Lady MacLennan's lap and showed her how to make the steam tent.

After the lad had breathed the steam for a while, Elizabeth said, "Now, little man, show yer mama the proper way to breathe deep and cough."

He smiled. "Ye do it like this, Mama." He breathed in and out deeply and after the third breath in, he gave one strong cough, clearing more phlegm.

Elizabeth smiled at him. "Well done. Now do that several times and have a little more to drink, then I want ye to rest again."

When they had him tucked into bed, Lady MacLennan sat next to him, rubbing his back lightly until he fell asleep. When she looked up at Elizabeth, her eyes were bright with unshed tears. "Thank ye, Elsie."

"Ye're very welcome, my lady. He isn't completely better, and it may be a while before he is, but I think things are moving in the right direction."

"I think so too. I was so frightened, but now...well...I believe he'll be all right." As if really seeing Elizabeth for the first time, her brows furrowed. "Oh my, ye're just a lass."

Elizabeth smiled and gave the answer she knew she

would likely have to give over and over again, "I've been studying the healing arts for over eight years now and have learned quite a lot."

Lady MacLennan smiled. "It seems ye have."

Elizabeth's stomach took that moment to growl loudly.

"Oh, my dear, Revelin brought ye straight up here when ye arrived. I'll warrant ye've had nothing to eat since midday yesterday."

"Ye needn't worry about me, my lady."

"Nay, ye need to eat and have a wee rest too. I'll wake Barabal—"

"Oh, please don't do that. She's as exhausted as ye and the laird. Let her rest. I'll be fine."

Lady MacLennan grew stern in a motherly sort of way. "I appreciate yer thoughtfulness but ye must eat. Go down the stairs and out the back of the great hall. Ye'll see the kitchens. It won't be long until sunup. Someone will be there soon if they aren't already. Tell them I sent ye."

Elizabeth's stomach growled again. Lady MacLennan gave her a *don't-even-think-about-telling-me-ye-aren't-hungry* look.

Elizabeth smiled. "Aye, my lady. Thank ye. I'll find the kitchen. I am a bit hungry."

Elizabeth had started towards the chamber door, when Lady MacLennan stopped her. "Lass, ye'll need a candle to see yer way to the hall, and I expect ye'll want yer mantle. 'Tis a bitter night and without it ye'll chill even on the short walk to the kitchen."

Walk to the kitchen? It must be outside the keep. "Aye, my lady." Elizabeth left, taking her cloak and one of the candles from the mantel. *Okay, creeping around a medieval a castle, in the dark, with only a candle is a little spooky.* She did manage to find the stairs that Laird MacLennan had brought her up. When she reached the great hall, she was surprised to see people sleeping on the floor. She moved to the back of the hall as quietly as she could to avoid waking anyone before slipping through the back door. The wind instantly extinguished her candle. Snow had fallen all night, accumulating about eight inches. A path had been worn in the snow to a building just beyond the keep. *That must be the kitchen.* When she reached the building she knocked hesitantly and listened.

"Come in," a voice called.

She pushed the door open. An elderly woman stood stirring a pot over the hearth.

"Pardon me. Lady MacLennan said I should find something to eat. I came with the MacKenzies. My name is Elsie."

"I know who ye are, lass." The elderly woman turned around.

"Gertrude?"

"Aye, lass."

"What are ye doing here?"

"We have a few things to discuss, but Lady MacLennan was right, ye need to be fed. I've made some porridge. Sit here with me and eat while we talk."

Stunned, she sat as Gertrude ladled up a bowl of porridge, poured a liberal amount of honey and cream into it and placed it on the table in front of Elizabeth.

"Is this yer home? Is this why ye sent me here— wherever or whenever here is? To save that lad?"

"Nay, lass, this isn't my home. I told ye, I am a citizen of the universe. But, I have friends everywhere. Ye're at Brathanead keep—it's in the Scottish Highlands northwest of Inverness—and 'tis the year of our Lord, twelve-hundred and seventy-nine."

"Twelve-seventy-nine? Are ye serious?"

Gertrude chuckled. "Absolutely serious. I assure ye, sweetling, the one thing I'm very good at is telling time."

"So, was it my purpose to save the lad? And if this isn't yer home, what are ye doing here?"

"I know Peg, the cook here, and I'm sure she won't

mind me whipping up a bit of porridge for ye. As for saving the lad—and rest assured, ye did save him—that was simply an added benefit."

"Can I go home now?"

"Not yet."

"But ye said I could go back anytime, I just had to say the word."

Gertrude arched a brow at her. "And what is the word?"

"I...I don't know. I can't remember what happened after I got into the cab."

"Aye, well, that's a problem. But the bigger problem is that ye don't have the watch."

"Well, not on me. I thought it might be in my bundle of things."

"It isn't, lass."

"How do ye know?"

"Because it didn't come with ye."

"But ye said it would."

"And normally it would have. But it didn't."

"What happened?"

"Several things actually. Ye say ye remember getting into the cab?"

"Aye."

"Do ye remember having the watch in yer hand in the cab?"

"Vaguely, aye."

"Well, several cars ahead of ye were in an accident. Yer driver avoided it, but other cars crashed into the cab. Ye hit yer head and lost consciousness. Thus, strictly speaking, ye fell asleep. Ye must have dropped the watch as it was happening, because the soul exchange occurred, but the watch stayed in the future."

"Then if I didn't tell it a word, as I should have before falling asleep—and by the way, I'm not sure I agree that losing consciousness constitutes *falling asleep*—how will I get home?"

Gertrude chuckled. "The watch makes the rules, not medical science. As far as it was concerned ye fell asleep and whatever word ye said last is the return word."

"But I don't know what that was. Ye said I hit my head? That must be why I'm having trouble remembering."

"I expect it is. At the moment, yer body and Elsie's soul are at NYU hospital center."

"How is that possible? Ye said a second would pass for every day I was in the past. I haven't even been here twenty-four hours. My body should still be in the cab."

"As I said, things didn't happen quite the way they normally do. Time has become equal."

"What does that mean?"

"One day here, is one day there. Time is equal in both places. I don't believe that has ever happened before. It might be simply because the watch stayed in the future."

"Ye said I'm at NYU. There's a trauma center there…was I seriously injured?"

"Not as bad as others in that pile-up. A broken arm, a couple of broken ribs and a few lacerations. The biggest problem is yer head injury. There seems to be no serious damage, but ye haven't awakened yet. For the moment that's a good thing. Ye—or Elsie, I should say—won't awaken until I am there with her. She will need help understanding what's happened."

"I'll say she will. Poor lass. She'll be all right?"

"Aye, she will. I'll make certain of that."

Elizabeth wasn't sure why she was confident in Gertrude's assessment, but she was. "Ye said several things went wrong."

"Now, 'wrong' is a strong word. Several things didn't go as they usually do."

"Fine. Things are different. There was a wreck so I lost consciousness instead of going to sleep and the watch stayed in the future. Did anything else unexpected happen?"

"Well, ye don't remember the word—but I expect ye will, given a bit of time."

"But I don't have the watch."

"Nay, still that shouldn't pose a huge problem. Once ye remember it, and Elsie wakes up, I can tell her. She'll be able to say it when the time comes."

"But why would she? Ye said she was destined to die."

"Aye, well, that's the other thing that didn't happen in quite the normal way. Ye arrived here a bit early."

"Why does it matter when I arrived?"

"For Elsie's life to be over, she would've had to have made a choice that would lead to her death. In this case, ye'd have had to arrive after Elsie had been ordered to pretend to be a skilled midwife."

"I don't understand."

"Did Laird Macrae threaten ye?"

"Aye, he said he'd have me beaten if I didn't comply."

"Well, Elsie would have chosen the beating. Her moral convictions would not have allowed her to lie to the MacKenzies about her abilities, or lack thereof. Sadly, that beating would ultimately have resulted in her death. But yer souls were exchanged before she knew what was happening—before she made her choice. So she did not set the events into motion. That may also be why time has become equal."

"So Elsie can switch our souls back?"

"I expect she can—if ye remember the word. However, don't worry about it for the moment. Ye have work to do."

"Did I ever have any real choice in this?"

"Of course ye did. Ye chose to accept the watch. Ye intended to try it. Would ye choose to go back right now if ye knew the word?"

"Nay."

"Why?"

"Because I think I may be able to help Lady

MacKenzie."

"So there's another choice ye've made. I suspect by the time ye need the word, ye'll remember it."

Again, Elizabeth wasn't sure why Gertrude's assurance gave her confidence, but it did. "So, what happens now?"

"Ye eat yer porridge."

"Nay, I mean what are the next steps?"

"There is the chess player again. Elizabeth, for now, live in the moment. Ye're a smart lass, and a wonderful doctor."

"How do ye know that?"

Gertrude laughed merrily. "Do ye believe our meeting was left completely to chance?"

Elizabeth shook her head, but smiled. "I really didn't have a choice."

"Of course ye did—but I knew ye'd make the right one."

Chapter 6

Cade hadn't seen Elsie since she had followed Laird MacLennan into the keep. For that matter he hadn't seen Laird MacLennan either. MacLennan servants had provided him and his men with food and sleeping quarters the previous evening. Now the sun was well up, the snow had tapered off and the sky was clearing. They had long since finished their morning meal. Cade would tarry a few days—if it were necessary for Elsie to help the lad. But if she was unable to do anything more than the MacLennan healers, he was anxious for them to be on their way.

Perhaps sensing Cade's disquiet, Eric asked, "What do ye suppose is happening?"

"I wish I knew."

"I suspect we would have heard something if there were a problem."

"Aye, we probably would've. Still…we really know nothing about her."

Eric laughed. "We don't, but I doubt she's gotten us into a clan war…yet."

Cade shook his head but smiled. "We can only hope."

They waited at least another hour before Laird MacLennan emerged from the stairs to the upper levels, smiling and relaxed. "Sir Cade, I don't believe I've ever thanked the Almighty for a snowstorm, but yesterday's was truly fortuitous. Had it not been for the storm, ye would not have sought shelter at Brathanead."

"I take it, the Macrae healer proved to be of benefit?"

"Aye, very much so."

"Yer son is better?"

"Not completely, but he is significantly improved and with time and care we're confident he'll recover fully."

Cade was relieved to hear that. "Is she still needed here? It's rather urgent that she see Lady Wynda as soon as possible." This was especially true now he knew he wasn't just relying on instinct. She had proven she had some healing skills at least.

Revelin frowned. "Well...she has taught our healer what needs to be done."

"So we can prepare to leave?"

"I'd prefer ye stay. At least until tomorrow."

"But ye said she isn't needed."

"Cade, she was awake, working to help clear the child's lungs all night. Just after daybreak I insisted that she lie down. She's exhausted and deserves a little rest.

"With all due respect, Laird MacLennan, it seems she's had several hours rest already and surely ye understand it's vitally important we get her to Carraigile as soon as possible. The weather's clear today, but if we tarry too long, we could be delayed by another storm."

"But she'll do ye no good if she falls ill from fatigue."

"She's young and healthy—and completely unable to sit a horse. She'll ride the whole way on my lap anyway. If we leave now we might still be able to reach the Matheson holding tonight and seek shelter there. Then if the weather holds, we can be home late tomorrow."

Revelin did not look pleased but he nodded. "I understand yer urgency. I don't believe one day will make a difference, but after the blessing ye brought us, I won't insist ye stay. Excuse me. I'll return with her shortly."

It was easily another half hour before Laird MacLennan arrived with Elsie. Cade suffered a brief stab of guilt. She did indeed look tired. He consoled himself with what he had told Revelin—she wouldn't be overtaxed by riding on his lap.

Laird MacLennan saw them off. Before Cade lifted

Elsie onto his horse, Revelin took both of her hands. "I'll never be able to adequately thank ye for what ye've done, Elsie."

"Ye're very welcome. I'm glad I was able to help."

"Well know this—I am in yer debt. If ye ever find yerself in need, please seek me out."

Elsie nodded. "Thank ye, Laird."

To Cade he said, "Tell yer father I am indebted to the MacKenzies as well."

Cade thanked him, thinking his debt was probably to Laird Macrae for giving Elsie leave to travel to Carraigile in the first place, but he held his tongue. Being owed a favor by a strong clan was a very good thing.

As they rode out of Brathanead, Cade had another surge of guilt when Elsie rested her head against his chest and closed her eyes. "I know 'twas a hard night and ye're very tired. I would have liked to have allowed ye to stay and rest—"

"Don't worry—I understand. I'm anxious to see Lady MacKenzie too. There may be something I can do, so the sooner I see her the better. But ye don't mind if I just close my eyes for a bit do ye?"

He chuckled. "I have never minded having a beautiful woman sleep in my arms."

She huffed in exasperation. "Ye're incorrigible."

He leaned down until his lips almost touched her ear. "Ye have no idea," he whispered, delighted to see a blush rise in her cheeks.

Elsie did seem to doze some, although only lightly. Not wanting to disturb her, they rode in silence. However with no other distraction, his attention remained focused on the lovely woman in his lap. At one and twenty, she would have been long married by now, if she had been born a noblewoman. Peasants didn't marry at quite as young an age. They also could follow their desires and choose their own spouses. She wasn't married but had she given her heart to someone? Did she leave a lover behind who pined for her return?

Cade frowned. He wasn't sure why it mattered, but he hoped not.

After several hours Elsie stirred. She blinked her eyes open. She looked confused, even a little scared for a moment, but recovered her composure immediately.

"Ye look surprised. Were ye expecting to awaken in some other man's arms?"

"Frankly, I'm not in the habit of waking in anyone's arms, but if I have to, you'll do."

Cade threw back his head and laughed. "Elsie, ye're unexpected."

"Ye have no idea," she echoed his earlier words back to him.

He laughed again.

Elsie repositioned herself several times over the next few minutes.

"Are ye uncomfortable, lass?"

"Nay. I mean, well, I…uh…need a bit of privacy."

"We're nearing a river and will need to stop for a while to rest and water the horses. Ye'll have yer moment of privacy very soon."

When they reached the river a few minutes later, he pointed Elsie in the direction from which they had just ridden. "Go back a little, into the trees, and find yer *privacy*."

As they tended their mounts, Stephan asked, "Do ye think we can reach the Matheson holding by dark?"

"Nay, I don't. We started too late," Cade answered.

"We might be able to reach Castle MacDonnell if we take a more westerly route," said Eric.

"We probably could," said Sully, "but even if we left there at first light tomorrow, we'd be hard pressed to reach Carraigile by dark."

Cade nodded. "Aye. With this much snow on the

ground, I doubt we could. And if we're destined to spend one cold night out of doors, tonight is the best choice. The sky is clear and it should be dry. If we stop as the sun sets we'll have an hour or so of gloaming to make camp."

~ * ~

Elizabeth was exhausted when Cade and his men stopped just as twilight fell. She thought they must be resting the horses again, but surely their destination wasn't that much farther away. She stood, watching the activity around her, completely confused. Sully had gathered dead wood, brushed the snow off a wide area and was building a fire. Stephan and Eric were removing the horses' tack and Cade was cutting and stacking boughs of fir.

"Make yerself useful, lass, gather some more wood," said Sully.

Elizabeth hadn't slept for more than a few hours in three days. She realized Elsie might have had a good night's sleep on Friday, but even so, she was bone-weary now. All she wanted was to get to where they were going and find a bed. "How much wood do we need?"

"A lot more than this if we intend to have a bit of warmth through the night."

Through the night? "We're staying here?"

Sully looked at her as if she were a total idiot. "Aye, lass. That would be why we're making camp."

Sleep outside, in frigid weather, with little more than the clothes on her back?

As if reading her thoughts, Sully ordered, "Go! Ye'll be no happier about this if the fire burns out in the night."

Shaking her head, she walked away from them, looking for dead wood. By the time she had brought back several armloads, she was ready to drop. Cade had made piles of fir boughs around the fire. The blanket that had been wrapped around the bundle of Elsie's belongings ad been spread over one pile. The fir branches must be makeshift beds.

She started to go get more wood but Cade stopped her. "That's enough, lass. Ye look exhausted. Come, sit and have something to eat before ye drop."

He guided her to where her blanket was spread and she sank onto it. The remainder of her bundle was there too, as well as another folded blanket. The boughs were springy and there were enough of them to keep her off the damp ground. Not a bed exactly, but not bad, all things considered. When she was seated, he handed her a costrel of water, a piece of dried meat and what appeared to be a dense, dry bread made from oats.

Before she had finished eating, Cade sat beside her with his food. The other men seemed to be settling down on the fir boughs too. Elizabeth realized there were only four piles. Clearly Cade intended to sleep next to her. She opened her mouth to voice an objection and shut it just as quickly. There were worse things than snuggling next to a big, strong, handsome man on a cold night.

When she finished eating, she drew her knees to her chest and rested her head on them. The warmth of the fire on her face was pleasant and she closed her eyes. She had never been good at doing nothing, so her thoughts drifted to the cab ride from the airport. She tried to remember what the cabby had looked like. If she could get an image of him in her head, she might be able to recall what they had talked about.

"What troubles ye, Elsie?" Cade's question startled her.

She opened her eyes to see his bright blue eyes twinkling in the firelight and looking intently at her. "Nothing. I'm just tired."

"I expect ye are, but tired people usually look relaxed. Yer brow was furrowed as if something worried ye."

"I…I…well, I was thinking about…home."

"Home in general, or perhaps someone special?"

She frowned. *There's no one special* was on the tip of her tongue until she realized she wasn't sure if there was or not. Laird Macrae had said she had no family and nothing held her there. She didn't think she had someone special, but a vague sense of longing from deep within her made her stop. Perhaps it was one of Elsie's memories leaking through. "Just home."

Cade captured her gaze for a moment. "Well, put whatever ye're worrying over aside now. There is nothing ye can do about it and ye need to rest. We all do." He turned his attention to his men. "Sully, ye take the first watch, then Eric, me and the last watch will be Stephan's."

"Since I'll be sitting up, ye can have a kip here on my bed," said Sully.

Cade grinned. "Nay, since the lass feels certain she can *restrain* herself, and thus I'm in no fear of my virtue, I think I'll avail myself of her warmth tonight."

Elizabeth rolled her eyes. "I'm not sure why ye find that so amusing."

"Because ye believe it's true."

Elizabeth laughed. "I'm going to sleep." She laid down on her blanket, reaching for the far edge to wrap around her.

Cade stopped her. "Nay, lass. There is a much better way to keep each other warm." He laid down beside her, pulling her to his chest and wrapping his plaid around her. Then he covered them both with the other blanket.

She pretended to be unaffected by this intimate arrangement, grabbing her bundle and putting it under her head for a pillow. However, if truth were told, she wanted to melt into his embrace and never leave. *Spooned by a Highland Warrior*. She smiled to herself. It sounded like a romance novel. A *hot* romance novel.

Once she was settled he nearly undid her forced composure. His warm breath caressed her cheek as he whispered, "Good night, Elsie," and then planted a kiss behind her ear.

She should have scolded him for his inappropriate behavior, but all she could muster was, "Good night, Sir Cade."

Wrapping his left arm around her, he pulled her even tighter against him, then casually rested his hand on her right breast. Elsie was beginning to understand why no lass had ever said no. He was a tsunami of scorching masculine sexuality. If they had been alone, she was not sure she would have turned him down.

She closed her eyes and for just a moment thought about what it would be like to make love with him. Even as she reveled in the delightful imaginings, she realized she could never give in to those desires. She wasn't Elizabeth Quinn the independent, responsible, twenty-first century woman. She was a twenty-one year old, unmarried, medieval girl.

If the pocket watch had worked as it was supposed to, Elizabeth would have been less worried. No harm could be done; Elsie's life would have been over anyway. But now it appeared that wasn't the case. Once she had taken care of Lady MacKenzie—and remembered the word—she and Elsie would switch places again. It would be irresponsible and morally wrong to make a decision of that magnitude, and risk pregnancy, when she wouldn't be the one to have to deal with the consequences.

That thought was sobering enough to quench her rising desire. She sighed and gave in to sleep.

Chapter 7

The sun was setting at the end of their third day of travel. While riding horseback on the lap of a drool-worthy warrior, had its appeal, Elizabeth was ready for the trip to end. They had risen before dawn, eaten a breakfast of oatcakes and cheese, and were on their way as the first rays of daylight breached the horizon.

Elizabeth had slept surprisingly well. Cade had kept her comfortably warm most of the night. She smiled thinking back to her college days when the other girls—all significantly older than Elizabeth—had said that the best heater for a chilly dorm room was an "Armstrong" heater. Then they would laugh and say: *two strong arms to keep me warm*. That variety of Armstrong heater had kept her warm as they rode as well. By midmorning the skies had turned leaden and the damp cold wind penetrated her many layers of clothing.

She had been too tired the previous day to form cogent thoughts, much less carry on a dialog. But a great deal earlier in the day, in an attempt to pass the time, she had tried to engage Cade in conversation. She found it somewhat one-sided as she asked questions and he gave short answers.

"Where exactly is Carraigile?"

"It is on the west coast of the Highlands."

"Is it actually on the coast?"

"It's on a mountain loch but ye can see the ocean from the upper battlements."

"I'd like to see that." Elizabeth loved the ocean and she missed it. She had grown up in Maryland, but did her

residency in Cincinnati, and—at least for the time being—
had decided to stay there.

"Is this the first time ye've left the Macrae village?"

"Aye." Very technically it was the first time Elizabeth
had left Macrae land because two days ago was the first
time she was ever on Macrae land. But deep within, she
knew that Elsie had never travelled beyond her clan's
territory.

He said no more. After several minutes, she tried
again. "So, I am assuming the current Lady MacKenzie is
not yer mother."

"Nay, she isn't."

"How old were ye when ye lost yer mother?"

"Three."

"And how old were ye when yer father remarried?"

"Twelve."

"How old is Lady MacKenzie?"

"Thirty-five. Ye are very full of impertinent questions
today."

She went silent, realizing that she had been firing off
questions like a doctor gathering information, and it might
have seemed rude. It reminded her of the cabbie who drove
her from the airport.

Holy cow, that's it. The cabbie had asked tons of
questions and Elizabeth had tried to shut him down with
one-word answers. She just needed to remember the things
he had asked. One of the answers had to be the return word.

"Lass, ye are very bold, but I was teasing. Ye can ask
what ye wish."

"Nay, that's fine. I'll find out what I need to know
from Lady MacKenzie." She didn't want to talk anymore
anyway. She wanted to think about the cab ride. She
remembered telling the man she was a doctor and hoping
that telling him she was an OB-GYN would make him stop
asking questions.

She had been lost in thought when Cade whispered, "I

truly didn't mind answering yer questions."

"Then maybe ye shouldn't have suggested I was being impertinent."

That comment had put a fairly quick end to any more conversation. Perhaps it too was impolite, but having remembered the cabbie, she had wanted to figure out what she might have said to him. His wife had had a baby and he asked a lot of questions about labor and delivery, but the last question she remembered answering was: "Hey, what does the 'C' in C-section stand for?" The word might be *Caesarian*, but she thought more had been said.

Now, hours later, she had been unable to remember any additional details and her head hurt from trying.

The wind was picking up sharply and it started to snow. She closed her eyes and rested her head on his chest.

"Are ye sleepy, lass?"

"Not exactly. Just a bit travel weary, I guess."

"Well, ye'll be glad to know, Carraigile lies just ahead of us."

Elizabeth opened her eyes and, through the swirling snow, she could just make out the shape of a castle in the distance. It stood on a hill, on the opposite bank of a small loch. It took nearly an hour to reach the castle after they had spotted it. Elizabeth guessed that was probably a good thing from a defensive standpoint. The inhabitants of the castle could see invaders well in advance of their arrival.

When they finally rode into the inner bailey, Elizabeth just stared in wonder. It appeared to be considerably larger than either the Macrae keep or Brathanead

Cade said, "Welcome to Carraigile." He dismounted, then lifted Elizabeth down. Giving his mount to a waiting stable hand, he led her to the hall, followed by the men who had accompanied them. Before entering he said, "While I have found yer bold manner amusing, my father will not. Hold yer tongue, lass. Only speak if ye are spoken to. Do ye understand me?"

Elizabeth couldn't hold in the exasperated huff. "Aye. I understand."

They entered the hall to find the evening meal well underway. Sully and Stephan took seats at the trestle tables, but Cade led Elizabeth to the laird's table, followed by Eric.

The man who sat at the head of the table was an older, more somber version of Cade. As soon as he saw Elizabeth, he frowned. "Son, welcome home. When ye hadn't returned earlier today, I began to worry."

"All is well, Da. The weather slowed us a bit but we were successful. Laird Macrae allowed Elsie, here, to return with us."

Elizabeth bobbed a curtsy instinctively. She kind of hated that she did that, but she supposed it was expected and she'd be considered "bold" if she didn't.

"That…that…*lass* is the famed Macrae midwife? What is Macrae trying to put over on us?"

Here we go again.

"I had the same doubts about her, but both she and Laird Macrae assured me there was no one better able to help Lady Wynda."

"He lied to ye."

"Ye might think so, but she has already demonstrated remarkable healing skills. We stopped at Brathanead to shelter from the storm two nights ago. Young Kelvin MacLennan was dreadfully ill."

A very slender, dark-haired woman, sitting on Laird MacKenzie's left appeared instantly concerned. "Oh, no. They've lost so many bairns. Maeve must have been beside herself with worry."

"They both were, my lady, but Elsie spent the night caring for the lad and turned things around. He is expected to fully recover. Laird MacLennan said to tell ye he is in yer debt, Da."

"This child saved young Kelvin's life?"

I am not a child, was on the tip of her tongue. Cade gave her a quelling look before answering, "Aye, Da."

Laird MacKenzie turned his attention to Elizabeth. "Ye're Macrae's famous midwife?"

Technically, no. "I have been training for over eight years in my profession."

"Ye didn't answer my question."

"Laird MacKenzie, it's clear ye won't believe me regardless of my answer. The truth is, there's no one in Scotland who is better able to attend Lady MacKenzie than I am, but ye've already judged me unworthy simply because of my age. Nothing I can say is likely to convince ye otherwise."

Laird MacKenzie's eyes narrowed with anger.

Cade scowled. "Elsie, I warned ye—"

"Ye warned me not to speak unless I was spoken to, and yer father spoke to me." Elizabeth turned to Lady MacKenzie, ignoring the two men. "My lady, I believe I might know what the problem is and how to manage it. I can stand here and waste my breath trying unsuccessfully to convince yer husband that I know what I'm doing, or ye can let me examine ye and draw yer own conclusions."

Laird MacKenzie looked stunned.

Cade looked irritated.

Lady MacKenzie canted her head and considered Elizabeth for a moment. "Come with me. Lilliana would ye come with us too? Angus, my love, please send someone for Morag."

"Wynda, this lass—"

"May be dissembling. I know, and ye're right. But so is she. Her assertions will not be enough to convince ye. The only way to know for sure is to let her prove it."

Laird MacKenzie scowled at Elizabeth and then looked into his wife's eyes. The love and concern Elizabeth saw in his gaze was unlike anything she had ever witnessed. What must it be like to be adored? In a gentler tone she asked,

"Laird MacKenzie, please let me help yer wife."

He softened a little. "Wynda, if this is what ye wish, I will allow it."

Lady MacKenzie gave him a heart-melting smile.

"But, lass, be warned, if I find out this has all been a ruse, ye'll regret it. And there isn't a deep enough pit in hell to hide Laird Macrae from my wrath."

Lady MacKenzie shook her head as she stood. "Angus, cool yer temper until we know more." Another woman stood too and together they guided Elizabeth out of the hall and up the stairs.

"Elsie, this is Lady Lilliana, my sister by marriage. Her husband, Sir Hamish, is Laird MacKenzie's younger brother."

"Good evening, my lady. Are ye Sir Eric's mother then?"

The lady smiled. "Aye, Elsie, I am."

"It's lovely to meet ye both."

"I trust Eric and Cade behaved themselves on the journey?" Lilliana's eyes danced with mirth, suggesting that she suspected the contrary.

Elizabeth smiled. "Sir Eric was a perfect gentleman."

Amused, Lady MacKenzie added, "And Cade was a bit of a rogue."

"A bit. But I've handled worse."

Both women laughed.

When they reached the bedchamber, Lilliana lit candles. Lady MacKenzie asked, "How would ye like to proceed, Elsie?"

"First, I'd just like to ask ye some questions." She motioned towards a table and chairs near the hearth. "Shall we sit?"

Lady MacKenzie nodded, taking one of the chairs. Elsie too sat and Lilliana joined them once the room was sufficiently well lit.

"My lady, when did yer courses come last?"

"The middle of November. But they don't always come as they should, thus I didn't think anything about missing them in December. But when I realized I was more tired than usual and they didn't come in January, I suspected I was carrying. Morag confirmed it."

Elizabeth asked her about her other pregnancies and although she knew generally what had happened, Lady MacKenzie told her the sad story. Elizabeth probed for details as sensitively as she could. Learning that Wyna had carried the first baby into the seventh month and that he lived for a few hours was heartbreaking. With twenty-first century technology, it was highly likely that son would be alive today.

By the time Elizabeth had learned Wynda MacKenzie's full history, Morag, the midwife, had arrived. Elizabeth had been a bit worried. She had feared that Morag might see her as a threat, but she was pleasantly surprised. Morag was a sturdy, no-nonsense, older woman who only wanted the best for her lady. She seemed fully prepared to give Elizabeth an opportunity to prove herself.

"Thank ye for answering my questions, my lady. It is important for me to know all that has happened so far."

"I understand," said Lady Wynda.

"I promise ye, I'll do everything possible to keep it from happening again. May I examine ye?"

"Aye, lass." Lady MacKenzie gave her a small sad smile. "That is why we've brought ye here is it not?"

Elizabeth smiled. "Aye, it is."

Elizabeth helped her onto the bed and examined her gently. When she was through she sat beside her. "My lady, just as ye suspect, ye are about three months pregnant and I expect the baby is due near the end of August. I think I know what the problem in the past might have been." How was she going to explain an incompetent cervix to three medieval women?

"The problem?"

"Aye. The opening to a woman's womb usually remains firm and closed until the baby is ready. Then it softens and opens, allowing the baby to be born. But sometimes this softening happens early. Then the weight of the developing baby pushes on it, forcing it open too early."

"And this is what's wrong?"

"Aye, my lady. The opening to your womb isn't strong enough to hold the baby under normal circumstances."

"How do ye know that?" asked Morag, appearing truly interested.

"The number of miscarriages she's had and the fact that they have occurred well into each pregnancy is the most telling. However, even now the opening to her womb is beginning to shorten."

Tears filled Wynda's eyes. "So there is nothing ye can do?"

There were lots of things Elizabeth could do in the twenty-first century. However even if she had the proper equipment, they were not without risk. But thankfully there was something very basic they could try. "Actually, we can do something. It's simple really. It's the pressure of the baby as it grows that opens the womb. If we put ye on strict bed rest—I mean lying in bed, flat or on yer left side, not even sitting up—the pressure is removed."

"Lie in bed? For six months?"

"My lady, if ye had carried all of yer pregnancies into the fifth month or later, I might be comfortable waiting a bit, but ye lost the last one at barely four months. If ye go into labor, there is nothing I can do, so we must do everything possible to delay labor as long as we can."

"What do ye think, Morag?" Lady Wynda asked.

"I've never heard anything like this. But it makes a certain kind of sense."

"So, Elsie, if I stay in bed, the bairn will be all right?"

"If ye stay in bed, there is a chance, a good chance that ye can carry the babe long enough. Mind ye, ye can only get up to use the chamber pot. Also, ye must not...uh...have marital relations. And when the babe is bigger we may need to put blocks under the foot of the bed. That will take more of the baby's weight off of the opening to yer womb."

"That's all?"

"Aye, my lady, I'm sorry."

"Sorry? Why? Ye have given me hope and I agree with Morag, what ye say makes sense."

"It still may not be enough, but I know it can work."

Lady Wynda's gaze locked with hers. "Elsie, I would do nearly anything to keep from losing this bairn. I have prayed constantly to the Blessed Virgin since the first moment I suspected I was carrying. I am willing to believe ye are the answer to my prayers."

That statement nearly took Elizabeth's breath away. No one had ever said anything like that to her.

Turning to her sister-in-law, Wynda said, "Lilliana, would ye help manage the running of this household for the next six months?"

"Wynda, ye needn't even ask. Of course I will."

"Would ye start by seeing that Elsie is given a chamber?"

Before Lilliana could answer, Morag said, "My lady, she is welcome to stay with me in my cottage."

"That is kind of ye, Morag. And I am happy for her to help ye in yer work, but I'd prefer if she stayed within the keep. Honestly, Lilliana, I would like her given a room on this floor."

Lilliana nodded. "If that would give ye peace of mind, I'll see it done."

"Now, lass, ye were barely through the door and we brought ye up before ye could eat even a morsel of supper. Lilliana will see that ye're fed and I expect after three days on the road, ye might like a bath."

"Aye, my lady, I would. Thank ye." Elizabeth was sure

she had never needed a bath more in her life.

"I'll see to it, Wynda."

"One more thing," added Elizabeth, "since Lady MacKenzie must stay flat, I would be more comfortable if someone is always with her."

"Aye, that's wise. I'll send Alice up to help ye."

"Thank ye, Lilliana. I too think I would feel better if I wasn't alone and if Elsie wants me to lie down, I may as well start now."

Lilliana reached out and squeezed Wynda's hand. "By the Grace of God, these months will fly and, come harvest time, we will celebrate a new life."

Wynda nodded, holding onto Lilliana's hand as if it were a life-line.

Elizabeth was awed by the love and friendship between the two women. She couldn't think of anyone in her life with whom she felt that kind of closeness. She was suddenly struck with the single-minded desire to bring this baby into the world. *Get that thought out of your head, Elizabeth. You will return to the twenty-first century long before then.*

~ * ~

"Cade, by all that's good and holy, how could ye possibly believe that lass was a midwife?" his father asked.

"Da, ye saw her. Have ye ever encountered a young common lass who would speak to a nobleman as she just did? With the impunity of a peer? She firmly believes she can assist Wynda. And she was able to help Kelvin MacLennan."

"But she's a child."

"I know, and I can't explain it, but I'm certain she's telling us the truth. Still, we'll know more after Morag and Aunt Lilliana have taken the measure of her."

Nearly three quarters of an hour later, when the meal had been cleared and only his father, Eric and Uncle

Hamish remained at the table, Lilliana and Morag returned to the hall with Elsie.

"Well?" demanded Angus.

"Elsie thinks she knows what the problem is and she has told us what to do about it," answered Aunt Lilliana.

"Do ye believe her?"

"Aye, Angus, I do."

"Morag, do ye?"

"Aye, Laird. Elsie, perhaps ye should explain it to the Laird."

Elsie frowned and hesitated. "I would prefer not to talk about Lady MacKenzie's condition to others without her being present."

"Nonsense," roared Laird MacKenzie. "I'm her husband and her laird. Not to mention that for the time being I'm yer laird as well, and ye're trying my patience. Tell me now."

Elsie sighed. "All right, if ye insist." She proceeded to tell them about the problem.

Angus frowned. "The opening of her womb is weak? I've never heard of such a thing."

Morag jumped to her aid. "I've never heard it explained as she did. But it makes sense and I have known other women, seemingly healthy women, who couldn't ever carry a bairn past the sixth or seventh month. And just like it has been with Lady Wynda, the babes seemed to be perfectly normal too, just too small to live."

"All she has to do is stay in bed?"

Elsie nodded. "Aye. Flat in bed, and…"

"And what?"

"Now that I think on it, perhaps it would be better if Lady MacKenzie tells ye."

His father practically growled. "I asked ye to tell me and ye will answer me. *Now.*"

Elsie cocked her head to one side putting her hands on her hips and fixing him with a stern look. "Well, if ye insist. Ye and Lady MacKenzie must not engage in…marital relations."

Cade could barely keep from laughing at the shocked expression on his father's face. That slip of a lass had left him speechless. Uncle Hamish looked equally as shocked. Cade suspected that his father and step-mother's *marital relations* had never been so publically addressed. Still, his father had asked for it.

Aunt Lilliana looked as if she was having trouble containing her own mirth. It was Morag who stepped in. "Well now, Elsie hasn't eaten and would like a bath. I'll just show her to the kitchen on my way out." She took Elsie's elbow, guiding her quickly out the back of the hall.

They were barely out the door when his father finally found his voice. "Well, I'll be damned."

Cade grinned. "Nay, Da, ye won't be damned, just sorely vexed by a cheeky, young, midwife."

His Aunt Lilliana frowned, "Why is it if a young warrior arrived full of bold confidence and proved himself to be worthy, yer description of him would glow with praise, but when a lass demonstrates equally admirable skills, she's 'cheeky'?"

Her husband, Hamish, barked a laugh. "That's a silly question. It's because she's a lass not a warrior."

She just shook her head, saying under her breath, "Grant me strength," before adding, "pardon me, please, I must see that a chamber is readied for her."

"A chamber?" Angus asked.

Cade too was a bit surprised at that. He expected that she would sleep in the great hall as many of the people who worked in the keep did.

"Aye, Angus. Wynda wants her close."

That was all it took to stop any argument. Cade knew his father would grant Wynda anything that was within his power.

Chapter 8

"Did ye do that a'purpose, Elsie?" Morag asked, after they were out of earshot.

"What?"

"Embarrass Laird MacKenzie."

"Oh, I didn't do that. He managed it all on his own. I tried to keep it all private and he pushed for details."

Morag stifled a chuckle. "Perhaps so, but ye might want to avoid giving him those opportunities in the future. He is a good man and a good laird, but I suspect ye might not see much of that side of him if ye goad him like that."

"Then I suspect he should be careful pushing me for details he might not want to hear in front of others."

She did chuckle at that. "Ye are an odd lass, Elsie. But ye've given Lady MacKenzie some much needed hope."

Like Brathanead, the kitchen at Carraigile was a separate building outside the keep. Morag introduced her to Ellen, the head cook before saying, "I'll leave ye now. Ellen will see ye fed and show ye to the bathing room."

Bathing room? Before Elizabeth could think too much about that, Ellen ushered her into a chair at the kitchen table and sat a bowl of rich stew in front of her. "There, lass, eat up. There's plenty more if ye're still peckish when that's done."

The stew was warm, filling and, while she wasn't certain what the meat was, it was delicious. She'd had nothing warm to eat since the porridge Gertrude had made for her at Brathanead early yesterday morning.

She was just finishing her last few bites when a girl of about nineteen came through a door in the back of the kitchen, holding the bundle of Elsie's things. The girl smiled shyly at Elizabeth.

"Deirdre, lass, do ye need something?" asked Ellen.

"Nay." She just stood there holding the bundle, looking confused.

Ellen shook her head—a bit exasperated. "Deirdre, if ye don't need anything, what have ye come for?"

The girl blushed furiously. "Oh…right…Lady Lilliana asked me to bring the new midwife her belongings. She said I was to help her get a bath and then show her to the chamber she's been given. I've started heating the water already."

"Well then, Elsie have ye had yer fill?" Ellen asked.

Elizabeth smiled. "Aye, thank ye, it was delicious."

The cook beamed at her. "I'm glad ye liked it.

"And—Deirdre was it? I'm Elsie, thank ye for bringing me my things."

"If ye'll come with me, I'll show ye our bathing room."

Elizabeth had worried about what a medieval bath might be like, but a bathing room sounded promising, and she didn't think she'd ever wanted a bath more. The bathing room turned out to be a room behind the kitchen. It was built over a well, which was evidently the water source for the castle. There was a huge fireplace that shared the same chimney as the kitchen. Iron hooks held pots of water over the flames.

Deirdre showed Elizabeth how to draw cold water from the well to partially fill the tub. When the pots were boiling, she added hot water until the bath was pleasantly warm.

The maid gave her linen toweling and a crock filled with a liquid. Sniffing it, Elizabeth found it had a very pleasant, lavender aroma. "What is this?"

Deirdre's brow drew together, appearing confused by the question. "Do Macrae's not use soapwort for bathing?"

Soapwort? That was something a healer probably should have known. Elizabeth bluffed. "Aye, Deirdre, but it has something else in it. Lavender?"

Deirdre smiled and nodded. "Aye, sometimes we add lavender or rose petals when making it. Do ye like it?"

"Aye, I do. It has a lovely fragrance."

Deirdre beamed, clearly pleased. "Well, we'd best get ye in the tub before the water cools. I'll help ye."

Help her? "I don't need help bathing."

The maid blushed. "I'm sorry. I forgot ye aren't a noblewoman. Ye seem so important. I'll just bank the fire and leave a couple of pitchers of hot water here beside the tub to rinse yer hair with."

That was good; Elizabeth had no idea how to bank a fire. "Thank ye."

"Do ye need anything else?"

"Nay, I don't think so. Thank ye."

"When ye're done, ye can pull this plug." Deirdre showed her a wooden plug stoppering a hole on the back side of the tub. When the plug was pulled, it would empty in to a curved wooden channel that sloped downward and through an opening in the wall.

"Where does the water go?"

"Outside."

Elizabeth smiled. "That much is apparent. Where does it go after that?"

Deirdre blushed. "Of course, that was silly of me. The channel carries the water far enough away from the building to where it can drain into the ground."

Elizabeth nodded. It was a relatively good way to discard "grey water" and certainly made emptying the tub easy.

"If ye don't need me, then, I'll wait for ye in the great hall. It is probably best if ye go there to dry yer hair. The fires are larger and hotter, it'll dry more quickly. Then I'll show ye to yer chamber. I expect ye're tired after traveling for so long."

"Thank ye, Deirdre, I am tired."

When Deirdre had left, Elizabeth undressed and climbed into the tub. The hot bath was a little slice of heaven after three days of travel. She had a large soaking tub in her bathroom at home that, with the push of a button, became a whirlpool. She had never actually used it but as she closed her eyes, enjoying the tranquility of soaking in this little wooden tub, she wondered why.

Sadly, the water began to cool too soon. She sighed, opened her eyes and began to wash with the soapwort solution. She was struck again by how very willowy Elsie was. Elizabeth had never thought of herself as beautiful, at least not by twenty-first century standards. She was too short and much too curvy. She marveled at the feel of Elsie's long, slender legs and the delicate curve of her hips to a narrow waist. She had given up a bit of real-estate in her bust, but what she had now could only be described as *perky*. That was certainly different. She giggled to herself. Elsie had the kind of body most modern men loved. Of course she might not have a particularly attractive face— Elizabeth didn't know since she still hadn't seen her own reflection—but Cade had certainly been interested. Smiling, she thought that probably said more about his intense sexuality than it did about her appearance.

Still the idea of such a beautiful man making love to her was tempting. *Nay, Elizabeth, don't even let yourself imagine that*. This wasn't her body and she would not make casual decisions that might have far-reaching consequences.

She sighed and finished her bath by washing her hair and rinsing it with the pitchers of hot water. Elizabeth climbed out of the tub, chilling almost instantly. She wrapped herself in the linen toweling and grabbing her bundle, moved close to the fire. She removed the belt and blanket. She had used the blanket the previous evening but hadn't delved into the rest of Elsie's things. As it turned out the girl had very little—a few clothes, a pin that appeared to be silver and a comb. Elizabeth put on fresh undergarments, wrapped the blanket around her shoulders and sat by the fire to comb out Elsie's long chestnut colored hair. The air was getting cold as the fire died low, so she worked quickly, getting as many tangles out as she could before braiding it loosely. She would do as Deirdre suggested and finish drying it in front of a warmer fire. She put on clean outer garments, pulled the plug on the tub, and rerolled the bundle of Elsie's belongings before leaving the bathing room and making her way back to the keep.

~ * ~

At the sound of the rear door opening, Cade glanced towards it. He smiled as Elsie stepped tentatively into the hall. This was the first time he had seen her looking unsure of herself. She clutched her bundle to her chest and glanced around nervously, until her eyes lit on Deirdre.

The young maid hurried towards her. "Elsie, come sit close to the fire to dry yer hair. There's no hearth in the room that's been prepared for ye—only a small brazier. Ye'll take a chill if ye go to bed with wet hair." She ushered Elsie to the hearth on the opposite side of the hall. Elsie loosened her damp braid and leaning her head towards the fire, worked a comb through it. The women were too far away for him to hear their conversation, but he found it oddly erotic to watch Elsie comb her wet hair as it dried into a rich brown cloud touched with gold. She was beautiful and very desirable.

Long after the evening meal was over, Cade had stayed at the table drinking ale with Eric. Before Elsie returned, he had glanced towards the rear door every time someone came through it.

After he had done this several times, Eric nudged him. "Are ye expecting someone?"

Cade frowned. "Of course I am. I intend to caution her one more time about her sharp tongue."

Eric had been clearly amused. "Ah, it's her sharp tongue ye're thinking about."

"Aye, if she doesn't rein it in—around Da at least—ye can be certain there will be consequences." Cade grinned at Eric's skeptical expression. "I won't deny also being intrigued by her. She is...unusual."

Eric had snorted at Cade's choice of words. "That's an understatement. She's very pretty—if a bit too thin. Still, this is unlike you. You're usually drawn to the lassies who are first drawn to ye."

"Aye, usually. But she's perhaps the most alluring woman I've ever encountered, and I'm not sure I want anyone else to discover her charming wee self until I've had the chance to prove her wrong."

"About what?"

"About being able to restrain herself and resist my charms."

Eric had chuckled. "This is definitely going to be entertaining. She's not just going to fall into yer bed as most lassies do."

"Lassies don't fall into my bed."

"False modesty isn't becoming. Ye can't deny that ye've never had to work much to gain a lass's attention. But ye'll have to work for this one. Perhaps the fact that she won't be easy to win will make victory all the sweeter."

"Ye're an arse, Eric."

"I'm an arse because ye've let a lass get under yer skin?"

"Nay, ye're an arse because ye keep braying on about foolish things."

"Foolish things...now I'm glad ye mentioned that because enticing that bossy little bit into yer bed might be exceedingly foolish."

"Why, pray tell, do ye think it would it be different from a tumble with any other willing lass?"

"It probably wouldn't be if she hadn't gotten under yer

skin." Cade had scowled at him but Eric went on, ignoring his cousin's displeasure. "And frankly, it might not matter quite as much if she were a clanswoman. The romance would run its course, or if it didn't, yer da might be convinced to let ye marry within the clan."

Cade hadn't been able to keep from snorting. "*That* would be foolish, and highly unlikely."

"But still possible."

"Aye, I suppose it's remotely possible. So, since we are discussing the extremely improbable, why would she be different from any other common lass?"

"Because that common lass belongs to Laird Macrae, not yer da. She has to be returned to him, and likely very soon. It would seem that she's already done all she can do. Wynda doesn't require the attention of a midwife for the next six months—she just needs to stay in bed. And there's no chance under heaven that Laird Macrae will allow someone with her skills to stay here forever. She's a valuable asset to his clan. I expect he'd sooner marry ye to one of his wee lassies."

"They're bairns."

"My point exactly. He wouldn't make such a betrothal. And that's what daughters are for—making alliances."

Cade had arched an eyebrow at his cousin. "Ye might want to avoid ever saying that to the lass ye find yerself betrothed to."

"'Twas a jest, but ye know I'm right. Macrae won't allow her to stay here. So if ye do manage to win her, don't make more of it than it is."

"Why are ye worried? I haven't lost my heart to a lass yet."

Eric had shrugged. "This one seems different."

"Ye're daft. She's just an attractive lass."

"Perhaps, but never say I didn't warn ye."

"I won't because the warning was completely unnecessary. Make no mistake, Eric, I would never make a decision that would not be in this clan's best interests. I am intrigued by her, but I am in no danger of losing my heart."

Eric had barked a laugh. "I believe ye, thousands wouldn't."

"Arse," muttered Cade.

"Well, coz, after almost six days in the saddle and sleeping on the frozen ground most nights, ye can wait alone to tangle with that lass's sharp tongue," his innuendo was clear. "I'm going to bed. Good night," he had called over his shoulder as he left.

Now, as Cade watched the beautiful lass from a distance, it irritated him to admit, even to himself—his cousin had been right. He was drawn to Elsie in a way he never had been to any other lass before her. He'd spent much of the last three days in her company—hell most of that time, she'd been on his lap with his arms around her— and he'd quite enjoyed it. Perhaps it was just the thrill of the chase, but there was no question he desired her.

Elsie had evidently finished drying her hair, because she confined it once again in a long braid before picking up her small bundle.

That was his cue. He stood and crossed the hall towards the entrance to the tower stairs, reaching it just as Deirdre and Elsie did. "And where are ye lovely lassies going?"

Deirdre smiled shyly and curtsied. "Good evening, Sir Cade. I promised Lady Lilliana I'd see to Elsie. I'm showing her to her chamber."

"Ye needn't bother, I can do that. It's late, I'm going up to my own chamber and I need to speak with Elsie anyway. Which room did my aunt have prepared?"

"The small one at the end of the corridor, just down from the Laird's chamber, sir."

"Well then, Elsie, after ye." He motioned towards the stairs. "Good night, Deirdre."

"Good night, sir." She bobbed another curtsy.

Elsie frowned but didn't argue. He followed as she climbed the stairs. The enticing scent of lavender trailed in her wake. When they reached the landing, he placed his hand in the small of her back and guided her down the corridor, stopping in front of the last door.

Turning to face him with her back to the door she said, "Ye told Deirdre ye needed to speak with me."

His lips twitched as he suppressed a smile. She actually believed she was going to control this encounter. He leaned in close, gaining no small bit of satisfaction on hearing her breath hitch as he did. Reaching behind her, he lifted the latch and opened her door. "After ye."

She blushed but didn't move. "Ye don't need to come in to tell me whatever's on yer mind."

"Aye. I do." He took hold of her shoulders, turned her around and gently pushed her inside the room before closing the door behind him.

Once inside she spun to face him. "What right do ye have—"

He put a finger on her lips, silencing her. "Not another word."

"How da—"

He silenced her again. This time he put his hand behind her neck pulled her to him, crushing his lips to hers. She was warm and soft and tasted as sweet as he had imagined. When he felt her begin to respond, he broke the kiss, letting go and taking a step back.

He had to stifle a smile again at her flustered expression.

Her mouth opened once more, as if to speak, and he held up one hand. "Ye'll remain silent, or I'll give yer tongue something better to do until ye learn how to keep it still."

She scowled, her lips pressed into a hard line, but she said nothing.

"That's a good lass."

If anything, her scowl deepened.

"Now, over the last few days I've repeatedly told ye to mind yer tongue. This very evening, I'm certain those words were barely out of my mouth before ye stirred my father's ire. Ye told me ye hadn't spent much time in Laird Macrae's company but surely ye know better than to speak to him as ye did to my father. The Macrae is not known for his gentle nature and I'm certain ye would have paid dearly if ye'd shown him such impudence."

Elsie remained quiet but fear flitted briefly across her features.

If that's what it took, he would use it. "By contrast, my father is a much more tolerant man, but Lady Wynda's wishes are all that stayed his hand tonight. Since ye've sent her to bed for six months, it's unlikely she'll be able to stop it again and, as much as I might want to, neither will I."

He saw that flash of fear again and to his surprise, he felt guilty at having been the one to put it there. Still, he'd feel worse if she crossed Da again and suffered because of it. "Lady Wynda needs ye and for that reason, ye've been granted a measure of respect not normally given a lass of no standing. While something tells me 'tis yer bold self-assurance that gives yer clan confidence in ye, ye must remember yer place. Particularly around my father and for that matter, Uncle Hamish too. Elsie, please don't give either of them a reason to punish ye."

Suddenly she looked very young and vulnerable—he hadn't seen that in her before. It stirred something deep within him. He reached out and cupped her cheek in his hand. "I don't want ye hurt. Do ye understand?"

She gave a small nod.

He smiled. "Ye can speak now, lass."

"I have nothing to say."

"Well, that may be a first."

She looked away. He wasn't sure if she was angry or embarrassed. He lifted her chin to peer into her eyes. She had beautiful, silvery gray eyes, which at the moment were unreadable. "I don't know what to make of ye, lass. Ye intrigue me...nearly as much as ye irritate me."

There it was—that flash of spirit returned.

She stepped back, away from his touch. "Well, if I irritate ye so, feel free to take yer leave."

He chuckled. "Not yet. I have one more thing to tell ye."

"What is it?" she demanded with her hands on her hips.

He took a step towards her and pulled her close. "Only that ye might want to mind yer tongue around me too. I won't punish ye, but I'll be only too happy to silence it in my own way." He kissed her again. If he had felt any resistance he would have released her, but on the contrary, she seemed to melt against him. He deepened the kiss, plundering her mouth with his tongue. When he finally pulled away, her cheeks were flushed and, to his delight, she looked a little off balance and starry-eyed.

He winked at her. "I'm glad to see it works."

Regaining her composure, she huffed and rolled her eyes. "Good night, *sir*."

"Good night, Elsie." Cade grinned to himself as he left her chamber. Aye, he'd prove her wrong.

Chapter 9

As tired as she was, Elizabeth lay awake, her head spinning. She couldn't even begin to process her attraction to Cade MacKenzie. She had been in her last year of medical school before she had ever connected with someone enough to date him seriously. That had ended when they had accepted residencies in different cities. Since then she had dated a few men casually, and while she'd enjoyed their company, she had never been so befuddled by one. She wanted Cade's arms around her, his mouth on hers, but good Lord, when he kissed her, every mature, rational thought fled.

She supposed the realities of her presence in the thirteenth century were of more immediate concern. Although Cade had mentioned it several times, she really hadn't taken his cautions about her "boldness" too seriously. She had failed to realize the importance or perhaps more accurately, the lack of importance of her "place" as Cade had called it.

In the twenty-first century not only was she given respect as a doctor, she had also grown up with the privileges afforded by virtue of her family's wealth. But even without that, she was as free to speak to whomever she chose and in whatever manner she saw fit as any American.

However, in the twenty-first century, other than perhaps being snubbed or accused of having a poor "bedside manner," there were no real consequences if she were blunt or discourteous. Here, showing disrespect to the wrong person could apparently result in severe punishment.

As Cade had pointed out, the sad truth was that, as a "lass of no standing", she had *no* power, *no* voice and *no* rights. Pushing back, against that reality, could result in serious consequences.

How could she live like this, even for a short time? How could she assume the submissive attitude that seemed to be required?

Because you weren't asked to be submissive, just respectful.

Elizabeth thought more about her interactions with Laird MacKenzie. She had simply been honest. Well…bluntly honest. Although the things she had said to him were true, she could have been a bit more considerate and less dismissive. She had been angry at once again being judged by her age. But when she looked at it from his point of view, she realized he only wanted the best for his wife. Elsie was even younger than Elizabeth herself was. Could she really blame him for not having faith in an arrogant, sharp-tongued girl?

Furthermore, if she were being honest with herself, she would not have been so blunt when speaking to one of her parents or grandparents, or someone in a position of authority at work. But outside of that, she had to admit, she tended to be direct and probably wasn't always as considerate as she could be. She hadn't been particularly nice to Gertrude when she first met her. Then Elizabeth remembered the cab ride from the airport. The cabby had just been trying to be friendly and she had done her best to shut him down. She couldn't escape the fact that she had been downright rude and now felt acutely embarrassed.

He was a young curious father and had wanted to talk about delivering babies, the profession to which Elizabeth had devoted her life. She had done everything she could to end the conversation, until he finally asked if he could put on some music. She smiled to herself. Even that had become a drawn out affair as he had asked her about her preference in genres. There was one she had never even heard of. What was it? He had asked about Christian rock, salsa, gansta rap and…she knew there was more but she just couldn't remember.

She huffed in frustration. She had popped into the past, saved a little boy's life and offered a pregnant woman hope. Surely that was sufficient. She was ready to go home and have control over her life again.

Control. She gave a mirthless laugh. That was exactly what she and David had argued about after their brunch date.

They had been sitting in the car outside his beautiful home. He had asked her in, but she had declined. "I'm tired. I really should go home and go to bed."

He had said, "Elizabeth, I'm worried about you. You need to take some control of your life back."

"What are you talking about? I have always been in complete control of my life."

"No, you haven't."

"Of course I have. I've plotted my own course and worked single-mindedly to reach my goals. I didn't follow the mold. I graduated from high school at fifteen, when other students my age were just finishing their sophomore year. I received a bachelor's degree just three years later and was one of the youngest students ever accepted into my medical school. And once there, I worked relentlessly to stay at the top of my class."

"And why was that?"

"I wanted to excel, to be the best."

"Hmm. Break it down for me. Why did you work so diligently to finish high school early? You could, and almost certainly still would have excelled if you had taken things more slowly."

"But why take longer than necessary to complete a task?"

"Because it wasn't just a task—it was a life experience, a part of one's social development. So why rush through that? You still could have been the best student, but you might also have been involved in student government. You could have been a peer tutor. You could have been the slowest swimmer on the swim team. You could have sung in the concert choir. You could have taken ceramics."

"I didn't need those things. I wanted to be a doctor. Why plod through the unnecessary?"

"Because those things would have been fun."

"They were of no value to me."

"Look me in the eye and tell me you never longed for ordinary high school experiences."

Elizabeth had actually opened her mouth to say the words—but she couldn't.

David nodded. "That's just what I thought. So if you wanted to do some of those things, they had value to you. Why shun them?"

"Other goals were more important."

"To whom?"

"To me."

"Elizabeth, do you honestly believe that? Tell me, if you had come home one afternoon and announced that you had joined the swim team, what would have happened?"

"Nothing."

"Really? Absolutely nothing?"

"What are you implying? That my parents would have been angry with me or something? They wouldn't have cared."

"And *that* is my point. When your mother managed to pry herself away from her high-powered clients, she wouldn't have said, 'Excellent choice, Elizabeth; that sounds like fun.'? Your father wouldn't have left the hospital early a few times to cheer you on at a meet?"

"My parents work very hard at their careers. So do I. There's nothing wrong with that."

"That's debatable. Tell me this, what was their reaction when you enrolled in every advanced placement course your prep school offered?"

"They were pleased."

"And when you aced them all?"

"They were pleased."

"What does that mean, Elizabeth?"

Her temper was rising. "What do you think it means? They said, 'well done'."

"There was no little celebration for that perfect report card?"

"Of course not. Students are expected to work hard and do their best. I didn't get patted on the head for doing what was expected."

"I see. So the same thing was true in college. You worked hard, you made the highest grades in every class and your parents said, 'well done'."

"Yes, David. You come from the same world I do. Did your parents throw a gala for you every time you did what was expected?"

"No. But when I challenged myself and succeeded, no matter how busy they were, they celebrated that accomplishment with me. Tell me this—did your parents attend your graduations?"

"They were there when I graduated from medical school."

"That's not what I asked, but I have my answer."

"They planned to see me graduate each time, but emergencies came up. My grandparents were at the other graduations."

"Really? The lawyer or the surgeon?"

"Neither of them...but both of my grandmothers were there."

"Will you listen to yourself, Elizabeth? The only time your parents even looked up from their own careers to say 'well done' was when you excelled at academics and even then it was lackluster. You were valedictorian, weren't you?" It had been more a statement than a question.

"Yes."

"All three times?"

"Yes."

"Who doesn't move heaven and earth to see their daughter deliver a valedictory speech? Three times."

"You don't understand."

"The hell I don't. My parents had demanding careers too. You know that. My father is your mother's biggest client. Still, they managed to be at dance recitals and basketball games and concerts, and they were certainly at all of their children's graduations—and none of us were ever valedictorians."

"Look, David, I had a busy night and I'm tired. What exactly is the point of this?"

He shook his head in frustration. "You just very proudly stated that you have *always been in control*. You have *plotted your own course* and worked to reach *your* goals. But that simply is not true. You are the product of your parents' expectations. You said it yourself. Excelling at the hardest courses, getting the best grades, being the first in your class, all of that—it wasn't what you desired, it was simply *expected*. You worked relentlessly to reach your parents' goals for you—perhaps even to gain their approval."

"You're wrong. I wanted those things too."

"Really? I believe you, thousands wouldn't."

"I became an obstetrician. That was my choice."

"Oh, that's right. You broke your mother's heart by choosing medicine instead of law and then you pissed daddy off by not becoming a surgeon. I guess after twenty some years of doing exactly what they both expected, neither one of them were prepared for you to exert your own will in the smallest way. But ever since that little act of defiance you have worked unceasingly to be the best."

"What's wrong with that?"

"Nothing if it gives you satisfaction. But it doesn't. I

think you are still trying to prove something to your parents. You work constantly to show them that you are worthy. Can you deny that?"

She hadn't been able to, so instead of answering his question she countered, "Why are you pushing this?"

"Because I care about you—more than anything. I love you, Elizabeth, and want you in my life. I want to be in your life, but I fear if things keep going as they have been, there is no room for me—or anyone."

"You want me to give up my career? Are you crazy?"

"Of course I don't want you to give up your career. And if you truly loved your work, if it gave you joy, I wouldn't begrudge you a single minute. *But it doesn't.* You work around the clock, driving yourself relentlessly, and you aren't happy. Furthermore, if you continue to rely on your parents' approval to make you happy, you never will be."

Happy? Did she know anyone who was happy? She had been too tired to think about that. "What do you want from me, David?"

"I don't want anything *from* you. I want something *for* you. I want you to find some real control, some balance. I want you to discover what makes you happy—not what you think other people want from you. And once you find your destiny, I want you to embrace it."

"My destiny? I'm doing what I studied for years to do. That is my destiny."

"But is it what you wanted? Are you happy with your life as it is?"

"Of course I am." But even as she had said the words, she'd known they were untrue.

He'd shaken his head sadly. "Well then, there's nothing more to say. You haven't allowed any room in your life for anything but a job that drains you. I love you Elizabeth, but I want more for you. I want more for us. And I don't want to continue watching your futile efforts to be what your parents think you should be. It's sucking the life out of you."

"I don't know what to say, David."

"No, I suppose you don't and I'm sorry." He had taken both of her hands in his, and leaning in, brushed her cheek with a kiss. "I will miss you, my beautiful girl. And someday, I hope you work your way free of *expectations* and allow joy to enter your life." He squeezed her hands before letting them go and getting out of the car.

Now, sitting on a mattress stuffed with heather, in a small, cold, thirteenth century castle bedchamber, the horrible, painful truth of David's words hit her. While she had technically been the one making choices, her decisions had nearly always been dictated by her parents' expectations. She had never really been in control of her own life but had created a life that replicated theirs. Status and career was the sun in their universe. Happiness, joy, and love had never played any role. David had said he loved her, but she hadn't said it back. She had never said it to anyone. Frankly, she hadn't known if she loved him or not, because she wasn't sure she understood what it meant to love someone or if she had ever experienced it.

Well, that was no longer true. In the last few days, she had witnessed it over and over again. Starting with Elsie—out of love and respect for a woman she didn't even know—rather than lie, she would have taken a beating that ultimately would have killed her.

The MacLennans had loved their wee son so dearly, they would have done anything to ensure he lived, including pinning their hope to a stranger's confidence. And even under incredible stress, their abiding love for each other was clearly evident.

This evening she had seen Laird MacKenzie's deep love and concern for Wynda, and hers for him.

Even Wynda and her sister-in-law Lilliana shared a love and friendship that awed Elizabeth.

With the exception of her first boyfriend, she had never experienced anything close to the profound emotion each of these people had. Not even from her parents. Hell, she understood Laird Macrae's Machiavellian machinations more than she did love. But now that she had witnessed it, she came to the crushing realization that it was what she had been seeking forever. David had been right. The thing that had brought her to this point in her life was her frenetic, inexorable need to feel loved.

Bereft, she put her face into her pillow and sobbed until she finally exhausted herself and slept.

Chapter 10

Elizabeth woke the next day to the sound of someone knocking at her door. She sat up groggily, registering the frigid air and the bright morning light flooding through the narrow window. "Come in," she called.

Deirdre opened the door, carrying a large tray. Her shy smile was instantly replaced with concern. "Elsie, is something wrong?"

"Nay. I'm sorry, I guess I overslept."

"Don't worry about that. Lady Wynda said to let ye sleep. She knew ye might need it after three days of travel. Besides, tonight will be a late night—with the feast and all. But as it's well past terce now, she bid me bring ye a pitcher of warm water and something to eat. It's just, well, ye look terrible. Oh…I'm sorry, that's not what I meant…I mean…ye look as if ye don't feel well."

Remembering her terrible epiphany last night, Elsie forced a smile. "I'm fine. I guess I didn't sleep very well.

Deirdre deposited the tray on the small table and put the steaming pitcher of water on the washstand. She took a small cloth from the stand and dipped it into the pitcher of cold water that already stood there. "Here, put this cool cloth on yer eyes for a bit. Maybe the puffiness will go away."

"Thank ye Deirdre. Do I look that bad?"

"Ye look like ye cried half the night."

That's because I did. She couldn't very well tell Deirdre that. "I guess I miss home," was all she could say. In truth what she probably missed was her busy schedule, which prevented her from thinking about anything other than work.

"I'm sorry. But tonight will be fun. Ye'll meet a few

people and maybe feel more comfortable."

"What's tonight?"

Deirdre frowned. "It's Shrove Tuesday."

Shrove Tuesday? Oh, right, the day before Ash Wednesday when Lent starts. Elizabeth covered by saying, "What with travelling and everything, I guess I lost track of the days."

"The MacKenzies have a huge feast, with music and dancing." She proceeded to describe details of the coming fete as Elizabeth nibbled at the bread and cheese Deirdre had brought her.

Elizabeth had to admit, it sounded fun.

She had hoped that after a good night's sleep, she might be able to remember the last bit of her chat with the cabby. But she didn't feel all that well-rested and she could remember no more of the conversation. Frankly, she was more than a little curious about tonight's celebration. David had implied that she lacked life experiences, and she felt very certain a real medieval feast would be an experience unlike any other.

After Elizabeth had eaten her breakfast and washed up a bit, Deirdre said, "Ye're looking much better now. If ye're ready, I'll show ye the castle and village."

"I really should see Lady MacKenzie."

"Nay, she's the one who bid me to introduce ye around. Lady Lilliana is with her now."

So Elizabeth spent the rest of the morning exploring her surroundings and meeting MacKenzies, in the end winding up at Morag's cottage.

"I'll just leave ye here with Morag—I have some work to do before the feast. Ye know the way back," said Deirdre before hurrying back to the keep.

Morag ushered Elizabeth into her cozy cottage, clucked about the bitter cold day and had a hot herbal tisane in her hands in minutes. When she had made herself a mug of the warm brew, she sat down.

"Well, lass, I was hoping we would get a few minutes alone."

Elizabeth realized instantly why. Morag proceeded to grill her about how she would handle a variety of pregnancy related issues. Elizabeth felt as if she was sitting an oral exam and she suspected that was precisely Morag's intent. Some of her questions were so very basic, she couldn't imagine that an elderly midwife didn't know the answers. After her self-revelation the previous night, Elizabeth chose not to be insulted by the inquisition and she addressed every question with confidence, but more importantly with patience.

Morag's questions grew more complex, moving from broad, general queries to specific patient related issues. At some point, Elizabeth realized that the examination was over and Morag was truly seeking input.

"Now, lass, how would ye go about turning a babe?"

"That depends. How far along is the mother? Is this her first? How big is the baby?"

"Well the lass—her name is Jessie—is two and twenty, but she is a right wee thing. And while it's her second child, she had a lot of trouble with the first one and that wee lass came headfirst. Jessie has about a month more to go."

"It is possible to massage the babe into a better position, but I would wait until much closer to when it's due."

"Aye, I agree."

"The best thing is if the babe turns on its own. I have heard of a way to get the baby to move—and if it's moving a lot, there is a good chance it will oblige us."

"This method, does it work?"

"Honestly, I've never done it." According to reports Elizabeth had read, practitioners of traditional eastern medicine used a treatment called "moxibustion" which seemed to be effective at stimulating movement. But she had no first-hand experience with it. The standard way of handling a breech presentation in the twenty-first century United States was caesarian section. "But we could try it."

"What do ye do?"

Well, you go to a Chinese herbalist's shop and buy two moxa sticks. Clearly they couldn't do that, but maybe she could figure out a substitute. Although it was possible that the smell of the burning moxa sticks might have some effect, Elizabeth figured that the heat was the key element. "This is going to sound a little crazy, and like I said, I've never done it, but one puts a focused heat source—maybe a red hot fire iron would work—near the outer edge of each small toe. It should be as close as the mother can tolerate, without burning. The mother does this for a bit longer than a quarter of an hour, in the evening, before going to bed. I suppose, to keep the heat constant, it would be necessary to have several irons and keep changing them as they cooled."

"And this makes the babe move?"

"That's my understanding."

"Is there any risk of it harming the mother or the babe?"

"Nothing we do to try to reposition a breech baby is without risk. In this case there is a very small chance her labor could start early. We would have to weigh the risk of delivering a babe that might be up to a month early with the risk of this mother delivering with the baby as it is." Elizabeth knew with traditional moxibustion there was also the chance of an allergic reactions to the burning herbs, but that wouldn't be a concern here.

Morag nodded. "I fear that as small as she is and with the trouble she had the last time, Jessie will not be able to deliver the baby breech. She is close enough to term that the baby might be all right even if it came early. On top of which, if she did go into labor early the baby will be smaller. If it hasn't turned, she might have a better chance of delivering a smaller babe. Considering the risks of all options, I am inclined to try it. Will ye help me?"

Elizabeth would never have tried something like this in her own time. She was more confident in her ability to perform a caesarian than risking something she knew little about. However, in the thirteenth century a caesarian was not an option. "Aye, I'd be happy to." As long as she was here, she might as well help. This might take a few days but even if she remembered the word at this moment, she felt sure Elsie would be willing to wait a short time, if necessary, to help a pregnant women.

"I'll talk to Jessie about it tomorrow. With the feast and all today, I don't think we could get everything arranged this evening." Morag glanced out the window. "Oh dear, it's getting late, we should be getting up to the keep."

As they walked up the lane towards the castle together, Elizabeth glanced sideways at the old midwife. "Well, did I pass?"

"What?"

"Did I answer all of yer questions satisfactorily? Are ye comfortable I know what I'm doing?"

Morag chuckled. "It was so obvious I was testing ye?"

Elizabeth smiled warmly. "Aye it was."

Morag smiled back. "Well then, aye, ye did very well. Ye aren't insulted?"

"Nay, Morag. 'Tis apparent ye care very much for Lady MacKenzie. I realize I'm young and it's hard to believe that I could be very skilled. Ye wouldn't have her best interests at heart if ye didn't satisfy yerself about me."

Morag shook her head. "Ye're clever beyond yer years, lass, that's a certainty."

~ * ~

Cade's mind had drifted to the cheeky, little midwife all day. Her lips had been so warm and sweet; he wanted to taste them again. He half hoped she would be just as full of sass at the feast as she had been for days. He would quite enjoy kissing her into starry-eyed bewilderment as he had promised he would if she didn't mind her tongue. When the clan began to gather and he didn't see her among the people in the hall, he frowned, a little disappointed. He supposed she was with Wynda, but he would have enjoyed dancing with Elsie.

Other matters drew his attention during most of the feast, and he thought no more about her. When the food was cleared and the trestle tables taken down to make room for the dancing, his mind returned to their unusual guest. He scanned the crowd again, this time finding her chatting merrily with a few of the young clanswomen who worked in the hall.

He frowned when several men joined the group—among them Laird Archibald Chisholm's youngest son, Rory, who was in training at Carraigile. Both handsome and charming, Rory left his fair share of lassies swooning in his wake. Eventually the other lads pulled Elsie's companions onto the dance floor, leaving her alone with Rory. Cade's frown deepened as Rory leaned down, appearing to whisper something in her ear that made her laugh.

Eric, noticing what held Cade's attention, said, "Seeing as how ye didn't want anyone else to *discover her charming wee self* until ye'd proven her wrong, either she gave in to her unquenchable desire for ye last night, or ye're failing miserably."

Cade glared at him. "Have you always been this annoying?"

"Annoying? Me? Nay, I'm not annoying—just insightful. And insight is only annoying when it's painfully true."

Cade just shook his head, turning his attention back to Elsie and Rory. A slow smile spread across his face as one of the kitchen maids, Shauna, approached the pair. Shauna was no great beauty but neither was she unattractive, although she paled in comparison to Elsie. However, Shauna enjoyed a good tumble and thus never lacked for company. Cade expected that she would have Rory's complete attention and be dancing with him in a matter of moments. But uncharacteristically, Rory didn't seem too anxious to accept what she offered.

Eric chuckled. "Now that is odd. The lads rarely turn Shauna away. Perhaps Rory has found greener pastures."

Cade laughed. "Quit trying to goad me. I'm not worried about Rory Chisholm or any other man in this hall."

"What makes ye so confident?"

"Because I haven't accepted failure at anything yet."

Eric gave a nod of acquiescence. "Fair point."

With a confident smile, Cade rose and crossed the hall to where the three stood. "Good evening, Rory. How is it ye've managed to garner the attention of two fair lassies?"

Shauna curtsied, batting her eyes coyly. "Good evening, Sir Cade."

Glancing sideways at Shauna, Elsie too bobbed an awkward sort of half-curtsy but said nothing.

Rory inclined his head. "Ah, 'tis likely the other way 'round, Cade. These lovelies have taken pity on me."

"I see. Shauna, lass, since 'tis pity ye're dishing out, see if ye can find it in yer heart to give poor Rory here a dance."

She pouted prettily. "He's already turned me down, but ye look in need of a partner."

"Now, lass, I'm sure he only turned ye down because he didn't want to abandon Elsie, but never fear, I'll keep her company while the two of ye enjoy yerselves."

Rory arched a brow and gave Cade a wry smile before taking Shauna's hand and pulling her towards the dancers. "Aye, pet, with Elsie in *good hands*, I'd love to dance with ye."

Cade turned his attention to Elsie. Now that he was close to her, he frowned when he noticed the faint bluish circles under her eyes. "Are ye enjoying the feast, Elsie?"

"Aye, thank ye."

"Did ye sleep well last night?"

She looked amused by his question. When she smiled, one side of her mouth went a little higher than the other in an adorably lopsided way. "Aye, Sir Cade, and ye?"

He gave an exaggerated sigh. "Well enough, I suppose, although I daresay I slept better the night before."

"On the frozen ground?"

"Was the ground frozen?" He leaned close. "All I remember was the soft, warm lassie snoring in my arms."

"I do not snore."

"Maybe 'twas Sully then."

"Ye slept with Sully in yer arms?" she teased.

He laughed. "Nay, lass, 'twas Sully snoring. I'm fairly certain 'twas ye in my arms." He added in a whisper, "I'd recognize that soft, round backside anywhere."

She blushed. "Ye're a prime rogue, Cade MacKenzie."

"Ah, ye wound me with that wee sharp tongue. And I recall warning ye that there would be consequences. Perhaps I can be convinced to grant ye leniency if ye agree to dance with me."

The amusement fled her features and she took a step back. "Nay, I can't."

"Of course ye can."

"Nay, I'm sorry, I really can't. I mean, I don't know how to dance."

Cade frowned. "How is that possible?"

"I…I…I suppose I never took time to learn."

"Well, that little problem must be rectified. Now." In spite of her protests, he took her hand and pulled her towards the dancers. "Just watch me and do what I do—as if ye're my reflection."

She blushed and glanced nervously at the other

dancers.

He put a finger under her chin, turning her face towards him. "I said watch me. Don't worry about anyone else."

She nodded and he proceeded to guide her through the steps of the dance. She hadn't lied; she really couldn't dance. But, she didn't take her eyes off of him—something he realized he quite liked—and after the pattern repeated a few times, she seemed to be catching on.

When the song ended, she took a step back. "Thank ye. It was kind of ye."

She started to turn away, clearly intending to leave the floor, but he caught her by the hand. "And where do ye think ye're going?"

She looked flustered. "I…well, the song is over."

"But another one is about to start."

"And I'm terrible."

"Do ye always give up so easily?"

"I'm not giving up. I'm just—"

"—afraid?"

She frowned. "I'm not afraid."

"Nay? Then why are ye giving up?"

She put her hands on her hips and scowled. He stifled a grin. It was fun to tease her.

"Oh all right. I'll just stumble through dance after dance until everyone is laughing at me."

The music started again and he guided her through another dance. She really was terrible but he had more fun teaching her than he had ever had with the most skilled dancer in the clan.

When she tripped and fell into his arms at the end of the dance, she asked, "Will ye let me stop now?"

"Nay."

"Ye don't think I've embarrassed myself sufficiently yet?"

"Elsie, ye're taking this much too seriously. Besides,

no one is laughing at ye. On the contrary, every lass in the room wants to *be* ye."

"That's ridiculous."

"But it's true."

"Why would ye say that?"

"Because, sweetling, ye're dancing with me." He laughed when she scowled, adding, "And what's more, every man in the room wants to be me, because I have the bonniest lass present falling into my arms."

~ * ~

Elizabeth was dumbfounded. No one had ever infuriated her one moment and said something so incredibly wonderful the next.

"So are ye brave enough to try it again?" he asked.

How could she possibly say no? "Aye, I'll try it again."

She laughed and stumbled through dance after dance with Cade until he finally said, "I think, my lovely lass, ye've earned a bit of refreshment." Grabbing her elbow, he maneuvered her to one of the benches set up along the walls, grabbed two tankards of ale from a passing serving maid and sat beside Elsie, handing her one of the tankards.

Elsie took a sip. She was surprised by the flavor and the fact that the alcohol content seemed quite low. That explained why everyone, including children, seemed to drink the stuff without becoming intoxicated.

After Cade had taken a long pull from his tankard, he captured her gaze, considering her for a moment before asking, "Tell me, Elsie, how is it ye never learned to dance?"

She shrugged. "I guess I spent most of my time learning my trade." That was absolutely true. While it was understandable that Elizabeth didn't know how to dance the sometimes complex medieval country dances, she would have fared no better in a nightclub. She hadn't gone to dances in school, not even her high school prom. Back then she had considered it a waste of time. She supposed David would say it was just another life experience she had missed out on. Now, with a tankard of ale in her hand, her sides aching from laughter and sitting next to a beautiful man whose strong arms had kept her from falling several times—she had to agree. This had been more than just fun. It was a pinnacle moment that she would never forget.

"Ye've gone very quiet on me, lass."

"Aye. I suppose I'm a bit sorry I've never learned to dance before tonight."

"I'm not."

"Why?"

"Because then I wouldn't have had the joy of teaching ye how."

She raised her eyebrows skeptically. "Joy?"

"Aye, joy. I consider any evening passed with a lass in my arms, time well spent—even if it is to keep her from landing on her soft round backside."

"Ye seem to pay an inordinate amount of attention to my—"

"—soft round backside?" He winked. "That's because I spent the last three days with it nestled up against me, and I've grown rather fond of it."

She blushed. "Like I said, ye're a prime rogue."

"Now there's that wee sharp tongue again. This time it must be taught a lesson." He cupped her cheek in one hand and leaned down to give her a kiss.

The world around her dissolved as his lips explored hers, first gently teasing, then more demanding. When he finally pulled away from her, she was breathless. No one had ever kissed her like that—or maybe it was that she had never kissed anyone back with quite the same ardor. Either way it stirred a deep aching need within her. She had no doubt giving into that need would be another pinnacle moment, but as much as she longed to, she knew she couldn't. *Not my life, not my body.*

She looked away, trying to gain some measure of control. "I...I should...I'm rather tired...I really should say good night."

He smiled seductively. "Ye don't have to."

She sighed and looked him in the eye. "Aye, I do. I had a wonderful evening. I can't remember ever having more fun."

"I'm glad ye enjoyed it."

"Thank ye for teaching me to dance."

"Ah, lass, 'twas my pleasure. But now that ye mention it, there is something else ye must learn to do and I think yer lessons should start soon."

She frowned. There were any number of things she would like him to teach her, but she had no idea what he was talking about.

He laughed. "Now put those wicked thoughts aside. I said ye needed to learn to ride a horse before we take ye back to Castle Macrae."

She blushed. "I had forgotten. Ye needn't bother."

"'Tis no bother. Besides, it's for the benefit of any horse ye may encounter in the future."

She smiled. There were no horses in her future but she thought she might like having him teach her...well...anything. "Then on behalf of the horses in my future, I thank ye."

"I'm thinking we should start yer lessons tomorrow— right after the midday meal. I suspect it will take a while."

She laughed. "Good night, Sir Cade."

"Good night, Elsie." He leaned in and gave her another kiss that set her head spinning and left her breathless.

With tremendous effort, she pulled away. "Good night," she whispered, forcing herself to turn and walk towards the stairs.

Chapter 11

The next morning, Elizabeth rose early, washed and had just finished dressing for the day when Deirdre knocked at her door.

"'Tis Ash Wednesday. We'll go to Mass before starting the day's work."

Mass? While nominally Episcopalian, Elizabeth's family wasn't very religious. She had been baptized, received first communion and was confirmed. But in recent years she had only attended church on major holidays. She knew people in thirteenth century were very religious. She figured she probably should try to fit in, but how was she going to fake ancient Catholicism? Perhaps she could learn enough to manage by watching.

She thought it might be interesting, but she expected no more than that. However, she found the experience moving in a way that surprised her. As she entered the small church, she realized that all of the clan members who lived in the village or keep were there. Everyone. Morag, Ellen, Shauna, the other castle servants, villagers, men-at-arms, Lady Lilliana, Sir Hamish, Eric, even Cade and his father all came together to pray and worship. The sense of community was profound.

She tried to imagine going to church with her whole family, all of her coworkers, neighbors and by extension, all of her patients. She wondered what it would be like to see children she had delivered begin to toddle and walk—to grow. What would it be like to be so much a part of the community that she knew each soul she cared for? To see little improvements in those who had been ill or simply in passing to notice if things weren't quite right? To know and care deeply for each person she encountered, not just those sitting in a paper gown on an exam table?

The feeling was overwhelming. She remembered Gertrude's words: *"There was a time when doctors, healers and midwives experienced exactly what ye say ye want. They knew their patients and spent time with them."*

That time is long gone, had been Elizabeth's response. And yet, now, for her, time had looped back on itself. This is what she had wanted to experience when she accepted the pocket watch. She didn't count on it igniting such a potent longing within her. As she walked back to the keep with Deirdre chattering away, she vowed to seize these days she had been given and immerse herself in this life.

David would approve.

Morag caught up with them. "Elsie, I have some rounds to make today and I thought perhaps ye'd go like to go with me."

I'd like it more than you can imagine. "Aye, Morag, I would. I do just need to check in on Lady MacKenzie first."

"You do that. Take yer time. I expect Lady Wynda would enjoy the company. When ye're done, meet me at my cottage."

"Aye. I will."

When they reached the keep, she hurried upstairs to Laird and Lady MacKenzie's chamber. Alice opened the door when Elsie knocked.

Lady MacKenzie called from the bed, "Oh, Elsie, dear, it's good to see ye. Come in. Can ye stay for a bit?"

"I'll be going with Morag on her rounds today, but I can stay with ye a while."

"Wonderful. Alice, since Elsie is here, ye should take a break."

"Aye, my lady. Shall I return in an hour or so?"

"That will be fine."

After Alice bobbed a curtsy and left, Lady Wynda looked at Elizabeth as if she were sizing her up. Elizabeth suddenly had the feeling that she was about to get another grilling along the lines of the one Morag had given her the day before.

But after a moment, Wynda looked directly into Elizabeth's eyes and said, "I asked Alice to leave because I want to talk to ye alone. I need for ye to tell me the truth."

The truth? "My lady, I don't understand. I assure ye, what I've said about yer condition is true."

"I'm not talking about my condition. I am oddly confident that everything ye've said is precisely true. However, I am also dead certain ye aren't the midwife my husband sent for."

"But, my lady—"

"Nay, lass. I need to know. Morag, one of the finest midwives I know, has never heard of this weakness in the opening of a womb. But ye're little more than a child and not only do ye know about it, ye're supremely confident about what to do. Ye cannot be the woman we sent for. Ye must tell me the truth." She fixed Elizabeth with a serious look. "Now."

Elizabeth wasn't sure what to say. Laird Macrae had threatened her with a beating if she told anyone the truth. What's more, the truth was nearly impossible to believe and could get her accused of witchcraft or some dark art. And yet, what Laird Macrae had done was wrong—even if it turned out to be very much for the better.

"Now, Elsie," Lady Mackenzie insisted.

Elizabeth sighed. "I will tell ye the truth, my lady. But what I'm going to tell ye will sound fantastical. Please promise ye'll listen to the whole story before ye make any judgment."

"I so promise."

"If ye want the whole truth, I also need the promise of yer protection from Laird Macrae."

"From Laird Macrae?" She arched a brow but nodded. "Ye have it."

"All right. I guess it all starts with the idea of time. Most people believe that yesterday is followed by today and then tomorrow. They believe that time is a line that goes ever forward. But it isn't." Elizabeth proceeded to tell her about the pocket watch and the essence of soul exchange.

Lady Wynda didn't seem as shocked as Elizabeth expected. She simply asked, "So what had Elsie done that would have resulted in her death?"

"As it turns out, nothing...yet. Ye see, Laird Macrae did intend to deal falsely with ye. Elsie was the niece of the woman ye sought. Evidently she was training to be a midwife, but just like all of the rest of ye, I too doubt she had the experience to deal with anything very unusual. But Laird Macrae didn't believe there was a single chance anyone could help ye. It was his opinion that some women simply can't carry a child to term. He figured since no one could help ye, it didn't matter who he sent. If he passed an apprentice off as a master, the outcome would be the same. All he needed was for Laird MacKenzie to believe Elsie was indeed a master to gain a powerful ally. To her credit, Elsie would not have agreed to the ruse, but she would have been beaten for her disobedience and the beating would have resulted in her death."

"Oh, the poor child."

"As it turns out, we actually changed places before any of that happened. Gertrude—she's the old woman who gave me the pocket watch—she thinks that's why the watch stayed in the future with my body and Elsie's soul. And it's also probably why time is equal in both places."

Wynda looked mildly surprised at the mention of Gertrude, but made no comment.

"And Laird Macrae didn't know any of this about ye?"

"Nay, my lady, he believes I'm Elsie."

"Tell me, how is it ye know so much about pregnancy? Are ye a midwife in the future?"

"Not exactly. I'm a doctor—but one who specializes in pregnancy and women's health, similar to a midwife."

"A doctor from the future? It seems when ye said, 'there is no one in Scotland who is better able to attend' me, ye spoke the absolute truth."

"Aye, I believe I did."

"But I suppose this means since ye have a little less than sixty days left, ye'll not be able to attend me at delivery."

"Aye, but ye won't need me. Ye don't need me now. I've told ye everything ye need to do—what's left is up to ye. But, I won't be leaving immediately. I haven't remembered the word that will switch us back yet. Gertrude believes that I will when the time is right, but I confess, I'm worried about this entire situation."

"I too expect ye will remember the word. What has ye worried?"

"Like I said, ye don't really need me here, but I'm concerned about going back to Elsie's home. I was only at Castle Macrae for a few minutes before leaving with Cade. No one had time to notice that I had no memories there. I'm new here so there's no memory loss to explain. If ye send me back, the Macraes will likely think I've lost my mind if I can't remember anything."

"Put that out of yer head. I'll see that ye're not sent back for as long as ye need to stay."

"Thank ye, my lady. But what if Laird Macrae demands that I be returned?"

"I don't think he will. The whole reason for sending ye was to fool my husband into thinking he was trying to help. Since Laird Macrae believes ye aren't even a fully trained midwife, he has no reason to push for yer return right away. At least as long as Angus is happy."

"I'm not certain Laird MacKenzie is very happy with me."

Lady Wynda laughed. "Aye, he is a bit put off by yer

boldness, but this bairn means the world to both of us. He won't send ye away as long as I want ye to stay."

"Thank ye, my lady. I'll try my best to curb my tongue and not upset him."

Wynda's smile was warm. "I would appreciate that. 'Twill make all our lives a bit easier."

"I expect so," Elizabeth said wryly. "It's just that things are very different for me. Women in the future have more of a voice, more power."

"I suspect that's a very good thing."

Wynda's complete acceptance of the concept of time-travel astounded her. "My lady, may I ask ye something?"

"Anything, lass."

"Ye believed my story without hesitation or question. Why?"

"As it happens, there's an old woman who passes this way every now and again." She smiled broadly. "Her name is Gertrude. She told me ye'd be coming; ye wouldn't be what I expected and that if I pushed, ye'd tell me something that was nearly impossible to believe. Regardless of that, she asked me to believe it and trust that ye knew what ye were doing, despite the fact that ye'd look very young."

"Gertrude beat me here?"

Wynda chuckled. "It seems so."

"Where is she? I need to talk to her."

"She isn't here now. She came right after Cade and my husband's other men left for Castle Macrae."

"How's that possible? I only met Gertrude four days ago, the same day Cade arrived at Castle Macrae."

Wynda laughed merrily. "Now lass, didn't ye just tell me time is not linear?"

Elizabeth smiled. "I did. But ye should know, my lady, even in my time, most people don't know that. Having only just learned it myself, I'll beg yer forgiveness."

"Ye have nothing to worry about, Elsie. Oh, I guess that's not really yer name."

"Nay it isn't. My name is Elizabeth. Elizabeth Quinn."

"It's lovely to meet ye, Elizabeth. I am infinitely grateful that ye decided to try the pocket watch. For the first time in years I have hope."

Hope. I may have no real voice here, but I have the power to give hope where there was none. "I am so glad I was able to help. I'm also finding being here a blessing in ways I didn't expect."

Wynda smiled. "I daresay that was Gertrude's plan."

Elsie laughed. "I suppose it was."

"Well, Elizabeth, I suspect the best way to keep ye safe is to keep all of this between the two of us. As angry as I am about Laird Macrae's duplicity, I fear that if Angus knew the truth he would be furious, and ultimately Laird Macrae would find out that we knew the truth. If that happens, I'm not certain we could keep ye safe from him forever."

"Aye, I expect that's best. It's probably also best that I just go by Elsie. I'm getting used to it anyway."

"Elsie it is then."

~ * ~

As Elsie walked to Morag's cottage after leaving Lady Wynda, she felt lighter than she had since arriving in the thirteenth century. The knowledge that someone else here knew who she really was and how she came to be here—and perhaps more importantly, believed the story—was a comfort. She didn't feel quite so alone.

Morag's rounds consisted of a walk through the village, stopping at every cottage where there was a pregnant woman or a newborn. It felt very casual but Elsie noticed how Morag mixed the occasional health related question in with ordinary conversation. She smiled to herself when she realized Morag asked each woman what she was making for dinner.

After about the third time Morag had done this, when

they left the cottage Elsie asked why.

Morag smiled. "'Tis Lent. I firmly believe the eating of flesh is important to a woman who is with child but during the days of fast and abstinence it is forbidden. However, Father Henry says that the birds of the air and the fish of the sea were created on the fifth day. While the creatures of the earth were created on the sixth day. Therefore, eating fish is allowed. I always like to make sure a lass knows not to be too strict with herself."

Elizabeth saw this as an opportunity to add a little twenty-first century nutritional information. "Aye that seems prudent. I've also found a number of plantstuffs to be very beneficial."

"Have ye? Like what?"

"Actually, eating any fruits and vegetables has value. Nuts, peas, lentils, and beans are very good as are root vegetables like carrots and beets. Anything dark green is wonderful—but I suppose that is hard to come by in the winter."

"About the only dark green plantstuffs available in the winter are some dried seaweeds."

"Aye, kelp is excellent. Milk is too."

"Ye mean almond milk?"

Almond milk? Who knew it was medieval? Elizabeth thought it was a trendy new fad from her own time. Well at least it had a little protein. "Aye, almond milk."

Still, she thought modern Catholics consumed milk and eggs on Fridays during Lent and she was certain they ate fish. But Morag seemed to have to defend that choice. Maybe the rules were different in the middle ages. She would have to ask Wynda.

"Have ye found anything else to be particularly helpful?"

"Well, now that you mention it, I've found mothers and newborns succumb to fever less if you keep things very clean. I wash my hands a lot."

"How could that possibly make a difference?"

Elizabeth said the first thing that came to her mind. "Dirt."

"What about it?"

Where was she going to go with this? "Uh…things grow in dirt…and, uh, things rot in dirt. I think dirt helps festering to start. So I try to keep things very clean."

"Really?" Morag sounded skeptical.

"Aye, really."

Morag shrugged. "It is a bit of nuisance, but it can't hurt."

Woohoo! Score one for germ theory.

By the time Morag completed her rounds, it was well after midday. Morag took Elizabeth to her cottage for a bannock and a mug of herb tea, which she called a *tisane*. While they sat at the table, Morag said, "Tell me more about this heat treatment ye want to try. What do we need?"

"We'll need something that will provide a small focused heat source. Yesterday I said that hot fire irons might work but I am a bit worried that their length might make them hard to manage. Do ye suppose the blacksmith could loan us eight iron spikes and tongs to handle them with?"

"Aye, I'm sure he can. Why so many?"

"I expect it takes a while to heat them, but they'll cool fairly quickly. If we have several heating we can switch them out often."

"Ah, I suppose ye're right."

"We also need three blocks of wood."

"That won't be a problem. I'll get all the things we need. Ye said it's best to do it at night?"

It would still be several hundred years before Sir Isaac Newton described the laws of gravity. She had to make this simple. "Aye. It's best to do it just before the mother goes to bed for the night, because when she is lying down, it's easier for the baby to move." She smiled. "Its little bottom isn't sitting down so firmly in her pelvis."

Morag laughed. "I guess that's right. So come back 'round to my cottage after the evening meal and we'll try this."

Chapter 12

Elizabeth spent some more time with Wynda that afternoon. The laird's wife gave her a quick summary of Lenten practices, so Elizabeth wouldn't make any serious gaffes that might raise eyebrows.

Then, after the evening meal, Elizabeth met Morag at her cottage as she had said she would. "Were ye able to get everything?"

"Aye, I was. The wood was no problem. Jessie's husband, John, is a bow maker and fletcher. However, when I asked our blacksmith, Gil, for eight spikes and a pair of tongs I'm sure he thought I'd lost my senses." She grinned, "But he's Jessie's uncle and when I explained why I needed them, he gave them to me. He said to make sure the fire is burning hot and to prop the spikes so their tips are in the white part of the flame because it will be hottest. He said he'd help us if we need him."

"That's kind of him. If we can't get the spikes hot enough, can we send for him?"

"Aye, of course we can. He only lives a few cottages away."

Elizabeth smiled. "Well then, let's see if this works."

Morag led her down several village lanes until they reached the right cottage.

A young woman ushered them in. Morag introduced Elizabeth to Jessie and her husband. When Morag asked about their wee daughter, Flora, Jessie explained that she was at John's oldest sister's cottage for the night. "I figured we should sort out how to do this without having to worry about her this first time.

Elizabeth agreed. "That's a very good idea."

"John thinks once we learn how to do it, he can help

me so ye don't have to come every evening."

"We'll see how it goes but that might work. So, I understand Morag has explained what we want to try?"

"Aye, she has."

"Would ye mind if I examined ye before we start?"

"Nay, that's fine."

"Morag, maybe we should go ahead and put the spikes in the fire to begin heating them, and we should probably have a bucket of water close by too."

Elizabeth had Jessie lie down and assessed the baby's position, confirming that it was still bottom down. Jessie was indeed a very small woman, but Elizabeth knew that really didn't matter as much as people once thought. Still, delivering a baby that isn't head down is hard and Jessie'd had difficulty delivering her first child.

"Does the baby move a lot?"

"Aye, it kicks something fierce. Every now and then it feels as if the baby is stretching, pushing up and down at the same time."

Elizabeth smiled. "Aye bairns have no respect for the fact that their mamas only have a limited amount of space for them."

Jessie laughed. "I suppose not."

"Morag explained to you that this heat treatment is supposed to cause the baby to become active?"

"Aye."

"And just by making it active, it might turn over, but it might not."

"Aye, that's what she said. She also said there is a chance it could start labor early."

"That's right. But we think ye are far enough along that the risk of going into labor is smaller than the risk of delivering the babe as it currently lies. I will show you some body positions that may encourage the little one turn over too. Even if ye decided not to try this heat treatment, you can do those and they still may help."

"I understand, but I do want to try. My last labor…well I'm a little afraid."

Elizabeth nodded. "I understand. But Jessie, try to put yer fears to rest. Each labor is different and the first ones are often the hardest. Still, it would be nice if the little one would oblige us and turn, so we will give this a try. When the spikes are hot I am going to have you stand on this block of wood. Maybe we should take your outer garment off and make sure that yer léine is pulled up and out of the way. We wouldn't want it to brush against the irons and catch fire."

Once Jessie was in place, Elizabeth placed the other wooden blocks on either side of Jessie's feet. These were to hold the hot spikes and keep them positioned near her little toes. "We'll rest the spikes on these, with the hot part off the edge. Then we'll move it as close to yer small toe as we can. I do not want it to burn you, but I do want it to be as hot as you can comfortably tolerate."

"I understand."

When the spikes were hot, they started. The blocks were large enough to fully support the spike and they could move the whole block as needed to get the right position. When one spike cooled, they replaced it with a hot one to keep the heat as constant as possible. After about a twenty minutes, Elizabeth said, "I think that's enough for tonight."

"Now what?" asked Jessie.

Elizabeth showed her some of the positions that might help. "You can do these intermittently throughout the day. For now, just go to bed. You may notice the baby moving more and hopefully it will turn over," said Elizabeth. "We will do this every night for a week or so. If nothing happens, when we're a little closer to your due date, we will try moving the baby from the outside."

"All right. This was easy enough."

John picked up one of the blocks of wood on which they had rested the spikes. "I think if I carved out a groove, we could rest the spike in the groove and there would be less risk of it falling off and burning something. It might also make it easier to position."

"I think that is an excellent idea," said Elizabeth.

Morag nodded her agreement. "Elsie and I will come back tomorrow evening and maybe one more time after that. But if everything goes well, John should be able to take over."

Elizabeth concurred. She and Morag bade the young couple good night and walked back up the lane towards Morag's cottage and the castle gates.

"I've heard of healers and midwives using all sorts of bizarre things to treat one thing or another, but this may be one of the oddest."

"Aye. I have to agree. And even if the baby turns, it isn't necessarily because of this, but I figured it was at least worth a try."

"Well, now we just have to stick to it and wait I suppose."

Elizabeth laughed. "I've never been very good at waiting."

"And ye're a midwife? It seems we spend much of our lives waiting. But I suppose since ye know other healing arts, ye're kept busy enough."

Elizabeth nodded and simply said, "Aye." She couldn't tell Morag that in the twenty-first century, schedules are booked and over-booked and it is ever on to the next patient.

When they reached Morag's cottage, Elizabeth bade her goodnight and continued on to the castle. The people who were beginning to bed down for the night in the great hall called greetings as she passed, lighting a glow within her. Each, "good night, Elsie," or "sleep well, Elsie," caused the light to grow a little warmer and brighter. By the time she started up the stairs, she was sure it had spilled out onto her face as a joyful grin.

Halfway up the stairs she met Cade coming down. He filled the stairwell—all broad shoulders and devastating good looks. She nearly stumbled over her own feet. "Ah, Sir Cade. Good evening."

"Elsie, I was looking for ye." When his eyes met hers, his face split into a megawatt smile that made her knees go weak. "Ye look very happy. What has pleased ye so?"

If anything her smile broadened. "Nothing in particular. It's just been a very good day."

"Has it?"

"Aye. At least I think it has."

"Now, ye see, I was thinking my day could have been significantly better."

"I'm sorry. Did something happen?"

"Nay, lass, something *didn't* happen."

Her brows drew together. "I don't understand."

"I haven't seen ye all day."

"Oh," was all she could manage to say. She had never be so discombobulated simply by being in someone's presence. Of course, she had to admit, her discombobulated years were spent with her nose in books.

He chuckled, moving closer. "Aye, lass. Over the last few days I fear I've grown quite used to having ye nearby." He brushed her cheek with the back of one hand. "Very nearby."

When he was this close and touching her, she could barely form thoughts. "Well...I..." *what had he said*?

"Missed me too?"

"Aye," she sighed. "Nay...I mean...I was busy today with Morag."

"I see. However, I'm certain I was to begin teaching ye to ride right after the midday meal. But ye were nowhere to be seen."

"I was with Morag. We didn't dine in the hall."

"Are ye avoiding me for some reason?"

"Nay, of course not. I was just—"

"Then if ye had no reason, ye must have simply chosen to defy me."

"Defy ye? I didn't defy ye."

"Didn't ye? Did yer memory fail ye? Do ye not recall our conversation last night?" The mischievous grin on his face suggested he was teasing.

"I didn't think ye were serious."

"Oh, sweetling, I was very serious." He leaned close, speaking low. "And I don't like being defied."

Her breath caught. Why did she find this so seductive? "Nay?"

"Nay." He brushed his lips across her cheek, stopping at her ear. "I fear ye must learn not to do that," he whispered.

She swallowed hard, too overwhelmed by his nearness to process what he had said.

"But how am I going to do that?" He pulled back a little and, placing a finger under her chin, tilted her head up to look at him.

"Do what?"

Cade laughed. "Oh little midwife, ye are a pure delight—for someone who was so certain she could resist my charms, that is. But to answer yer question, I'm wondering how best to teach ye not to defy me."

Elizabeth frowned. "I didn't defy ye."

"Oh but ye did."

"I just misunderstood ye."

"Do ye think," he kissed her lips lightly, "if I make myself very clear," he kissed her again, "ye might remember to meet me after the midday meal tomorrow?" He captured her lips in a demanding, all-consuming kiss.

She wasn't sure of much of anything at the moment. But she was confident his kisses were more likely to leave her brain a complete blank than solidify any memory. "Cade, ye don't need to teach me to ride."

"Nay, lass, that was the wrong thing to say." He kissed

her deeply again.

She realized he had wrapped his arms around her and she was fairly sure she would have melted into a puddle at his feet if he let go.

"Let's try this again. I expect ye to begin learning how to ride tomorrow after the midday meal. Is that clear?"

"Aye."

"There's a good lass. Don't forget." He kissed her again.

When he broke the kiss, Elizabeth sighed. "I'm not sure kissing me does much to improve my memory. Frankly, I fear the opposite is true."

He chuckled. "Let's hope not. While I quite enjoy this, I'm sure teaching ye to ride will be equally as entertaining. So, ye won't want to forget tomorrow."

Dear God, if it was any more entertaining than this, Elizabeth didn't think she could stand it. "Nay."

"Excellent. Until tomorrow, then." He kissed her one last time, slowly and more sensually than before. "Good night, Elsie." He let go of her, stepping aside so she could pass.

She swayed slightly. "Good night, Sir Cade."

He chuckled as he continued down the stairs.

It took Elizabeth a moment to compose herself and make her way up to her bedchamber.

Chapter 13

After a hard morning of training, Cade returned to the great hall for the midday meal. He frowned when he didn't see Elsie among those gathered at the trestle tables. He continued to be out of sorts as he ate, until he saw her emerge from the tower stairs just as the meal ended. He stood and crossed the hall to her. "When I didn't see ye in the hall, I feared ye had defied me again."

"Nay, ye made yer point well last eve. I was sitting with Lady Wynda this morning."

He grinned at the memory of how he'd *made his point*. "Well, I'm glad my methods worked." He was rewarded with her lopsided smile and faint blush. "Speaking of Lady Wynda, is she well?"

"Aye, she is. I fear lying flat in bed all day is much more difficult that she first imagined."

"I'm sure it is. But even so, she is happier and more hopeful than she has been in weeks—years even."

Elsie smiled. "It's good to hear that. Though I would like her to have some meaningful distraction. I am trying to figure out ways that she can do some of the things she enjoys, like needlework, and still remain flat. I want to speak with a carpenter. Perhaps we can build something that will hold her tapestry frame above her, so she can work it lying down."

"That's a brilliant idea, Elsie. I know just the person to ask. Leave it with me."

She shrugged but looked pleased. "Thank ye, Sir Cade. Six months is a long time."

"Aye it is, and it might take that long to have ye sitting a horse properly if we don't get started."

She laughed. "Well lead on then."

They went together to the stables and he saddled Edda, the palfrey he had taken to Macrae for her to ride. "Today we'll stay in the rear bailey and just review basic skills."

Elsie cast a wary glance towards the horse. "Are ye sure she's the best horse for me to learn on? She didn't seem to be all that easy to ride."

"The problem was the rider—not the horse. She is a well-trained, gentle mount. Any other might have dumped ye on yer soft round backside that day."

She frowned. "What do I need to do to get yer mind off my backside?"

He grinned salaciously. "Any number of delightful things, lass."

She huffed and shook her head. "Forget I asked."

Cade laughed. Once again he realized how much he enjoyed teasing her. "Ah well, then, I suppose I'll have to settle for teaching ye how to stay on this beastie's back."

She rolled her eyes at the innuendo, causing him to laugh again.

When they reached the rear bailey, he helped her into the saddle and asked her to ride in a wide circle around the bailey. He had assumed she would know a few basic skills, but as soon as he told her to urge Edda into a trot, it became evident that she didn't. As hard as it was to believe, it seemed as if she'd never been on a horse in her life. She bounced stiffly, pulling every which direction on the reins, causing Edda to toss her head irritably. Then Elsie compounded the problem by leaning forward and digging in her heels.

He stepped in. "Whoa, Edda, easy there, lass." The horse, clearly aware that she had an incompetent rider, followed his command. He took her reins. "Elsie do ye have no experience at all?"

"I told ye I didn't."

"Nay, ye told me ye didn't ride *much*. It's as if ye've never sat a horse."

"Well, I have ridden before...a long time ago...and only at a walk."

He shook his head, but couldn't keep from smiling. He had to start at the beginning, and this was going to take much more time than he had expected. The thought actually pleased him. It was a perfect excuse to spend time with her. "Well I suppose we should start with the basics. I told ye Edda was a very well trained horse. She will respond to the slightest command."

"What does that mean? What commands do I give?"

"Elsie, ye give commands with the reins and yer body. Her mouth is extremely sensitive. When ye yank the reins it is as if ye're screeching at her. To make matters worse, ye're pulling them first one way and then the other so she has no idea where ye want her to go."

Elsie looked both shocked and contrite. "I'm sorry." She patted Edda's neck. "I'm sorry, lass, I didn't mean to confuse ye."

Her instant compassion for the beast was sweet and told him she would put an effort into learning, as much for the sake of the horse as anything else. "So, I think today we will just work on what ye're telling her with the reins...I'll teach ye how to whisper."

He spent the next hour and a half teaching her the absolute basics while only walking. Elsie did learn quickly and had improved tremendously but he couldn't resist needling her a bit. "We'll call it a day now, lass. Edda has served valiantly and deserves a bit of peace." He lifted her off Edda's back.

Elsie frowned. "Was I that bad? I was trying as hard as I could. I don't want to hurt her."

Her concern for the beast was admirable. He lifted her chin to peer into her eyes and saw sincerity there. "Nay, Elsie. Ye did well." She gave him her sweet, lopsided smile and he simply couldn't resist. "And never fear, Edda cares much less about yer lovely backside than I do. She'd have dumped ye on it before she suffered mistreatment."

She huffed but the smile didn't leave her face. "Ye're incorrigible."

He grinned. "Nay, lass. I simply have good taste in bonny backsides." He captured her lips in a quick kiss before she could react, and was delighted to see how it knocked her off balance.

"I—I—I need to go find Morag. Thank ye for the lesson. Hopefully I'll be able to ride back to Castle Macrae when the time comes."

"Oh, nay lass, ye haven't improved that much. Ye'll need quite a few more lessons before Edda will be able to stand ye on her back for three days. We'll do this again tomorrow. Meet me here after the midday meal."

"Ye can't be serious."

"Oh, but I am. Be here tomorrow afternoon." He grinned. "Or there will be consequences."

"Consequences?" She asked incredulously.

"Aye, lass. Shall I demonstrate?"

"Uh…nay…that won't be necessary." She stepped away from him. "I'll see ye tomorrow."

~ * ~

Although Cade imagined it would have been fun to teach her the consequences of ignoring his requests, Elsie did meet him every afternoon just as he'd asked. When she had a better understanding of the basics, he moved on to trotting. That was an entirely new challenge and for a while he wasn't sure which one of the three of them was more frustrated. As soon as Edda began to trot, it was as if everything Elsie had just learned flew from her mind.

"Elsie, how many times do I have to tell ye not to lean forward? Ye can grip the saddle, or Edda's mane—she won't mind that—but when ye lean forward and dig yer heels in, she thinks ye want to run."

"Oh, dear God, nay. I don't want to do that."

"Then stop leaning forward."

"But, I don't like bouncing—I'm afraid I'll fall off."

"Edda doesn't like ye bouncing either, and it's worse when ye hold yerself so stiffly. Relax a bit; keep your back and pelvis supple. Your body will absorb the shock better and it will be easier on both of ye. Now try again—just a slow, sitting trot. Ye need to give a very subtle signal. A little click of yer tongue is all she needs. Any more than that and she'll think ye want to go faster."

She tried again, but after Edda's first few steps, Elsie tensed, leaned forward and let the reins go slack. It took nearly an hour for her to be able to progress from a walk to a sitting trot and stay relaxed enough to remain upright.

Cade decided it was best to stop while they were ahead. "That's enough for today," he called.

Elsie gave a gentle, "Whoa," and Edda stopped smoothly. The lass smiled, looking inordinately pleased with herself.

He helped her down from the saddle but kept his hands on her waist. "Ye're getting better."

She blushed. "That isn't saying much, is it?"

He chuckled. "Aye, ye still have a fair amount to learn. But ye're not going anywhere for a while—so there's time."

An odd expression that he couldn't quite read crossed her face briefly before she answered, "Aye, I suppose there is time."

He leaned down, catching the lavender scent of her hair. She was intoxicating. "That's a very good thing." His voice sounded low and husky even to his own ears. It pleased him to hear her breath hitch. He was certain she felt the same attraction he did.

"Aye...uh, well...I..."

"My thoughts exactly," he whispered.

She blushed profusely. "Excuse me, Sir Cade. I...I...must check on Lady Wynda."

She twisted sideways, and hurried across the bailey to the keep.

She might feel the attraction, but she was doing an extremely good job of not giving into it.

He led Edda back to the stable.

Eric was there saddling his own horse. "Since when have ye taken to riding palfreys?"

"I wasn't riding her. I've been teaching Elsie to ride."

Eric barked a laugh. "I know that, Cade. Everyone does."

Cade arched a brow. "And ye find it amusing?"

"What's amusing is how days ago ye assured me ye were, what was the word? Intrigued. Aye, that was it. Ye said ye were intrigued by her and that ye were in no danger of losing yer heart."

"By the saints, Eric, I'm just teaching her to ride—so she can ride back to her home...when the time comes."

"Keep telling yerself that each time ye can't take yer hands off her."

"Ye're an arse."

"Ye've said that before, but it doesn't stop me from being right. What's remarkable is her ability to resist yer charms when she is equally as attracted to ye."

Cade sighed. He really couldn't deny it. "Aye, she's a challenge."

Eric laughed. "A challenge is good for ye." He sobered. "But I've warned ye—pursuing her will have a price. One that could be hard for both of ye to pay. Perhaps she has considered that and is simply being sensible."

Cade frowned.

"And then there's always the possibility that she is simply a good lass who wants love and marriage to a lad who is worthy of her."

"Love?" He could love her. Loving her would be easy—marriage was the problem.

As if reading his thoughts Eric said, "Aye, Cade, love.

Ye have to follow Uncle Angus's wishes. She can marry whomever she desires. She might even have a lad pining for her at this moment."

"Nay, she doesn't." His tone was more vehement than he intended.

"Ye're certain?"

"Aye, I'm certain." On their journey to Carraigile, when he had asked her if she was thinking about home or someone special, she had said *just home*. But an annoying little voice whispered: *that doesn't necessarily mean there isn't someone special*.

Eric shrugged. "Still, she's a smart lass and knows as well as ye do that there's no future for her with ye."

Cade knew Eric was right. Winning Elsie's affection would ultimately mean hurting her, but that awareness fled anytime she was within an arm's length. "Then I expect it's best to finish teaching her to ride so she can return home."

"Keep telling yerself that."

Chapter 14

As hard as Elizabeth was finding learning to ride, she did look forward to her lessons. She liked spending time with Cade more than she wanted to admit. He was so easy to be with, but she couldn't quite put her finger on why. He was never deferential and had no trouble offering criticism. He clearly enjoyed teasing her mercilessly. She laughed a lot when she was with him—more than she ever remembered laughing with anyone else. Oddly, these things all lent an air of comfortable compatibility to their interactions. Then too, there was the scorching sexual tension between them that often left her breathless and longing.

She could fall in love with this man. She could imagine spending the rest of her life as his wife. He might frustrate the devil out of her regularly, but she could absolutely love him. It was only her concern for Elsie that held her back.

Occasionally, as she lay in her bed at night, she allowed herself to imagine what it would be like to stay here…and marry him.

That was until she learned marriage to Cade MacKenzie would never be an option.

Almost a week after her first riding lesson, she discovered a little fact about medieval life that she hadn't previously understood. During the evening meal, she sat at the trestle tables with Deirdre, Shauna and several of the other young women who worked in the castle.

"How are yer riding lessons coming?" asked Deirdre.

"I suppose that depends on who ye ask. Sir Cade says I'm getting better, but I feel like I'm still bouncing along hopelessly."

Shauna laughed. "I suspect Sir Cade wants ye to finish

learning to ride a horse so he can teach ye to ride something else."

Several of the young women tittered at her bawdy suggestion.

Elizabeth shrugged. "That isn't likely."

Shauna raised an eyebrow. "Ye don't think he wants ye in his bed?"

"It doesn't matter if he wants it or not. It won't happen."

"Well, that'd be a first. Most lassies he sets his eye on are more than willing to end up in his bed and he's never given them cause to regret it."

"That's because he usually sets his eye on lassies who are already so inclined," said Deirdre. "Elsie isn't ye, Shauna."

"She isn't ye either. Not every lass is so particular, looking for undying love and marriage. I suspect she's open to a bit of fun. Ye might want to consider it too—ye aren't that great a catch."

Deirdre flushed, embarrassed.

Elizabeth couldn't let it pass. "If by *open to a bit of fun*, ye mean willing fall into just anyone's bed, nay, I wouldn't say that. And have ye never heard that a man's not likely to buy a cow when he can get the milk for free?"

The other maids at the table laughed. It was no secret that Shauna was not in the least particular. She warmed the bed of nearly any man who glanced in her direction. It did surprise Elizabeth a little to learn that evidently Shauna had been *open to a bit of fun* with Cade.

Shauna scowled at her. "Well, if ye're so particular, ye'd do well to stay away from Sir Cade—or any of the young noblemen that sniff after ye. Although they're good for a cuddle, not a single one of them is going to marry a serving maid or even a midwife."

"Well, that's the truth," said Kirsty. "Even sons of younger sons are destined to marry whoever is chosen for them. Give me a handsome crofter or guardsman any day."

Shauna gave them all a smug smile. "Even the son of a younger son can make a lass's life a tad easier if he wants to. Lots of noblemen keep mistresses, and keep them well. I'd prefer a man who adores me and showers me with presents to a poor farmer or guardsman."

Elizabeth shook her head. "That's an interesting perspective, but I think Deirdre has the right of it. Choose once, and choose carefully. I'd rather have a partner for life. Ye can't cuddle up to costly gifts on a cold night."

"Lovers are just as warm as husbands," observed Shauna.

"Perhaps, but a husband will still be keeping ye warm come dawn," countered Elizabeth, garnering nods from several women.

Shauna shrugged. "No worries. I'll just have my lover build up the fire before he goes."

The women laughed and the subject moved to a less coarse topic.

However, when Elizabeth retired that night, her thoughts strayed back to that conversation. She hadn't realized that noblemen didn't choose their own wives. She guessed Cinderella really was a fairytale. Based on what she had learned tonight, even if she weren't so protective of Elsie's body, the chemistry she felt with Cade was destined for nothing. To Cade, Elizabeth—or rather, Elsie—would simply be another lass with whom to enjoy *a bit of fun*. Even so, Elizabeth decided, if the opportunity presented itself, she would get Cade's perspective.

~ * ~

As fate would have it, the opportunity presented itself the next afternoon during her riding lesson. When she'd arrived at the stable, Elizabeth had been surprised to find Cade had not only saddled Edda, but his own horse as well. "Ye're riding with me today?"

"Aye, ye've learned all ye can while riding in circles in the bailey. We'll ride out of the castle today so ye can learn how not to bruise yer soft round backside when Edda trots a little faster."

She rolled her eyes but chose not to comment.

Of course then she'd spent the next hour giving that part of her anatomy a pounding.

Cade had explained that a trot was a two beat gait. "The right front leg and the rear left leg move together, then the left front and the right rear. To keep from bouncing, ye rise up a little on the first beat, then sit on the second beat."

"That sounds exhausting—and hard on yer knees."

"It shouldn't be. Yer knee is part of it, but most of the motion should be in yer pelvis. Yer lower leg should maintain gentle pressure and yer heels still need to be pointed down. It's taken ye long enough to learn that." He winked, "But ye'll see now it will help ye maintain balance at the faster gait."

"Still rising up and down with every step seems tiring."

"It isn't as bad as ye think. Ye use the motion of the horse to rise out of the saddle. Watch." He clicked his tongue and his horse sped to a trot.

Elizabeth had never paid attention before, but now that she watched closely she could see that he rose slightly on every other beat. "Ye see, it's not a huge motion, ye don't want to stand up in your stirrups."

He turned and trotted back to her, dismounted, secured his mount and moved to stand beside her. "First, I just want ye to practice the rising motion."

He placed one hand on her knee and the other on her hip.

"Are ye sure this isn't just an excuse to put yer hand on my knee?"

"I see no reason not to have a little fun myself

whenever possible. But if ye like it, I'm sure I can touch ye other places that ye'll enjoy more." He moved his hand slightly, starting to slide it up her inner thigh.

She grabbed his wrist to stop its journey upwards.

He tsked. "Nay, lass, ye must keep yer hands still."

"Then, ye must limit yerself to touching my knee."

"Alas, I fear we'll have to save those delights for another time then and get back to the lesson at hand. I want ye to just practice the rising motion. Keep yer lower legs still and yer hands down."

After he was satisfied that she had grasped the basic concept, he had her try to trot. That was the moment the pounding started. It was not nearly as easy as Cade had made it look. After about an hour, exasperated, Elizabeth finally said, "I'm sorry, I don't think I'm going to be able to do this."

He went to stand beside her, taking Edda's bridle in one hand. "Are ye giving up?"

His voice held a challenge Elizabeth was hard pressed to ignore, but her thighs and backside ached.

"Nay. But I don't seem to be doing anything right."

He canted his head. "Ye think not? Do ye remember riding out of Castle Macrae?"

She felt a hot blush rise in her cheeks. "I'll not forget that anytime soon."

"Neither will I." He grinned. "That was my first introduction to yer soft round backside." She huffed and he laughed. "Elsie, do ye not think yer riding's improved since then?"

She frowned. "I guess. A little."

He captured her gaze. "More than just a little. Ye've come a long way. Learning to trot properly is not terribly easy. It will take a while." Then he winked and put his other hand on her knee, sliding it up to her hip. "And I intend to enjoy every minute teaching ye."

She shook her head, "Ye're absolutely incorrigible."

"Ye've made that observation several times. Ye might want to mind that wee sharp tongue of yers, lest it require a few lessons in manners."

She laughed. "I'll try to be careful."

He winked again. "Don't be too careful, I quite enjoy those lessons too."

She chuckled but decided it was better to remain silent.

"I'll help ye down." He lifted her to the ground. "We'll give Edda a rest and I expect yer soft round backside could use a bit of a rest too."

"Why are ye so preoccupied with my posterior? Everybody has one."

"Aye, but not everyone has such a lovely one."

Elizabeth rolled her eyes, took a few steps, stopped and groaned.

He laughed, secured Edda where she could graze and took Elizabeth's hand. "Ye'll feel better if ye walk a bit."

Elizabeth liked the feel of her hand in his. It struck her that holding hands was both innocent, and at the same time incredibly intimate.

They hadn't walked far when Cade said, "Ye confuse me, Elsie."

Her eyebrows shot up. "How so?"

"Ye're not naïve. Ye don't exactly spurn my advances. In fact, ye give every indication that ye enjoy my kisses."

"Aye, I do. Ye're rather good at it."

"But ye let it go no further."

"Aye."

"That's what confuses me."

"Why? I should think it's perfectly clear. I like yer kisses, but I don't want it to go further."

He arched a brow at her. "That much was clear. What I want to know is why? I have never felt such a strong attraction to a woman. Ye must feel it."

"Aye, I do."

"But…"

"But I'm fully aware of the potential consequences of that choice. I don't want to be the subject of unkind gossip and I don't intend to bring fatherless children into this world. But mostly I believe that kind of intimacy should only happen between people who respect each other and can choose to spend their lives together."

"I respect ye."

Elizabeth couldn't hold back the snort. "Nay, ye don't. Ye're intrigued by me. Ye desire me. But ye don't respect me, nor can ye choose to marry me."

"Nay, I can't marry ye, but people can spend their lives together who aren't married. It's true that noblemen marry for political reasons but because of that, they are often condemned to loveless marriages. A great many of them keep mistresses who they adore."

"And that, Sir Cade, is proof that ye don't respect me. For that matter, I can assure ye, I'll never be intimate with a man who I must address as 'sir'."

"Ye wouldn't have to address me as 'sir' when we're alone."

Elizabeth laughed. *Bless his heart, he believes that resolves the issue.* "Perhaps I should clarify; I will not be intimate with someone who could never marry me, who would suggest I become his mistress, ultimately making me an adulteress when he married someone else, and who I must *ever* address as 'sir'."

Cade pulled her close, lowered his head and captured her lips in an ardent kiss that left Elizabeth weak in the knees. "Tell me ye don't desire me as much as I do ye."

She rested her forehead against his chest as she tried to catch her breath. Finally she pulled away, looking him in the eye. "I can't, but that was never the issue. I respect myself and the man I will marry someday too much to give in to momentary desire."

"And I desire ye too much not to keep trying."

"That's yer choice, but I assure ye, I will not change

my mind."

"Ah, my beautiful, cheeky, lass, challenge accepted."

She laughed. "I suppose every man needs to learn the taste of defeat at least once in his life."

"Defeat? Don't be so certain it'll be my will that's defeated."

He kissed her again, more deeply and passionately than before.

It was a shame that he could never marry her. He might have been worth staying in the thirteenth century for.

Chapter 15

Elizabeth had seen several of the pregnant women clan with Morag, but the story of how she had helped Laird MacLennan's heir fight a lung infection also circulated through the clan. A few clansmen and women began to seek her out to treat illnesses and injuries, making word of her skill spread even farther. However, it was the unusual heat treatment intended to make Jessie's baby turn that was the real talk among the MacKenzies.

After the first few times, Jessie had been doing the treatment each evening with her husband's help. She did seem to think the baby was more active over the next few days. But when it had been a full week and nothing more than that had happened, Elizabeth feared it was not going to work. But to her surprise and delight, the morning after the eighth treatment Jessie arrived at the keep during the morning meal, with Flora on her hip. She hurried across the great hall towards the table where Elizabeth sat.

"Elsie, I think the bairn turned. Last night I was in the position ye showed me and it felt as if the wee one was having a grand time, stretching and kicking, then it gave an almighty lurch."

"Really? It does sound as if it might have turned." Excited by the news, Elizabeth stood up. "Do ye mind if I check?"

Jessie grinned. "Nay, that's what I came up here for."

Deirdre, who had been breaking her fast with Elizabeth stood and reached for Flora. "Come to Auntie Deirdre, poppet."

Elizabeth cocked her head. "*Auntie* Deirdre? Are the two of ye sisters?"

Deirdre shook her head, looking a bit confused. "Nay."

Jessie laughed. "Nay, I don't have any sisters. Deirdre is John's youngest sister."

"Are ye? Ye never mentioned that," said Elizabeth.

Deirdre's brow knitted. "Should I have? Should I tell ye who all my relatives are?"

Elizabeth laughed. "Nay, Deirdre, I just thought ye might have mentioned it when—" at the confused look on Deirdre's face, she just smiled. "Nay, never mind." One glance at Jessie's amused expression told Elizabeth that even her family found Deirdre's scatterbrained behavior humorous.

Elizabeth stepped towards Jessie. "I can give ye a quick check." She felt the top of Jessie's belly with both hands and smiled. "There does seem to be a wee bottom here now. I'll need to check while ye're lying down to be sure the babe is in the right position, but aye, it seems to have turned."

This news spread through the clan faster than lightning and very soon, Elizabeth's days became filled with caring for pregnant, ill or injured MacKenzies. Not filled as they had been in the twenty-first century—back to back patients one blending into the next. Here she could take as much time as she needed with each person, or perhaps more importantly, as much time as they needed. She had never fully appreciated the value of letting a patient talk if they wished to. Not only was it sometimes therapeutic for a person just to have a sympathetic ear to listen to them, she also found she learned details that she might have missed otherwise.

Cade continued to teach her to ride, taking her out riding nearly every afternoon. It probably had ceased being necessary. She had become skilled enough to not risk injuring herself or her mount. But Cade insisted there was still much for her to learn. Of course he also took every opportunity to steal a kiss while they were alone.

Elizabeth supposed she should have just put her foot

down and stopped it, but truthfully, she didn't want to. He enjoyed their time together as much as she did. So as long as she didn't let it go too far, the time she spent with him was a guilty pleasure she was unwilling to give up. She tried to tell herself this was just like a vacation romance. She imagined returning to her own time with fond memories of the feel of his hands and the heat of his kisses, which she would be able to cherish for the rest of her life. Oddly this made her heart ache a little. Deep down she knew he wasn't really a quick fling and leaving him would hurt. Her feelings were much deeper than she wanted to admit.

These thoughts often swirled through her head as she lay alone in bed. They kept her awake imagining "what ifs" well into the night. That was why she was still awake when a knock sounded at her door, late one night, a little over a month after she had arrived at Carraigile. She was curled up under her covers trying to quiet her thoughts and drift off to sleep when the noise pulled her back from the edges of slumber. She rose and wrapped a blanket around her shoulders, before opening the door. "Oh, Stephan, it's ye. Is something wrong?"

"Nay, Elsie, Morag sent for ye. Jessie's bairn is coming and she'd like ye to be there."

"Of course. I'll just dress and go straight away. Thank ye for coming to fetch me."

"'Twas nothing." He turned to leave, but stopped, turning back to her. "Elsie, please take good care of her. She's my little sister and ever since the trouble she had with Flora, I know she's feared this. It's one reason I asked to come Cade to fetch ye."

Elizabeth's breath caught. She was certain that the medieval warrior in front of her wouldn't shrink from any foe, but the naked fear in his eyes gripped her heart. This wasn't just a fear of the unknown or unexpected, encountered regularly in her practice but easily minimized with the confidence of modern medicine. Stephan was terrified that his sister might not live through this night—a fear that was all too real here.

Elizabeth put a hand on his arm. "I will do everything in my power to help her, Stephan. I promise."

He nodded. "Thank ye, Elsie."

Elsie dressed quickly and hurried out of the keep. Everyone still awake in the great hall called to her as she passed, sending their prayers and good wishes for Jessie. Once again the sense of community moved her deeply.

When she reached the cottage, John waited outside with two older men. One she recognized as William, one of the MacKenzie guardsmen.

John looked like a classic worried father. "Elsie, thank ye for coming. This is my da, Lars, and I suspect ye know William. He's Jessie's father."

Surprise number two. But now that she knew, she was amazed she hadn't noticed before. The resemblance he bore to Stephan was striking.

"Good evening." She nodded to the men. "Is everything well?"

John frowned. "Aye, I suppose well enough."

"Flora is with yer older sister?"

"Aye."

She smiled at him. "And ye'd rather be out here?"

"Oh, by the saints, if I could be on the other side of the village I would be. Hearing Jessie's cries rends my heart."

Elizabeth frowned. "Has she been in a lot of pain then?"

John shook his head. "Nay, but if it's anything like the last time, she will be."

"Well, I'll go in and see what's what. I'd tell ye to stay calm, but I fear I'd be wasting my words."

Both older men chuckled. "Aye, I expect ye would be," said Lars.

Before Elizabeth entered the cottage William said,

"She's my only daughter, Elsie."

His message was as poignantly clear as Stephan's had been. *I'm afraid of losing her.* Elizabeth turned back to him and placed a hand on his arm. "I'll do everything in my power to bring everyone safely through this night. I promise."

He nodded.

She gave him as reassuring a smile as she could before entering the cottage. She found Jessie, clearly in the middle of a contraction, standing and clutching the edge of the table, while her mother, Sorcha, rubbed her back. A birthing chair stood to one side.

Morag sat in a chair near the hearth. "Elsie, thank ye for coming, lass."

Elsie gave her a warm smile. "I would have been very disappointed if ye hadn't sent for me. How long has she been laboring?"

"She's had the odd pain since late afternoon. They became regular about two hours ago. I sent for ye once they were stronger and closer together."

"Has her water broken?"

"Nay, but I expect it will soon."

When the contraction had passed, Jessie drew in a deep breath and blew it out before letting go of the table. She gave Elsie a hug. "I'm glad ye're here."

"Nothing could keep me away. How are ye doing?"

"I'm fine, so far. I've been trying to breathe like ye showed me to. I think it helps. A little at least."

Her mother nodded her agreement. "I wouldn't have thought it, but so far it does seem to make things easier."

"Good. Jessie, can I examine ye quickly before the next contraction comes?"

Jessie nodded. "Come with me into the bedroom." When both her mother and Morag started to follow, Jessie said, "Oh Mama, ye and Morag take a bit of a rest. We'll just be a minute."

Morag nodded knowingly and linked her arm in Sorcha's. "It'll be a long night, taking a moment to rest is a good idea."

Elizabeth suspected there was something Jessie wished to tell her privately, and clearly Morag did to. It didn't take long to find out what it was. As soon as they were in the little bedroom, Jessie turned to her and, gripping her by the arms, whispered, "I'm afraid, Elsie. I don't want mama and Morag to know. But I don't think I can do this. The last time…well, I can't live through that again."

Elizabeth put her arms around the other woman. "I know ye're frightened, but ye must remember, every birth is different and the first one is usually the most difficult."

"But, Elsie—"

Elizabeth guided her to the bed. "Nay. We are not going to borrow trouble. Ye're doing very well. Lie down so I can check ye and perhaps we can put a few of those fears to rest."

Based on the pattern of Jessie's labor so far, Elizabeth suspected she was in the latter stages of active labor and this was confirmed with her physical assessment. Jessie's cervix was dilated to about seven centimeters and the amniotic sac was bulging.

Jessie moaned just as Elizabeth finished her exam. "Another one is coming."

"Hold my hand and I'll breathe through it with ye."

Jessie squeezed her fingers so hard, Elizabeth feared they'd break. *Note to self, grip thumbs next time.* The contraction was strong and Elizabeth estimated that it lasted a little less than a minute.

When it was over, and Jessie had taken a deep cleansing breath, Elizabeth smiled. "Well done. Ye'll be happy to know, the baby is in the perfect position and things seem to be moving along very nicely. I don't think it will be much longer."

"Really?"

"Really. Yer womb is opening and yer contractions are strong and getting closer together."

"Should I stay lying down?"

"Not unless ye're more comfortable this way."

"Truthfully, I'm not."

"Then let me help ye up and we can go into the other room if ye wish."

"Aye, Mama will worry if we don't."

When they returned to the front room, it was to find that two more women had joined them. Sorcha introduced them. "Elsie, this is John's mother, Mary, and this is Stephan's wife, Kat. They've come to help.

"It's nice to meet ye both." Elizabeth wasn't sure how much help they needed, but Jessie appeared very pleased to see them. Then again, when Elizabeth stopped to think about it, there were always lots of people attending a modern birth—the obstetrician, nurses, sometimes an anesthesiologist and maybe even a neonatologist. Most of these people were strangers to the parents but their goal was to help the mother and newborn. These women were here for the same reason. They all cared deeply about Jessie and wanted to support her and do whatever they could.

After years of practicing as an obstetrician, for the first time in her life, Elizabeth joined in the ancient ritual of waiting for a child to enter the world instead of just swooping in at the end.

For the next couple of hours, things continued on has they had. Strong contractions came every five minutes or so and lasted close to a minute. Between contractions the women kept Jessie distracted. Elizabeth learned that Morag had delivered Jessie, John, Kat and all of their siblings. Elizabeth wondered what it would be like to know a woman from the day she was born to the day she delivered her children and perhaps their children.

During contractions, they breathed with Jessie as Elizabeth had suggested, rubbed her back, and offered quiet encouragement. Jessie still found it easier to stand when she was in the grips of pain, but she was becoming weary and often sat to wait for the next one.

Finally, her water broke. Sorcha and Kat helped her clean up and change into a dry shift. Then the contractions were more frequent, stronger, and lasted longer. After several of these, she cried, "Mama, I'm tired, I can't do this."

Sorcha put her arms around her daughter. "Of course ye're tired, sweetling, but ye can do this. Come sit with me and rest." Sorcha led her gently towards the bedroom. She sat on the bed with her back against the wall and helped Jessie sit in front of her, between her legs. Wrapped in her mother's arms, Jessie's back rested against her mother's chest. Sorcha crooned a soft song that sounded like a lullaby. Mary moved to sit beside the bed, holding Jessie's hand.

Elizabeth watched from the doorway as these two women who loved Jessie, helped her through the next several contractions with calm, quiet strength.

Morag sat in her chair near the hearth, taking a brief rest herself. "I expect it's nearly time."

Elizabeth turned to her. "Aye, it likely is."

"I'll get things ready," said Kat, who busied herself collecting linen toweling, positioning the birthing chair and hanging a pot of water to warm over the fire. She also put a large wooden basin, a spool of thread and knife on the table.

Elizabeth reckoned that the thread was to tie off the cord and the knife for cutting it. "Morag, I know I have mentioned how important it is to keep things very clean. I've found it to be helpful to wash the knife well and pour boiling water over it before using it to cut the cord."

"Have ye? I can't imagine what it would do, but I see no harm in it. Kat, lass, can ye do that?"

"Aye, of course, Morag."

When the water was boiling, Elizabeth poured some into the basin and when it had cooled, she washed her hands meticulously. At Kat's questioning look, Elizabeth explained. "As I said, I've also found if ye keep anything that comes into contact with the mother or the baby very clean, they both stay healthier and are less likely to take a fever."

Kat shrugged and washed her hands. Morag did too.

Jessie was no longer able to keep from crying out during contractions, and after another long, keening wail, Elizabeth went into the bedroom.

"Elsie, the pressure is terrible. I need to push."

"Let me check to see if yer womb is fully open." She examined Jessie quickly and smiled. "Aye, ye're ready. Ye can push with the next contraction."

"Do ye want to stay here or sit in the chair?" her mother asked.

"The chair," said Jessie.

She had barely made it to the chair when she was gripped by another strong contraction.

"All right, Jessie, push while I count to ten," said Elizabeth. When she reached ten, she said, "Take a deep breath and push again." They repeated this one more time until the contraction left. "Now take a deep breath and let it go."

Jessie pushed in this manner for about twenty minutes before the baby started crowning, a little more of its head appearing each time.

After several more contractions, Elizabeth said, "We're almost there. This next one should do it."

Sure enough, the baby's head was out with the next push. "Stop pushing now for a moment." Elizabeth slipped a finger to the baby's neck to be sure the cord wasn't around it.

Morag handed her one of the clean linen towels. "All right, one more push, lass and we've a new MacKenzie."

The Midwife

Within moments a newborn's cry rent the air. Elizabeth wrapped the babe in a towel and smiling broadly, placing him in Jessie's arms. "Ye have a wee son."

Jessie laughed and cried, as did the other women in the room.

Elizabeth did not cut the umbilical cord immediately. Although it was the common practice in western medicine, it only began in the eighteenth century. She had read several articles recently suggesting that there was no harm in waiting a few minutes, so she elected not to shock her medieval friends by cutting the cord too soon. She waited until after she had delivered the placenta before tying off the cord and cutting it.

The other women took over caring for the baby and Jessie. Soon she was clean and tucked into bed with her newborn son suckling at her breast. Elizabeth and Morag tidied up all evidence of the birthing. When things were finally put to rights, Morag said. "Well done, Elsie."

Elizabeth smiled at her. "Was this another test?"

Morag chuckled quietly. "Aye, of course it was, and it's perfectly clear, ye may look like a bairn yerself, but ye're a skilled and capable midwife."

"Thank ye, Morag." Elizabeth hugged her. She had come to respect and admire the old woman immensely over the last two weeks. Now that she had received it, Elizabeth realized that gaining Morag's approval had been as important to her as passing her medical board exams had been.

"Now, lass, let's go tell John, he has a son and ye can walk me home. Things are well in hand here."

They stepped outside together and when she saw the worried men, Morag's face split into a broad grin. "Good news, Jessie is well and ye have a braw new son." John looked profoundly relieved. His father and father-in-law slapped him on the shoulders, offering their congratulations.

"Ye can go in and see her now, lad."

"Thank ye, Morag. Thank ye, Elsie. For everything." John hurried into his little cottage without another word and after thanking the women themselves, William and Lars followed.

Elsie walked Morag back to her cottage and then went alone the rest of the way to the keep. As she walked, she thought back to her last night on call, before Gertrude had given her the pocket watch. She remembered feeling exhausted that morning but now she realized it was more than that. She had felt numb. She had delivered six babies that night and couldn't remember a single detail about any of the women, the course of their labor or the infants she brought into the world. The miracle of birth had become mundane for her.

Now, as she trudged wearily through the cold, dark, pre-dawn hours, she was just as tired as she had been that morning. But this morning she was not numb—far from it. Every detail of the birth was brilliantly sharp, colored with the array of emotions she had witnessed and experienced. She had not only brought a new soul into the world, she had been a part of a sisterhood: the women who, throughout time, supported, encouraged, and loved a woman through one of the most painful, frightening and yet awe-inspiring moments of her life.

Elizabeth knew that this birth, out of the hundreds, perhaps thousands, she had attended, was different. It was exactly what she had imagined every day of her life as an obstetrician would be. It was what she had wanted. Gertrude's words came back to her yet again, *There was a time when doctors, healers and midwives experienced exactly what ye say ye want.*

When she reached the keep, Stephan was one of the men on watch. "How is she?" he asked, his tone as rife with worry as it had been hours ago.

She smiled broadly, thrilled to be able to deliver

wonderful news. "Everything went well. She's fine and the babe is a strong, healthy boy."

"Oh, thank God." Relief flooded his expression.

"Yer parents and Kat were still with her when I left."

"Aye, I expect they were, I'll stop by when the next watch comes on. Thank ye, Elsie."

She nodded. "Ye're welcome."

"Now, ye should find yer bed, ye look weary."

"I will. Good night, Stephan."

She slipped into the keep as quietly as possible. Most of the people bedded down in the great hall still slept, but a few roused as she passed and asked about Jessie.

The news, "She had a son and all's well," was always met with joy and prayers of thanksgiving.

When she reached her chamber, she didn't bother starting a fire in the brazier. She removed her outer garment and climbed into bed, pulling the covers over her. She sighed, satisfied with her night's work, and gave in to sleep.

Chapter 16

Elizabeth was jarred awake suddenly by the sound of metal crashing into metal and an intense pain in the back of her head. She sat up in bed, confused for a moment. She had been dreaming about being in the cab when the accident happened. She blinked several times in early morning light, taking in the room around her. *Right. The pocket watch. Thirteenth century Scotland.*

Not ready to venture beyond the warmth of her bed, she lay back down, snuggling under the covers. She tried to remember the dream. The cabbie had been asking her about music. He'd asked her what kind of music she liked, but he didn't want to listen to country-western. He asked her about *Christian rock, salsa, gangsta rap and...something obscure.* Why did she think it had something to do with video games?

She took a deep breath, closed her eyes and tried to relax. Maybe she could remember the whole conversation. After he shot down country-western he had asked if there was anything she didn't like.

"I don't think so."

"Christian Rock?"

"That's fine."

"Salsa?"

"Whatever."

"Gangsta rap?"

"I guess I don't really care for gangsta rap."

"How about Nintendocore?"

Nintendocore. That was it. That was the last word she'd said. She hadn't heard of it before and remembered thinking it might have something to do with video games, but the accident happened before she could ask the cabbie.

Nintendocore was the return word. She just needed to tell Gertrude and she could go back to the twenty-first century. For some reason, this thought made her sad.

She had been in the thirteenth century for nearly four weeks. From the moment she'd arrived, she'd struggled every day to remember the word. Now that she had, why did her heart feel so heavy?

Because the truth is, you haven't struggled every day to remember the word. You stopped thinking about it after the first few days.

What had changed? What had quieted the desire to go back to her old life? And when did she start thinking of it as her *old life*, instead of home?

She didn't want to think about the future. She had five weeks before she had to go back. Besides, she couldn't do anything until Gertrude sought her out anyway.

Elizabeth rose, dressed and ventured downstairs. She must have only slept a few hours, as it appeared many people were just beginning their work.

She popped into the kitchen to get a bannock and the herb tea that had become a replacement for her morning coffee.

Ellen and the other women working in the kitchen had heard the news about the baby and greeted her exuberantly.

"Come, sit down here at the table and I'll make ye a bowl of the sweet porridge ye like."

The words 'nay thank ye' were on the tip of her tongue but she couldn't say them. Ellen wanted to do this for her and Elizabeth wouldn't deny her that.

So she sat in the kitchen chatting with the women and eating her breakfast. They wanted details of how Jessie's labor had gone. They were all aware of the trouble she'd had bearing Flora. Elizabeth, the modern doctor who didn't wish to break confidentiality, found a way to offer vague details without divulging more than she was comfortable with. The women seemed satisfied.

After Elizabeth had finished her breakfast, she said, "I should be going and get out from underfoot."

"Ah, lass, ye're always welcome here," Ellen assured her. "But are ye going to see Jessie this morn?"

"Aye, I intend to go there now."

"Well then, would ye mind taking her some fresh bread? I expect neither Sorcha nor Mary will have time to bake today."

"Aye, I'd be happy to."

Ellen wrapped several loaves in cloth and placed them in a basket. Then she tucked a small covered crock in between the loaves. "Raspberry preserves," she said by way of explanation. "I know Jessie loves it."

Elizabeth smiled. "That is so kind of ye. I'm sure she'll be pleased."

Ellen beamed.

Elizabeth delivered the basket and checked Jessie and the babe over. Knowing that infection—childbed fever— was one of the illnesses that took many young mothers' lives, Elizabeth reemphasized the need for keeping everything as clean as possible. Although they didn't understand the connection, they were willing to believe Elizabeth.

Satisfied that the new mother and baby were well, Elizabeth bid them farewell and John showed her out of the cottage.

"Elsie, I can't thank ye enough for all ye've done."

"'Twas my pleasure."

"I pray the laird and lady will be as fortunate."

Elsie smiled at him. "As do I. Only time will tell, but I'm hopeful." She looked momentarily towards the keep.

"Are ye heading back to the keep now?"

She knew she should probably go back, but she hadn't been able to sort out her jumbled emotions since remembering the word that morning. The day was fine and bright. A light breeze whispered the promise of spring, enticing her to take a walk.

"Nay 'tis a lovely day. I think I'll go for a walk by the loch."

He nodded. "Aye, it's a grand day for a walk."

She bid him farewell and reaching the edge of the village in just a few minutes, she continued on until she reached the shore of the loch. All was still and very peaceful. That's exactly what she needed, a bit of peace. So she walked along the shore, towards the forest on the northern edge. Eventually she came to several large boulders. She climbed up to sit on one. Looking out over the loch, she tried to quiet her mind and simply absorb the wild beauty surrounding her.

She failed miserably.

She had been troubled from the moment she remembered the word this morning but she couldn't figure out why. She should be happy knowing Elsie could rearrange their souls again. The events of the last month swirled in her brain as she searched for some logical explanation for her disquiet.

Elizabeth wasn't sure how long she had been lost in contemplation when she heard the crunch of footsteps on the gravel at the loch's edge. Somehow, she knew who it was even before she looked up.

"So, ye've remembered the word?"

"Aye, Gertrude, I have."

"Ye don't seem happy. I expected ye to be champing at the bit, thinking three moves ahead. What's wrong?"

"I haven't thought three moves ahead for days. I have no clue what's happening to me."

"Do ye not? Truly?"

"Maybe it's as ye suggested, the powers that be have stepped in to slow me down."

"Aye, well that's certainly true. And what happened when ye were forced to live in the moment?"

What had happened? She brought hope to a frightened

woman—two frightened women. She made friends—not peers or colleagues—friends, for whom she cared deeply. She had learned to ride a horse. She danced—sort of. She experienced life.

Gertrude nodded sagely. "Ah, I see. Ye fell in love."

Elizabeth actually laughed. "Love? Nay Gertrude, I didn't fall in love. I mean I like Cade. I like him a lot, but I'm not in love."

"I didn't say ye fell in love with a man—although he would have turned my head a few years ago. Nay, ye might not have fallen in love with a man, but ye fell in love nevertheless."

"I don't understand."

"Do ye not? Then ye're ready to tell me the word and switch souls again?"

"Nay. Not yet. I…"

"Why?"

"Because I…I…"

"Ye're in love—with the people of this clan and the positive effect ye can have on their lives. Ye found the life ye've always longed for. What was it David said to ye? He wanted ye to find yer destiny and embrace it."

"How do ye know that?"

"Really, Elizabeth? Need ye ask?"

She smiled and shook her head.

Gertrude looked at her seriously for a moment. "Have ye found it? Yer destiny? Is it here among these people who you have come to love and who love ye dearly in return?"

Tears filled Elizabeth's eyes. "I don't know. How can I stay? What about Elsie? Even if she didn't want to exchange souls again, at some point I'll be expected to go back to the Macraes and I'll lose all of this anyway."

Gertrude laughed. "There ye go—thinking three moves ahead. I'm going to ask ye again and I don't want ye to consider what ye might believe is *expected* of ye. I want ye to give me the answer that is written in yer heart. It was yer desire to have an impact. Can ye do that here? Is yer destiny among these people? Caring for them, rejoicing with them, mourning with them, bringing them hope and comfort? Do ye want to stay?"

Leave everything behind and stay? Could she do that? The tears slipped down her cheeks, but even as she wiped them away, she knew they were for the people she would leave here if she returned to her own time. "Aye, Gertrude, I want to stay. These are the truly the dark ages, it's a hard existence. But ye're right, I've fallen in love with an entire community—a way of life. I love my parents, and I know they love me, but it's different here. Love is present in ways I've never experienced it."

"Elizabeth, when ye're always moving to the next thing, it's easy to miss the love around ye. I'm glad ye've finally found it."

"But I can't just ignore Elsie. I at least made the choice to accept the pocket watch. Elsie had no say in any of this. I can't decide to stay unilaterally."

Gertrude smiled. "Funnily enough, Elsie too has fallen in love. I haven't asked her whether she wishes to stay yet." Gertrude winked. "But I'm fairly sure she will."

"And what happens when the time comes for me to go back to Macrae?"

"Ye aren't the right midwife—or had ye forgotten?"

"But—"

"Have a little faith. If ye're meant to stay here, here ye'll stay."

"Ye're certain?"

Gertrude arched a brow at her. "Ye doubt me?"

Elizabeth gave a little laugh. "Nay, I guess not."

"Then believe that the universe unfolds as it should. If events transpire that take ye back to clan Macrae, 'twill be what's intended for ye—and them."

"But, Gertrude, ye said it yerself, I love this clan. I

don't know if I want to stay if I can't be here among the MacKenzies."

Gertrude narrowed her eyes. "Elizabeth, none of us are promised tomorrow. Can you imagine falling as profoundly in love with a man as ye have with the clan?"

Elizabeth's thoughts immediately went to Cade. She couldn't stop the slow smile that spread across her face. "Aye Gertrude, I can imagine it."

"Then, as ye are aware, loved ones are taken from us unexpectedly in every age. Ye're a doctor, ye know that's true."

Elizabeth nodded.

"Loving someone is not a guarantee that ye'll have them forever. The fact is, there's never enough time with a loved one. Couples who have been together for decades—fifty, sixty, seventy years or more—will tell ye even that's not enough time together. Knowing this, now that ye've experienced love in so many ways, would ye choose to protect yerself from the pain of loss by not falling in love? Would ye have held yer heart away from Morag or any of the other MacKenzies? If ye could, would ye go back to that moment on the plane and refuse the pocket watch?"

The events and emotions of the last month played in Elizabeth's mind like montage of movie clips. She shook her head. "Nay, I wouldn't trade this for anything. Every day has been a gift."

"And as long as ye wake each morning believing that, they will continue to be, whether ye're here or elsewhere. So will ye take the gamble? Do ye still want to stay here knowing ye have no assurances about tomorrow or next week, or next year?"

Elizabeth took a deep breath and nodded. "Aye. Whatever time I have here is worth it."

"Excellent. Tomorrow will come when it comes, bringing what it brings. So for now, live fully in the moment."

"I will. Or at least I'll try to."

"Good. Now, I have to go tell Elsie the good news."

"Do ye want to know the word? Just in case?"

"Nintendocore?"

"Ye knew? How did ye find out?"

Gertrude chuckled. "How do ye think I found out? I asked the cabbie."

"Why didn't ye tell me?"

"Before ye had time to find yer destiny? Nay, Elizabeth. Several weeks ago ye suggested that ye had no choice in any of this, but it should be obvious ye do. Still, things had to happen in their own time. I told ye, when the time was right, ye'd remember the word, and ye did. Ye needed to stay long enough to decide here is where ye belong. Once ye did, ye remembered the word so ye could make the choice to stay."

Elizabeth laughed. "I suppose there's a logic there."

"Of course there is. And now that ye've made yer decision and embraced yer destiny, I must be going. Come give me a hug." Gertrude opened her arms.

Elizabeth stepped into her embrace. "Will I see ye again?"

"Who knows what the future holds?" Gertrude laughed merrily.

Chapter 17

Cade had looked for Elsie that afternoon to take her riding. No one seemed to know where she was. She had been up most of the night, delivering John and Jessie's baby, but he had seen her earlier that morning walking towards the kitchens. Maybe she had gone to the village to check on Jessie and the bairn—the watch would know if she had left the keep. Cade strode to the castle gates.

"Affric, did Elsie pass this way?"

"Aye, several hours ago. I think she was on her way to see Jessie."

"Several hours ago? And she hasn't returned?"

"Nay she hasn't. Does Lady Wynda need her? I can send someone."

"That isn't necessary. Lady Wynda is fine. I'll go find Elsie myself."

"As ye wish, sir."

When he reached John and Jessie's cottage, John was outside, cutting wood.

"Congratulations, John. I understand ye have a braw laddie. Are Jessie and the bairn well?"

John grinned. "Aye, thank ye, Sir Cade. They are both in fine form."

"That's good to hear. Is Elsie with them?"

"Nay, she stopped in earlier, but as all's well, she didn't stay long. Elsie's mother and my own are helping out."

"Was she going to Morag's?"

"Nay, she said she was going for a walk."

"A walk? Alone?"

"Aye, she intended to walk to the loch."

Cade scowled.

John looked confused. "Is there something wrong with that, sir?"

Cade had to remind himself that Elsie was not a noblewoman who needed to be guarded. As a common lass she could walk outside the walls and village if she chose to. Still he didn't like it. "Nay, John, it's fine. Congratulations again."

"Thank ye, sir."

Cade returned to the castle stable to saddle a horse. As he did, he allowed himself to become irritated. Riding with her was his favorite part of the day. Ever since he'd started teaching her, he had claimed her nearly every afternoon. Ignoring this, she had simply gone off on her own. A little voice inside said, *ye only take her riding when ye're free to go, not to mention the fact that she didn't promise to ride with ye today.*

He shut that voice up. He'd rather be angry.

He left the keep, heading towards the loch. Seeing her nearly on the other side of it, walking towards him, he rode to meet her.

"What are ye doing out here alone?" He couldn't keep the annoyance out of his voice.

In her usual irreverent way, she put her hands on her hips and looked up at him. "Enjoying the lovely afternoon, until I encountered an ill-tempered man."

"I don't need yer cheek today." But in fact, he longed for her spirited responses.

She grinned at him. "That's odd. If I had to guess, I'd say ye were looking for me, so I reckon ye can either keep riding or put up with it."

Dear God, she was not like any other woman he had ever encountered. He leaned forward in his saddle, trying not to show his amusement. "Ye would try the patience of a saint." She opened her mouth but he put a hand up to stop her. "Before ye vex me more by pointing it out, nay, I'm not a saint."

She laughed. "I should say not."

He reached a hand down to her. "Ride with me."

"I was enjoying my walk."

"Nevertheless, ye'll ride."

"Ye're bossier than usual today. What's irritating ye?" Even as she said it, she took his hand and let him pull her up and onto his lap.

"A certain wee midwife who went wandering off instead of showing up for her riding lesson."

"We had no plans today and I needed some time alone."

"Why?"

"To sort a few things out."

"What things?

"It's none of yer business."

That was a challenge he could not resist. He stopped the horse, cupped the back of her head in one hand and turned her towards him. "That impudent tongue really is going to get you into trouble." Then he captured her lips in a demanding kiss. As ever, she didn't resist, but rather, returned his passion with fervor. When he broke the kiss, he rested his forehead against hers. "What is it ye do to me lass?"

She laughed. "Ye kiss me and it's my fault?"

"It must be. I don't seem to think clearly when ye are within an arm's length." Hell, he didn't seem to think clearly when she was anywhere in sight.

"That doesn't make it my problem." She turned to face front but leaned back, relaxing against his chest.

He put one arm around her waist, pulling her even more snuggly against him. "Ye're a puzzlement, Elsie."

She chuckled but gave no response.

They rode back to the village in comfortable silence. She was indeed a puzzlement. He had never worked so hard to win a lass's affection while at the same time feeling so closely connected with her. She had warned him that she would not let it go further. But he not only felt she belonged with him, it was nearly as if they had already been together for ages.

When they reached the inner bailey, he dismounted, then lifted her down. He stood her on the ground, between himself and the horse.

"I...I really should go see Lady Wynda."

"Not until ye promise to go riding with me tomorrow."

"As long as I am not needed elsewhere, I'll go riding with ye tomorrow."

"That isn't exactly the promise I was seeking."

She grinned. "Well, it's the only one I'm prepared to give."

He shook his head but smiled. Nothing with her was ever easy. "Then I suppose I'll have to take it."

She tilted her head to one side. "I expect ye'll have to if ye want to go riding with me at all."

"Bold lass." He leaned down and kissed her. Not as passionately as he wished to, because they had an audience, but he kissed her nonetheless. It did thrill him that she always seemed to be knocked as much off-balance by the kisses they shared as he was.

"Good day, Sir Cade." She hurried into the keep.

Sir Cade. He had begun to hate it when she called him that. He remembered the day he had pushed to know why she kept him at arm's length. She had said she wished to be respected. He firmly believed he did respect her. *But she had also said, "I'll never be intimate with a man who I must address as 'sir'."* There was absolutely no getting around the fact that he was a member of the nobility and she was not. He sighed and led his horse into the stable.

~ * ~

As Elizabeth entered the keep, she realized she hadn't fully thought out all the implications of staying in the thirteenth century—in Elsie's body. She no longer had to worry about her choices resulting in long-term consequences for the lass. She *was* the lass now. The consequences would be hers to manage.

She allowed her thoughts to roam towards the man who sent her senses reeling every time they were together. She had never met a man like Cade; at least she didn't think she had. Her thoughts flitted briefly to her first boyfriend, the first man she had ever slept with. He had been wonderful. Perhaps if the *powers that be* had stepped in to slow her down then, things with him might have been different. She had dated a few men since then and, even though she enjoyed their company, she had never been attracted to any of them as powerfully as she was to Cade. Maybe that's why all of her relationships had ended in precisely the same way as the one with David had. Her busy work schedule interfered, and eventually the man would bow out. She tried to imagine dating Cade in the twenty-first century. A pleasant heat blossomed within her. She couldn't imagine cancelling a date with him, even if she had worked twenty-four hours straight.

She gave a mirthless laugh. When she finally met a man to whom she was inexplicably drawn, he wasn't someone with whom she could have a permanent relationship. Rather like the complaint she had often heard before, *all the good ones are married.* He wasn't exactly married; he wasn't even betrothed. But he would be someday and to someone of his father's choosing. *Definitely not me.* Still, perhaps she could enjoy a casual friendship. She had before, and while not particularly fulfilling, it had been pleasant.

Ah well, she'd cross that bridge when she came to it. Now she realized she needed to speak with Lady Wynda. Other than Gertrude, she was the only person who knew the truth about the pocket watch and Elizabeth needed to tell her what had happened.

She went straight to Wynda's chamber and knocked.

Lilliana opened the door to her. A huge smile spread across her face. "Elsie, do come in, lass."

Wynda called from the bed. "Oh Elsie, I heard the wonderful news about Jessie and John's new bairn. I am so happy for them. I wish I could go see them."

Her excitement was palpable. Elsie suspected that on hearing the news of the birth, Wynda allowed herself to envision her own healthy child. Elsie had never been much for prayer, but she said a silent one in that moment. *Dear, God, please let this baby live.*

"I've been to check on them today, and both Jessie and the babe are well. As soon as Jessie has recovered a bit, I'm sure she'd be happy to bring him for a visit."

"Oh, I'd love that." Wynda practically glowed. "I normally go visit new mothers."

"Wynda, if Elsie can stay with ye for a while, I'll extend yer congratulations and invite Jessie to visit as soon as she is able," said Lilliana.

"That's an excellent idea."

"Aye, my lady. If ye wish, I'll stay with Lady Wynda for the rest of the afternoon."

"Perfect. Will I send Alice up when it's time for the evening meal?"

"I'd be happy to stay here and dine with ye Lady Wynda," said Elizabeth.

Wynda smiled. "That would be lovely. Thank ye, Elsie."

"Well then, I'll see to that, and send Alice up afterwards."

"Thank ye, Lilliana. I don't know what I'd do without ye."

Lilliana took Wynda's hand for a moment, giving it a squeeze. "'Tis my pleasure."

After Lilliana had left, Wynda motioned towards a chair near the bed. "Come sit. Ye look like something's on yer mind."

"Aye, my lady, there is something on my mind, and ye're the only one I can speak to about it."

A sad expression crossed Wynda's face. "Did ye remember the word? Are ye leaving us, Elizabeth?"

"Well, I did remember the word, but I'm not leaving."

"Will ye stay the full sixty days then?"

"My lady, I've decided to stay for good. It seems that Elsie wants to stay in my time too."

"If ye know that, ye must have seen Gertrude today."

"Aye, I did. She reminded me of why I accepted the pocket watch in the first place. It was because I wanted to experience what it was like to care for patients more completely. To feel that I make an impact on their lives. I can do that in this time and place."

Wynda looked at her seriously. "Aye ye can. Do ye not think ye could find a way to accomplish that in yer own time?"

Elizabeth nodded. "I suppose I probably could, but there is more to it than that. Gertrude asked me to consider whether this is my destiny. I think it is. I feel...complete here."

Wynda sighed with relief, tears filling her eyes. "I prayed...I'm sorry Elizabeth, I prayed ye wouldn't remember the word, but this is more than I had hoped for. Ye've *chosen* to stay here with us."

"Aye, my lady, that's precisely it. I want to remain at Carraigile. I know I'm supposed to go back to Macrae, but I hope I don't have to. I hope there is a way I can stay here."

"Don't worry about a thing. We will make it happen. I promise, ye."

Elizabeth wasn't entirely sure that was within Wynda's power, but it raised her spirits nonetheless.

Chapter 18

As the days passed, Elizabeth was surprised at how very happy she felt. She loved working with Morag. The old midwife hadn't been threatened by Elizabeth and her unusual ideas. She had been open to learning and trying new things. To her surprise, Elizabeth realized almost immediately there was quite a bit she could learn from Morag. The old midwife had an air that conveyed both calm confidence and grandmotherly affection. Elizabeth had always been direct and efficient, perhaps blunt, but she told herself she didn't have the luxury of time in her modern practice.

When Morag visited someone who needed her she took her time. She chatted casually, offered advice as needed but often she just listened. Elizabeth would have considered this to be time wasted until she had experienced it herself. The truth was, Morag learned things by simply allowing people to talk. She managed to subtly direct conversation in a way that resulted in her learning all she needed without simply firing off personal questions.

Elizabeth's admiration for Morag grew daily, quickly moving beyond a professional respect, even beyond friendship. She felt closer to Morag than she ever had to her mother or grandmothers. She suffered a little guilt knowing it had been years since she had spent any significant time with her family, but their lives had been as busy as hers. Family never seemed to be a priority to any of them.

On the other hand, Elizabeth visited Morag every day. Some days Morag had a patient to go see, other days, they just chatted over an herbal tisane. And so it was, the day after Elizabeth had decided to stay in the thirteenth century, she was drawn into a conversation that forced her to think long and hard about what it meant to be a medieval woman.

"Elsie, dear, ye are so much a part of life here it's hard to remember ye've only been with us a little over a month."

"Aye, it feels like home."

"I'm glad. Honestly, lass, I don't want ye to leave."

"That makes two of us. I don't want to leave."

Morag leveled a far too perceptive stare at her. "I would like nothing better than for ye to stay here. I'm getting older and it would do my heart good to know I was leaving my clanswomen in good hands. Moreover, I know it's what Lady Wynda wants, but how can ye stay? Laird Macrae is not likely to allow it is he?"

"I…well…I might be able to convince him."

"If ye belonged to Laird MacKenzie there's not a single chance under heaven that he'd just let ye up and leave. It was beyond generous when Laird Macrae let ye come here—being his best midwife and all. I cannot believe he will permit ye to stay."

"But maybe if I—"

"Nay, lass. *If* ye were Macrae's best midwife, ye would know I'm right. Ye're keeping something from me. Ye are little more than a child yerself and ye know more about delivering bairns and other healing skills than anyone I have ever met."

"But, Morag, I—"

"Elsie, I love ye, lass, but I know something isn't right. I'm afraid for ye. When the truth comes out—and I swear to ye, it always does—I fear for yer safety. My sweet lass, I might be able to help if I know the real story. Please, Elsie."

Words like sorcery and witchcraft were spinning in Elsie's mind. If Morag called her out—but nay, Elsie looked into the old woman's eyes and knew she'd never do that.

"Ye're right, Morag. I'm not who ye think I am. I'm not even who Laird Macrae thinks I am."

Elizabeth proceeded to tell her the whole story. When she had finished, Morag looked at her, not with fear but with something akin to awe. "So ye aren't a lass of one and twenty."

"Well, Elsie is, but nay, in my century I am older."

Morag canted her head, narrowing her eyes. "How much older?"

Elizabeth blushed. "Frankly, not all that much older. I am eight and twenty. I did start studying medicine younger than most people and I'm often judged by my age there as well."

"Yer story is hard to believe, but I understand now how ye know so many extraordinary things—and how there are ordinary things ye don't seem to know. Still, it seems ye're destined to leave anyway."

"Nay, Morag, I'm not. I finally remembered the word, the morning after Jessie delivered Caleb. But I don't want to leave."

"Ye'd choose to stay? What about Elsie?"

"Gertrude says she wants to stay in my time."

"Gertrude?"

"Aye, Gertrude is the name of the woman who gave me the pocket watch."

"I've known Gertrude for years. She passes through this way occasionally. There are folks who think she's odd, but I've always noticed good things seem to follow in her wake." She took Elizabeth's hands in hers. "I'd say this time is no different. Does anyone else know?"

"Lady Wynda knows. Gertrude told her I was coming—before I knew it myself."

Morag chuckled. "That sounds like Gertrude and since she's behind this, I expect she has some plan."

"Perhaps, although I do find it hard not to worry about it. At least Laird Macrae doesn't actually believe I'm a midwife, much less his clan's best."

"Hopefully that will be his loss. I'm glad ye told me."

"Please, don't tell anyone else. I fear that others may be less willing to believe the bizarre circumstances that brought me here."

"Aye, yer secret's safe with me lass." She grinned at Elizabeth. "Now that I know the truth, I suppose it explains yer boldness."

"I have tried to mind my tongue, but ye're right, things are very different in my time."

"They must be if lassies can be educated and become physicians just like men can."

"Aye, that's part of it, but honestly, where I live, there is no nobility. The idea that I would have to behave a certain way simply because I am a woman or wasn't born into a noble family is difficult for me to accept."

"Ah, about that. Lass, if ye're to stay here, there is something I want to discuss with ye. When I thought ye knew our ways and ye'd be leaving us, I didn't worry over much, but this changes things."

Elizabeth frowned. "What have I done now?"

Morag chuckled. "Nothing. Yet. But ye've clearly learned there's a sharp distinction between commoners and nobility."

"Aye."

"And Sir Cade is a nobleman."

Elizabeth sighed. She feared she knew where this was going. "I know that."

"Lass, there are whispers in the clan about how fond he is of ye."

"Is it that obvious?"

"Good heavens, he can't keep his hands off ye."

Elizabeth gave her a wry smile. "It is only with great effort that I keep my hands off him."

Morag chuckled. "Aye, there's no denying he's an attractive man. But, lass, he is destined to marry a noblewoman, creating a new alliance or strengthening an old one with another clan. Most noblemen are, although sometimes younger sons or nephews may have a bit more of a say in things."

"I do know that, but Morag, I'm not looking for a husband."

"Why? Are ye married to someone in yer own time?"

"Nay."

"Then it's something we must talk about. Now that ye're staying, ye need to think about getting married."

"Why?"

"Because, like it or not, men rule here. Everyone and everything is under the control of one man or another."

"I'm not and I won't be as long as I don't marry."

"Oh but, lass, ye are. Ye belong to Laird Macrae and he's loaned ye to Laird MacKenzie, so ye answer to him as long as ye're here."

"Ye're not serious. I *belong* to Laird Macrae? Am I some kind of slave?"

"Nay lass, ye aren't a slave, but ye belong to the Macrae nevertheless. Perhaps yer best way of staying here is to marry—then ye'll belong to yer husband, who would be a MacKenzie and thus bound by fealty to Laird MacKenzie."

"Morag, I'm not ready to be married. I'm too young."

Morag snorted. "Ye most certainly are not too young and whether ye want to or not, ye must marry to secure yer future. Ye need to accept that and plan for it. Ye'll need to choose carefully. The man who marries ye will need a tolerant nature and no small amount of patience."

Elizabeth frowned. "I'm not *that* bad."

"Ye aren't bad at all. But ye're different. Everyone knows it and ye'll want a husband who isn't threatened by that—who doesn't try to force ye to be someone ye're not."

Elizabeth sighed. She definitely hadn't considered this.

Morag laughed. "Don't look as if the world is ending. There are plenty of fine, sensible, MacKenzie men who'll fall over themselves for ye."

It was Elizabeth's turn to laugh. "I heartily doubt that."

"Don't. I'm certain of it. But I am also as certain that the best of the men available will not want a wife who has lain with other men."

Elizabeth was taken aback. "Morag, I haven't...I mean Elsie hasn't and I haven't since I've been in her body."

Morag arched an eyebrow at her.

Elizabeth shrugged. "Things are a bit different in the twenty-first century, but the fact remains, I haven't...well, you know...with Sir Cade."

"I think everyone knows ye haven't...well, *you know,* with Sir Cade." Morag winked at her. "But that isn't because he hasn't tried to woo ye into his bed. And ye certainly wouldn't be the first. Many a lass has...well, *you know,* with the young laird." It was clear that the old midwife found Elizabeth's difficulty chatting about this topic amusing. "It isn't as frowned upon as ye might think for a common lass. Nevertheless, many common men still prefer a pure bride or at least one who hasn't engaged in a widely known dalliance with the man who will be laird of the clan someday."

"So ye're saying to stay away from Sir Cade?"

"I'm saying, if ye plan to stay here at Carraigile, ye may want guard yer reputation well."

"What if I don't wish to be married?"

"Elizabeth, I assure ye that is not a choice ye want to make. Unmarried women are vulnerable and subject to gossip regardless of how careful they are. Nay, lass, if ye're staying in this time, not just in this clan, ye need to marry."

Chapter 19

Over the next few days, Elizabeth thought long and hard about the things Morag had told her. Although she didn't like to admit it, as Morag had pointed out, there were a number of very practical reasons why she should marry. It wasn't that she was opposed to marriage; it just hadn't been her primary focus. Just as she had told David, other goals were more important.

But now that she thought about it, although she loathed to admit it even to herself, marriage to a man with excellent prospects from a good family was yet another one of her parents' expectations of her. It was the reason she started dating David in the first place. His father was the owner and chief executive officer of a huge, multinational conglomerate that had subsidiaries in a wide variety of industries. And not coincidentally, he was one of her mother's most powerful clients.

She could only laugh at the irony of it. She had told Morag that there was no "nobility" where she lived, but she realized now that was just semantics. She wasn't Lady Elizabeth Quinn, but she was from a powerful, wealthy family. And although her parents couldn't force her to marry a man of their choosing, they still "made introductions" and expected her to "marry well." It was probably the reason she had avoided introducing them to her first boyfriend. It was one reason their relationship had ended.

Ironically, Cade was just the kind of man her parents would expect her to marry, but in this time, she wasn't a suitable wife for him. Even though she knew this, she had still harbored a small hope that, perhaps he would spurn convention, declare his love for her and ask for her hand.

She had to face facts. As much as she liked Cade and enjoyed his company, as much as she could love him if she allowed herself to, there was no future for them. Morag was correct, Elizabeth needed to find a husband, and that would never happen as long as she allowed the flirtation between herself and Cade to continue. She had to put her Cinderella dreams aside. So the next day, when Cade wanted to take her riding, she steeled herself and said no.

"Ye're refusing to ride with me?"

"I appreciate everything ye've taught me, but I ride well enough now and shouldn't take any more of yer time."

"My time is my own and not for ye to decide how I spend it. If I wish to ride with ye, it's my choice to make."

And there's the medieval nobleman rearing his head. She sighed. "Nevertheless, I don't want to."

He frowned. "Elsie, it's Sunday afternoon. Ye have nothing else pressing. I want ye to go riding with me. Ye've always enjoyed it." He held a hand out to her. "Come."

She tried again. "I don't wish to go today, Sir Cade."

His frown deepened to a scowl. "I've asked ye to accompany me on a ride. I don't care if ye wish to or not." He took her by the elbow and practically pulled her out of the great hall and across the bailey, towards the stable.

She tried to twist her arm out of his grasp. "I said, nay. Ye have no right—"

He stopped and faced her, still holding onto her arm. "Ye really do have trouble remembering yer place. I have every right to ask ye to do something and expect it to be done."

Incredulous, she asked, "Are ye saying I can't refuse ye? I thought it was a request, not a command."

"Today they are one in the same. Ye've never refused to ride with me. Something is wrong—I'm certain of it— and I mean to find out what it is, but not in the middle of the great hall. Ye'll ride with me today so we can sort this out privately."

Elsie had hoped to let whatever this was between them simply cool with distance. The only thing that truly brought them together on a daily basis was these riding lessons. Therefore, putting an end to them would create the separation she needed. Ah well, if she had to face it head on, she would.

She waited quietly while he saddled the horses. Then remained equally silent as they rode through the village. He urged his mount into a canter, something he had only just begun to teach her and at which she'd had very little practice. She could barely keep up and lost any semblance of good form.

When they reached the wooded area, out of sight of the village he reined in and turned to look at her. "Ye ride well enough do ye? I'd say the last few minutes are proof that isn't true, wouldn't ye?"

She bit her lip to keep from saying something he might consider cheeky. Clearly he wasn't in a mood to find it charming.

"Answer me," he demanded.

"I suppose it depends on one's definition of *well enough*." *Damn it all, Elizabeth, that qualifies as cheeky.*

His eyes narrowed. "Well, my definition includes cantering."

"A pace, if I recall correctly, at which we never rode on the way here from Castle Macrae. And since yer reason for teaching me to ride was so that I could ride back there, I'm not sure I agree." *For the love of God, shut up, Elizabeth.*

"I have had more than enough of yer impertinence. Do not push me farther."

Yup. Not at all in the mood to find it charming.

He dismounted, lifted her from Edda's back and secured both horses before turning his attention to her. "Now, explain to me why you didn't wish to go riding this afternoon. An activity which, until today, ye seemed to like."

She opened her mouth to answer and he put up a hand. "I'm warning ye, Elsie, think before ye speak. My patience has its limits."

She took a deep breath. Her patience had its limits too, but she knew better than to point that out. "I think it's better if we spend less time together."

"For whom is it *better*? Because it isn't *better* for me."

"It's better for me."

"Why? Has this been a chore for ye? Do ye not enjoy it?"

"Nay. Ye know it isn't that. I have quite enjoyed learning to ride."

"Then why is it *better* for ye if we stop?"

"I've told ye before, I don't wish to be the subject of unkind gossip."

"Who's been spreading gossip?"

"No one. Yet."

"Then it's not an issue."

"But people are noticing the amount of time we spend together."

He shrugged. "I don't see any problem with that."

"I suspect it isn't a problem for ye, but it could easily become one for me."

"I go riding with ye in the open. It's all very innocent."

She arched a brow at him but, considering the mood he was in, chose not to say anything.

He smiled for the first time since leaving the hall. "Fine. I taste yer sweet lips occasionally—far less often than I would wish—but where's the harm in that?" As if to prove it to her, he pulled her into his embrace. With one hand cupping the back of her head, he gave her an all-consuming kiss that came close to making her forget everything and left her breathless when he finally released her.

"Elsie, why are ye so set against this? I desire ye as I have never desired anyone before. And ye cannot deny that ye're drawn to me too. Yer body responds to mine instinctively. Yer lips answer my kisses with abandon."

"Sir Cade, I won't deny feeling attracted to ye."

"Then why do ye resist me so?" Some of his earlier irritation was back.

"I've told ye that already. There is much more than attraction to consider here."

"Nay, there isn't. I adore ye. I like spending time with ye. I even like yer cheeky tongue, most of the time. We are as well suited as any two people ever were."

Elizabeth sighed heavily, taking a step backwards. That was true. She had never met anyone whose company she enjoyed more and whose kisses so totally befuddled her. She blushed. "I agree. We are particularly well suited to each other—except for one minor detail."

"I'm Laird MacKenzie's heir. I've told ye before, that doesn't have to stop us from being together." His exasperation showed in his voice.

"Aye, ye're Laird MacKenzie's son and it does stop us from being together. We can't be married and I won't accept less. Ye're allowed yer minor dalliances. No one will find yer behavior scandalous. Which is unfair on so many levels, I can't even begin to explain it. But the fact remains, ye're allowed to give in to yer desires and I'm not."

Cade frowned. "Ye're not a minor dalliance. I told ye, I've never felt this way before."

"Be that as it may, even if ye declared that ye loved me, it wouldn't matter. The most I could ever be to ye, is yer mistress. Someday ye'll marry, I'll be set aside and my poor heart will be broken."

"It's far more likely ye'll go home to Macrae in a few months and leave my poor heart devastated. Why not take the pleasure we can from each other, in the time we have?"

Because I don't intend to leave. Nay, she couldn't say that. Not yet. She would go with the medieval approach. "Because I have nothing to offer my husband but myself— my innocence. I don't wish to give that away lightly."

Cade pulled her into his arms again. "I wouldn't take it lightly. Elsie, I want ye for my own. Forever."

"*As a mistress.* I'm sorry, no matter how I feel about ye, I will not agree to that."

He sighed and rested his forehead against hers. "I know, and I shouldn't even ask it of ye. It's a common enough thing, but ye deserve better than that. Nevertheless, I want ye in my life."

"So we're back where we started. A bird may love a fish, but they don't belong together any more than we do." She stepped backwards, out of his embrace, out of his reach.

He shook his head. "I don't want to accept that."

Elizabeth laughed. "Ye're a stubborn man, Cade MacKenzie."

"That can be a very good thing sometimes." His smile nearly melted her resolve.

"I suppose it can be. And I would love for ye to find a way around this. But until ye do, I have to protect myself. Please say ye understand and let me step away while my heart is still intact. I need some distance from ye."

He shook his head sadly. "I understand. I don't like it, but I understand."

"And ye won't order me to go riding with ye?"

He sighed heavily. "Nay." The pain in his expression mirrored her own, but she knew there was no other way.

Chapter 20

Easter morning dawned blustery and cold. It had been two weeks since Elizabeth had both made the decision to stay and asked Cade to maintain distance from her. During that time she had occasionally awakened in the cold pre-dawn hours and questioned her sanity, or at the very least her wisdom. The sights and smells that accosted her on a daily basis were not for the faint of heart. Still, each time she treated an injury or illness, or when she saw Jessie with her children or Wynda's happy smile as she waited, flat on her back for time to pass, Elizabeth knew she was impacting lives here. Then too, when people called warm greetings to her or stopped simply to pass the time of day, she had a sense of belonging unlike any she had ever experienced. And just as she had on Ash Wednesday, every time she attended Mass she realized this time and place, the entire community, was having an impact on her as well.

Easter was nothing like Elizabeth expected. In her own time, if she wasn't working, she went to church and either out to a nice lunch with friends, or on the rare occasion that she was at her parent's home, dined with the family. She gave into her sweet tooth and indulged in marshmallow chicks and egg shaped chocolates. But other than that, it was nothing terribly exciting.

That was not the case at Carraigile. After the Easter Mass, a feast began that was much more lavish than the one held before Lent started. There were even more minstrels, some of whom had just arrived during Holy Week.

Elizabeth was asked to dance numerous times. She tried to beg off, explaining that she couldn't dance, but each potential partner promised to teach her. She gave in to the few who were most persistent. Rory Chisholm was a glutton for punishment, pulling her into dance after dance.

Cade respected her request to maintain his distance and didn't ask her to dance as he had at the last feast. She knew that was for the best, but she didn't like it. And that, if nothing else, reinforced the wisdom of her decision. She cared deeply for him. If she had let things go on as they had been, she might have lost her heart to him forever. Still, she couldn't help glancing his direction occasionally, and each time she did, she found him watching her.

Elizabeth had to move past this and heed Morag's advice, but a little voice within her whispered that it was too late; she had already irrevocably given Cade her heart. She could not imagine a life with anyone else.

~ * ~

Cade couldn't remember ever being more miserable. He suffered through the Easter feast as well as he could, but he hated that Elsie was right there, in the same room, and he had agreed to stay away from her. From the day he met Elsie, he had made no secret of the fact that he desired her. He loved simply being with her. She was smart and funny. Her boldness amused him as much as her responsiveness to his kisses enflamed him.

And he couldn't have her.

He watched her stumble through dance after dance with other partners. He wanted her stumbling with him. He wanted to catch her when she tripped over her own feet. He wanted to be the one to see her lopsided smile even as the hot blush rose in her cheeks. And he certainly didn't want anyone else to kiss her as he desired to until she forgot her embarrassment.

Even Eric danced with her and to add insult to injury, when another partner claimed her, Eric took the seat beside Cade.

"What ails ye, coz?"

"Nothing."

"Ye haven't danced a single dance."

"Nay, I haven't."

"I'm surprised ye haven't had yer toes bruised yet by her *charming wee self*."

Cade just glared at him.

Realization dawned on Eric's face. "Ah, it happened didn't it? Just as I said it might. Ye lost yer heart to her."

It galled Cade to admit he was right. "Aye, I did."

"So why is she dancing with everyone else? She seemed as taken with ye as ye are with her."

"Because a bird can't love a fish."

Eric frowned. "What's that supposed to mean?"

"She doesn't wish to be my mistress."

"And ye can't marry her. Ah, I understand, a bird and a fish."

To his credit, Eric didn't gloat.

~ * ~

Robin had been earning his keep as a minstrel for over ten years, ever since he was ten and seven. He liked the life of a musician. He liked being responsible to no one but himself. Five years ago he met Paul and they had traveled and performed together since then. Paul met his bonny Jean nearly two years ago. She had been a servant in Laird Fraser's keep. Paul fell in love with her the moment he'd heard her sing. She had the voice of an angel. He begged her to marry him and sing with them. Minstrel groups usually didn't have women performers. But this set them apart and made them memorable.

They never had trouble finding employment. Occasionally they were joined for a short time by one musician or another, but inevitably they parted ways. Robin never cared over much. The three of them were fine on their own. That was until a few months ago.

They had been invited to stay at Castle Macrae for the winter. Minstrels could hope for nothing better than to be asked to stay at a noble house during the bitterest months. Just before Christmas, a number of additional minstrels arrived for the celebrations between Christmas and Epiphany. Among them was a young lute player named Geordie.

Robin knew talent when he saw it—Geordie was a gifted musician with an incredibly unusual style. Robin asked the lad to join them and together, Jean, Paul, Geordie and Robin, made music that was uniquely beautiful.

Then tragedy struck. Geordie fell in love with Elsie, a pretty lass from the village. At first Robin feared Geordie wouldn't want to leave with them in the spring. But then, Elsie disappeared. Laird Macrae said she had passed herself off as a skilled midwife and run away with some MacKenzie warriors. Geordie refused to believe that and feared for her safety. He decided he'd travel to the MacKenzie holding to find the lass. Robin had tried desperately to talk him out of it, even offering to go with him to Carraigile in the spring—perhaps at Easter. But Geordie insisted he could not wait. Unwilling to leave the comfort of a winter home, Robin agreed they'd join Geordie at the MacKenzie's castle for Easter.

When they arrived at Carraigile yesterday, Robin inquired about Geordie, learning that the young lute player had never arrived.

Now he didn't know what to think. Elsie was here, and she certainly didn't seem to be in trouble. On the contrary, she seemed happy. Perhaps it was exactly as Laird Macrae had said; she had chosen to run away with the MacKenzie warriors. But Robin wasn't sure what game she played. Elsie had loved to dance. It was what had drawn the lad to her in the first place. And yet, here she stumbled through dance after dance as one partner after another tried to teach her the steps.

Robin intended to find out all he could. God help her, if he learned everything Laird Macrae had said was true and Geordie had gone haring after the thoughtless lass.

Robin had always found serving maids to be the best source of information in any clan and he needed answers. A young woman named Shauna had served them ale during a break. As forward a lass as he had ever met, she wasn't particularly attractive, but Robin suspected he could get several things that he needed from her that night.

Other minstrels were playing a lively country dance, so there was no better time to make a move. "Shauna, ye'll break my heart if ye don't give me a dance, pet."

She grinned, sadly the smile doing nothing to improve her looks. "Aye, I'd love to."

He danced several dances with her before collapsing onto a bench and pulling her onto his lap. "Ye're an excellent dancer, pet."

"I do love to dance."

"I can tell. Ye're much better than most of the other MacKenzie lassies. Take that one for example," he motioned towards Elsie, "she's dreadful."

"Aye, she is, but she's not a MacKenzie."

"Nay?"

"Nay. She's a Macrae."

"Then why's she here?"

Shauna pouted, in a way that he supposed was meant to be coy, but on her bony countenance became an unattractive scowl. "Ye don't really want to talk about her do ye?"

"Nay, pet. But what I want to do, we can't do here. I was just curious. The Macrae holding is quite a distance from here. Did she marry a MacKenzie clansman?"

"Nay. She's a midwife, apparently a particularly skilled one. Laird MacKenzie sent for her to attend his wife."

"She's awfully young to be a midwife isn't she?" Robin knew that Elsie was not a *particularly skilled midwife*. She had only just begun to train under her aunt. It seemed Laird Macrae had not lied about what Elsie had done.

"Aye, everyone says the same thing, but she seems to know what she's doing."

"Well, that's a good thing. Now, let's get back to a more interesting subject."

"Like what?"

"Like what the lovely Shauna might have hidden here." He slipped his hand under her skirts and slid it up her leg.

She giggled, spreading her legs a little wider. "I'm not hiding anything, but if ye have something to hide, I have a lovely place to put it."

He gave a low growl. "Ah, lass, that sounds delightful and I might have the perfect thing to hide. Perhaps we can find a quiet nook and see if it fits."

Shauna led him down stairs to an empty storage room. Once he had availed himself of both *hiding places*, he found his way back to the fete. Glancing around the hall, he found Elsie, then worked his way through the crowd until he reached her side.

"Elsie, it's good to see ye looking well. We were worried about ye."

Chapter 21

Elizabeth froze. The man at her side, one of the minstrels who had played earlier, seemed to know her, but she had never seen him before tonight. He must have known Elsie at Castle Macrae, before Elizabeth's soul took up residence. Maybe she could bluff. "'Tis good to see ye too. How long has it been since ye were at Castle Macrae?"

"We only left a sennight ago, but Geordie left shortly after ye disappeared."

"Disappeared? I didn't disappear. Laird Macrae sent me here."

"That isn't the story Laird Macrae tells. He says four braw MacKenzie warriors were passing through the village and ye cajoled them into taking ye with them by saying ye were a midwife."

Why on earth would Laird Macrae have made that up? It had been his idea. "I don't understand, why would he lie?"

"He has no reason to lie that I can see, thus I'm not sure he's the one lying."

"Ye think I'm lying? Ask the MacKenzies. They arrived at Castle Macrae looking for a highly skilled midwife—my aunt, Dolina. Laird Macrae sent me instead."

"Ye're not a skilled midwife."

"I have more skills than Laird Macrae is aware of."

"Really? That'd be hard for anyone to believe but I know for a fact it's false—ye'd barely begun yer training. Ye said so yerself. What's more, it doesn't match the Laird's version of events."

"I don't care what story he tells—it isn't true. Laird Macrae sent me. He threatened to beat me if I disobeyed. I had no choice."

The musician frowned and shook his head. "Geordie was worried about ye, Elsie. God's teeth, he was barely more than a green lad but he fancied himself in love with ye and ye led him to believe ye were fond of him too."

"What?" *Dear God.* Elizabeth had no idea who the minstrel was talking about but she couldn't say that. "Wh-what happened?"

"He didn't believe Laird Macrae and thought ye were in danger. He followed ye on foot, but evidently he never arrived here. Most likely he's dead. I expect he froze or was attacked by wolves.

"Nay. By all the saints, I had no idea. I swear to ye, Laird Macrae forced me to go with the MacKenzies. I didn't imagine he'd lie about it to his clan. What does my aunt think happened?"

"She doesn't want to believe Laird Macrae's version of events, but there really is no other explanation. Frankly, now that I see ye here, I do believe the laird."

"Please, just ask Sir Cade or Laird MacKenzie. They'll tell ye the truth."

"Oh I have every intention of speaking to Laird MacKenzie." He grabbed her by the arm, dragging her towards the laird's table. "He needs to know that ye've been lying to him. Ye aren't the midwife he sought. Ye aren't a midwife at all and a fine lad has likely lost his life because of yer lies."

Elizabeth's mind was whirling. She could barely process what was happening. Why had Laird Macrae sent her here and then lied to his clan about it?

When they reached the laird's table, the man said, "Excuse me, Laird, I have information about this wench that I think ye'll want to know."

Laird MacKenzie, who had been laughing with his brother, turned his full attention on the minstrel. "What information?"

"She isn't who ye think she is. I understand ye think

she's a midwife, but I know for a fact, she's only an unskilled apprentice. 'Twas her aunt ye sought. She clearly chose to pass herself off as something she wasn't."

"What are ye talking about?" demanded Laird MacKenzie.

"She told yer men that she was a skilled midwife so she could leave castle Macrae."

Laird MacKenzie's eyes narrowed, clearly angry he turned on Elizabeth. "Is this true?"

"Laird, I—"

"*Is it true?*" he roared.

"Not exactly."

"What does that mean? Did ye lie about yer skills?"

"Nay, Laird, I did not."

"Ye're not a midwife, Elsie, yer Aunt Dolina is," said the minstrel. "Laird Macrae didn't send ye and yer lies have likely resulted in a man's death."

Cade had been on the other side of the hall, but the commotion drew his attention. "Da, what's wrong?"

"Robin, here, says that Elsie isn't a midwife, she sought ye out and lied to ye."

Cade frowned. "She didn't seek me out. Laird Macrae presented her as his most skilled midwife."

Robin frowned at this. "Laird Macrae told his clan she ran away with ye."

"Well she didn't. Laird Macrae sent her with us, assuring us she had the skills required to help Lady Wynda. Ask any of the men who were with me."

Laird MacKenzie turned his attention back to Elsie. "Are ye the midwife I sought or not."

Elizabeth swallowed hard. "Laird Macrae believed ye sought my Aunt Dolina. He thought there was nothing that anyone could do to help Lady Wynda and therefore it would be a waste to send someone with her skills. He threatened to beat me if I told ye what he'd done."

"*Ye lied?*"

"Laird Macrae lied, or he thought he did. He wasn't aware of the skills I have when he sent me."

"Ye lied. Even out of his reach, ye lied. Ye gave my wife false hope."

His accusatory tone ripped at Elizabeth's heart. "I did not lie. I absolutely know what I'm doing and I did not give her false hope."

"And what's this about a man dying?" Laird MacKenzie demanded of Robin.

"Another minstrel, a young friend of ours, had fancied himself in love with Elsie. He didn't believe Laird Macrae's story, was worried about her safety and followed her here but never arrived."

Cade frowned. "He didn't believe Elsie ran away, and he was right in that. But following us in the dead of winter, alone, was foolhardy. If he didn't reach his destination, it most certainly was not Elsie's fault. Da, Laird Macrae assured us Elsie was the most skilled midwife he had."

"Well, she isn't," insisted Robin.

"But, Da, if her Laird forced her to lie, she isn't to blame."

"Son, even after she was away from Macrae and in no danger, she still lied to us about her skills."

"Nay, Laird, I didn't. I swear I didn't. Robin doesn't know the truth and neither did Laird Macrae. I admit he thought he was trying to deceive ye. He believed nothing could be done and simply by sending someone ye would be in his debt. Now, if I am ever returned to him, he is likely to beat me to death. He would have if I had not agreed to his plan."

"I think I will send ye back to him—with a declaration of war."

"Da, please, ye can't do that," Cade insisted.

Morag, who had worked her way through the crowd, also came to her defense. "Laird, I don't care what this minstrel says. I assure ye, Elsie is more skilled than I am.

She knew how to get Jessie's baby to turn and she delivered the bairn expertly. Not to mention that her assessment of Lady Wynda's condition not only makes sense but seems to be working."

"*She lied to us!*" roared Angus.

Morag tried again. "Laird Macrae lied. She didn't. Before ye make any decisions, please speak with yer lady wife."

Laird Macrae shook his head. "She wants Elsie's lies to be true."

"Nay, Laird, she knows they aren't lies," said Morag quietly.

"Please, Da, ye know Morag is right. Talk to Wynda."

"I will not bother Wynda with this. It will crush her. What's more, until I decide what's to be done with Elsie, I want her kept away from Wynda." He scanned the crowd that had gathered, his eyes lighting on someone. "Sully, lock her in the dungeon."

Cade stepped forward, pulling Elsie behind his back. "Nay, Da. Ye're making a mistake. Please don't do that."

"Cade, I am at the limits of my temper and I will not tolerate defiance from anyone—not even my son." He motioned to two other guardsmen who grabbed Cade's arms, restraining him while Sully took Elizabeth by the arm, pulling her towards the stairs to the lower level and the dungeon.

Elizabeth didn't fight. She could barely believe what was happening. She hadn't lied about her abilities and had only helped since she'd arrived at Carraigile. She hadn't done anything wrong. *That's not completely true and you know it. You allowed Laird MacKenzie to believe Laird Macrae had helped him.* But what else could she have done? When she arrived, she'd had no choice. She'd had to ensure that Elsie didn't suffer a punishment because of Elizabeth's actions.

Sully finally spoke. "I knew Macrae was lying to us.

Ye weren't the midwife we went there for."

"So ye've said." Elizabeth's world was caving in and Sully's accusations were the last thing she needed.

"But, lass, ye told me ye were *absolutely, without a doubt, the best person to help* Lady Wynda and I believe ye weren't lying. Ye've done wonderful things here. William is so chuffed about his grandson, he talks of nothing else. If the baby hadn't turned—"

"—she would have had a more difficult delivery. That's all."

"That's no small thing. And ye know as well as I do, she might not have been able to deliver the baby breech. Ye're a blessing to us, Elsie."

Nothing could have shocked her more. "I...I...thank ye, Sully. Hearing ye say that means a lot to me."

"Aye, well it doesn't help this situation. I still have to lock ye in the dungeon. But I'll leave a torch so ye have light and I'll see that ye get a few items to make ye more comfortable."

Frightened and miserable, Elizabeth could only nod.

"I don't expect ye'll be here long. The laird will come around. If Cade and Morag don't convince him, Lady Wynda will."

"But he said he didn't want her told."

"He said that after Lady Lilliana had already slipped from the hall. I suspect Lady Wynda knows even now.

"I wish I was as certain and ye are."

"Ye wanted us to have faith in ye. Have a little faith in us."

"Aye, Sully, ye're right. I'll try. Thank ye."

He locked her in one of the cells. "I'll send someone down with fresh bedding shortly."

There was a low wooden platform in the cell that must have been intended to be a bed. She sat down on it, hugged her knees to her chest and in spite of her promise to Sully, she couldn't keep from giving in to despair and burst into sobs. She had never been in such a bad predicament. *You're an idiot Elizabeth. You chose to stay in the dark ages where you are little more than chattel and why? Because you wanted this life? I repeat, idiot.*

Ten minutes hadn't passed when she heard the sounds of footsteps hurrying down the stairs. She swiped at the tears on her face but couldn't suppress a sob just as Deirdre emerged from the stairs.

"Oh, nay, Elsie, don't cry. Please don't cry."

"I-I-I'm s-sorry, Deirdre. I'm sc-scared."

"I know ye are, and I'm going to stay with ye."

"That's kind of ye, but it's cold down here. I couldn't ask ye to stay. Ye'll miss what remains of the Easter celebration."

Deirdre, her sweet, scatterbrained friend smiled. "I don't care about the celebration. Not when ye're here. And I've brought some blankets, so we won't be cold."

Elsie sniffed. "I don't want the laird to be angry with ye."

"He doesn't know. Besides, Sir Cade is the one who sent me. I couldn't very well defy him could I?"

"Sir Cade?"

Deirdre grinned. "Aye, he didn't want ye to be by yerself while he tries to convince the laird to release ye."

Having Deirdre with her through the night was an incredible comfort. Even though Deirdre dozed while Elizabeth couldn't sleep to save her soul, it was just nice not being alone.

Hours later—it must surely have been morning—she heard footsteps on the stairs.

Deirdre woke and jumped to her feet. "Who do ye suppose that is?" she whispered. While clearly a little frightened, she stood in front of the cell door with her hands on her hips, as if to protect Elizabeth.

Elizabeth smiled even as tears welled in her eyes. Deirdre was a good friend and Elizabeth owed Cade her gratitude for sending the maid.

"*Gertrude?* What are ye doing here?" asked Deirdre.

Of all the people who Elizabeth thought might appear in the dungeon this morning, she would never have imagined it would be Gertrude, or guess that Deirdre knew her.

"Good morning, Deirdre. Ye're such a sweet lass to have stayed with Elsie as ye did. I know ye were a great blessing."

Deirdre blushed and said shyly, "She's my friend."

"Aye, I know that and that makes her very fortunate indeed. Now, shall I stay with her for a bit, while ye break yer fast? Then ye can bring something down for her as well."

Deirdre nodded but turned to Elizabeth. "Elsie, this is Gertrude. Is it all right if she stays with ye while I fetch our morning meal?"

"Aye, Deirdre. Gertrude and I have met before. I'll be fine while ye're gone. And, thank ye for staying with me. Gertrude is right, ye were a great comfort. I don't think I could have stood it without ye."

"Ye'd have done it for me."

Elizabeth gave her a broad smile and said, "Aye, I would have," knowing it was absolutely true. "But I hope I never have to," she added.

Deirdre grinned and called, "Me too," as she ran up the stairs.

Gertrude turned to Elizabeth. "Ye do have very good friends here. I understand why ye chose to stay."

"Aye, but now I fear I've made a terrible mistake."

"And why's that lass?"

Elizabeth arched an eyebrow. "Are ye trying to tell me ye don't know what's happened?"

Gertrude laughed. "Of course I know what's happened. Why do ye think ye've made a terrible mistake?"

Elizabeth looked at her, askance. "Oh, I don't know...I

suppose it has something to do with being locked in the MacKenzie's dungeon."

Gertrude pursed her lips. "Sarcasm does not become ye, Elizabeth. Ye chose to stay for a very particular reason. Ye loved the community and the difference you could make in it. Has that changed?"

"Well, I can't make much of a difference locked up here."

"Ye still have a little time left. Do ye want Elsie to say the word?"

Elizabeth thought about this for a moment. Gertrude was right. She still loved these people, well most of them—she wasn't overly fond of Laird MacKenzie right now. Even with circumstances as they were at that moment, the thought of leaving caused her heart to ache. Not to mention the fact that if she escaped, it would leave Elsie in a mess from which she had no ability to extract herself. She *wasn't* a midwife with special skills.

"Nay, Gertrude, I don't want her to say the word. It wouldn't be fair to her. I made this choice and I will see it through."

"That's what I thought ye'd say."

Tears welled in Elizabeth's eyes. "But I'm afraid." Her voice was barely above a whisper.

Gertrude reached through the bars of the cell and caressed Elizabeth's cheek. "Oh, my sweet lass, I know ye are."

"I don't understand what happened. I felt sure Elsie didn't have…anyone."

"Elizabeth, he was a minstrel. They had only known each other for a matter of weeks. She hadn't had time to do more than have the first flutterings of growing affection. Ye needn't worry. She is happy where she is."

"But the young man…it appears he lost his life trying to keep her—me that is, safe. No one knows what happened to him, and I feel responsible."

"Ye aren't responsible. Ye knew nothing about him."

"Is what Robin suspected true? Is he is dead?"

"Aye, Geordie is dead. Suffice to say, it was his time to leave and ye couldn't have changed that."

"But—"

"Nay, Elizabeth. If ye had known that by agreeing to come here, the young man would not have died, but ye wouldn't have helped Kelvin, or Wynda, or Jessie, would ye have chosen to stay?"

Elizabeth shook her head slowly. "Nay, I suppose not."

"The fact is, there is a time to live and a time to die. He made his choices. Ye made yours. That's all any of us can do. The universe unfolds as it should."

"That doesn't make it easy."

"Nay, it doesn't. Ye can only make the best decision possible with the information at hand. Looking back now and second-guessing those decisions serves no purpose."

"Aye, I suppose that's true."

"Of course it's true. I only speak the truth.

"What do I do now? What if Laird MacKenzie sends me back?"

"Do ye honestly think Wynda will allow that?"

Elizabeth smiled. "Nay, I don't suppose so."

"Just as Sully told ye, have a little faith in the people who love ye."

Gertrude was asking a lot, but Elizabeth reckoned she had to try. "Aye, I'll do my best."

"That's all ye can do, lass. I'll leave ye now."

"Thank ye for coming to see me."

"'Twas my pleasure." She started up the steps, calling back over her shoulder, "Take good care of yer clan, lass."

"Aye, I will."

A moment later Deirdre emerged from the stairs, carrying a tray. "Ye will what?"

"I was talking to Gertrude."

Deirdre looked around. "Where is she?"

"She left."

"Then why were ye talking to her?"

Elizabeth laughed. "She just left. She was on the stairs. Ye must have seen her on yer way down."

"Nay, she wasn't on the stairs."

"But—nay, never mind."

Chapter 22

Until this moment, Wynda had not resented having to lay flat for months. She looked at each day in bed as a gift to her child and her husband. If she'd had to hang by her feet for six months she'd have done it. But now the fact that she couldn't get up and force Angus to listen to her tried her patience sorely.

"Lilliana, please, go to him again and tell him I want to see him. I must see him."

"Wynda, I've told him repeatedly. He won't listen and he's already furious with me. After I'd left the hall to tell ye what was happening, he gave an order that ye weren't to be told anything. He didn't want ye to lose hope."

"I haven't lost hope. I have every confidence in Elsie. Angus is wrong."

"But, she did lie. She admitted it."

"*She* didn't lie."

"Fine, she allowed us to believe the Macrae's lies."

"Lilliana, ye don't understand. None of ye do. *I must speak to Angus.* I have something important to say and I can only tell him."

"Please don't get yerself so upset, Wynda. Wait a day or two until Angus has calmed down."

"Nay! He might decide to send her back and I will not allow that."

"I don't think he'll do that." Lilliana's tone of voice didn't convey any confidence.

"Ye don't know that. Please, try one more time. Make him understand how urgent this is. And before ye say he won't listen again, tell him if he won't come to me, I'll go to him."

"Ye're not allowed to get up."

"But I will. I swear I will if he isn't here within the hour."

That threat was all it took. Angus arrived to their chamber within minutes.

"Wynda, sweetling, I didn't want to worry ye with this."

"What's worrying me, Angus, is the way ye're treating that lass."

Angus opened his mouth to speak, but Wynda cut him off. "Nay, Angus, do not tell me again that she lied. I know exactly what happened. I have known since the day after she arrived. I know the complete truth about who she is and how she came to be here. Neither ye nor Laird Macrae can say that."

Her husband sighed. "Then tell me."

Wynda launched into the tale. When she had finished, Angus shook his head slowly. "From the future? *Soul exchange?* Surely ye don't believe that."

"I do believe it. She knows things that ye firmly believe a lass as young as she is can't know. She's shown us that repeatedly. That thing she did with Jessie to get the baby to turn? Morag is an extremely skilled midwife and she had never heard of it."

"That could be evidence that she *is* a fraud."

"Angus, it was yer idea to send a request to Laird Macrae. Ye knew nothing about the midwife ye sought. It's likely she was no more skilled that Morag. Most people believe that some women simply can't carry a bairn. Even Morag did until she met Elsie. It's understandable that Laird Macrae did too."

"But he sought an alliance through treachery."

"And Elsie, *the real Elsie* wouldn't have gone along with it even though it would have meant severe punishment that inevitably would have resulted in her death. The only reason Elizabeth agreed was because she knew she could actually help."

"But—"

"Nay! There is one thing I haven't told ye. Right after Cade left, Gertrude visited and told me the lass would be coming."

"Gertrude? Really?"

"Gertrude said even though she'd look very young, she'd know what she was doing. She also said if I pushed the lass, she'd tell me something that was nearly impossible to believe but that I should trust her."

Angus shook his head. "Someday, someone is going to call Gertrude out as a witch."

Wynda laughed. "Nay, they won't. She only brings blessings."

"Aye, my love. If Gertrude sent her, I will accept that she is what she claims to be."

"And ye understand why she feared risking Elsie's life by revealing Laird Macrae's lie?"

"Aye, I do. That she told ye immediately eases my mind." Angus stood to leave.

"Where are ye going?"

"To release *Elsie* from the dungeon."

Wynda was certain she hadn't heard correctly. "Did ye say dungeon? Tell me ye didn't put her in the dungeon."

"I...I thought Lilliana told ye what had happened."

Wynda gritted her teeth. "She failed to mention anything about the dungeon. Angus, how could ye?"

"Sweetling, everything indicated that she'd lied to us."

"But the dungeon?"

"Now, in fairness, Cade was as angry as ye are. He sent Deirdre to keep her company and see to her needs."

"Well at least one of ye had a modicum of sense."

"I would be happy to stay here and let ye explain how little sense I have, but I suspect ye'd prefer me to release her sooner rather than later."

"Aye, I do. Go get her and bring her here—there are things we need to discuss. But honestly, Angus, the dungeon?"

Her husband was out the door before she could say more.

~ * ~

Elsie paced her cell nervously.

"Elsie, ye must be exhausted. Perhaps ye should try to rest a bit. Ye've been up all night."

"I can't, Deirdre. I hate being locked up."

"Ye're going to make yerself ill."

Before Elizabeth could respond, she heard heavy footsteps on the stairs and moments later, Laird MacKenzie entered the dungeon. Elizabeth took a step back, away from the bars.

Deirdre hopped up from where she sat and bobbed a curtsy. "Good morning, Laird."

"Good morning, Deirdre. Ye can go back to yer other duties, I'll see to Elsie now." He unlocked the door and stood back, motioning for her to leave the cell. "Elsie, come with me. We have things to discuss."

Still more scared than she wanted to admit, she nodded. "Aye, Laird."

Laird MacKenzie headed back up the stairs. Elsie glanced at Deirdre, who shrugged and motioned for her to follow the laird.

Deirdre gathered the blankets and trailed after them.

When they reached the great hall, Laird MacKenzie took Elsie's elbow and guided her to the tower stairs. Elsie was acutely aware that everyone in the hall had fallen silent, watching. As she glanced around, she expected to see censure or disappointment, but she didn't. Most of the MacKenzie's gave her looks of affection or concern. Cade stood near the hearth and she briefly captured his gaze until he looked away. She couldn't read his expression, and above everything, that scared her.

Laird MacKenzie said nothing to her until they reached

the chamber he shared with Lady Wynda. When they entered, Alice jumped to her feet and curtsied. "Good morning, Laird."

"Leave us, Alice."

"Aye, Laird." Alice curtsied again, casting a worried look towards Elsie before leaving the room.

When the door closed behind the maid, Wynda said, "Oh, thank God. Elizabeth, I apologize for the misunderstanding. I'm so very sorry, but I had to tell Angus everything. He understands now. Tell her, Angus."

"Aye. 'Tis nearly impossible to believe, but I understand. I sincerely regret how I treated ye, Elizabeth. Still, ye must admit, it certainly appeared that ye'd lied to us, or were at least complicit in Laird Macrae's lie."

"Aye, Laird, I know it looked that way, but there was nothing else I could do. When I thought I was going back, I had to do what I could to protect Elsie."

"I understand that now, but what do ye mean? Are ye not going back?"

"Angus, Elizabeth would like to stay here with us. Evidently Elsie wants to stay where she is too."

"Stay?"

"Aye, Laird." She had done a lot of thinking as paced the cell after seeing Gertrude. "If ye don't wish me to stay here, I won't. But I want to stay in this time. Laird MacLennan said if I ever found myself in need I should seek him out. I could go there."

"Elizabeth, ye misunderstood me. I was just surprised after everything that's happened in the last hours—after the way I treated ye—ye would want to stay. I believe ye have some time left."

"Angus, the decision was already made and she told Gertrude that she wanted to stay. It's too late, thank God, because I want her to stay. Although, if ye still could go back, Elizabeth, I would understand and we would see to Elsie's safety on her return."

"Actually, my lady, Gertrude visited me this morning. I had the opportunity to change my mind but I truly do want to stay here. Not only just in this time, but here at Carraigile."

"Ye chose us twice?" Angus sounded a little in awe.

"Aye, Laird."

"So don't ye ever dare throw her in the dungeon again," warned Lady Wynda.

"Never, my love. Elizabeth, I'm…well ye're the boldest lass I have ever encountered, but I guess I understand a bit better why. I'm humbled that ye'd choose to stay here and I'm grateful. Ye'll be an asset to us. From now forward, I will consider ye a clanswoman and vow to keep ye safe."

"Thank ye, Laird."

"But, Angus, we have to sort out how to keep her. Elsie is a Macrae after all."

"Aye, that is a problem, but for now we'll remain silent. I suspect as long as Macrae thinks I believe his duplicity he won't seek to get Elsie back. That'll give us some time to plan. But speaking of Macrae, Elizabeth, what do ye know about the minstrel who followed after ye?"

"Only what Robin told ye. It seems that the young man had grown fond of Elsie and didn't believe the story Laird Macrae told his clan about me running away with Sir Cade."

"Ye don't remember meeting him?"

"Laird, my soul entered Elsie's body as she was practically being dragged to see Laird Macrae, after Sir Cade arrived. Moments later the laird told me what I had to do, threated to beat me if I didn't obey, and presented me as his most skilled midwife. I was riding out of Castle Macrae within minutes. I don't understand why he lied to his clan about sending me here. People saw me riding out of the village."

"Were there any servants within hearing when he told

Cade ye were the midwife we sought?"

Elizabeth closed her eyes, trying to remember. "I'm not certain, but I don't think so. I only remember seeing Sir Cade and his men."

"So there were no other witnesses?"

"Just the guardsman who dragged me to see Laird Macrae."

Laird MacKenzie's expression turned grim. "Elizabeth, the villagers who saw ye riding away with Cade have no way of knowing that their laird sent ye with him. It could be explained by the story he tells—that ye just left. He did what he did to get an alliance with me. He couldn't risk me ever finding out that he lied. If his clan knew the trick he'd pulled, word of it might eventually reach my ears and not only would there be no alliance, it would have resulted in a feud."

"But what would he have told them when I returned?"

Wynda smiled sadly. "I expect he would have lied again, and leveled another threat against ye in order to keep that secret."

"Or worse. He might have ensured yer silence by seeing that ye met with an accident before ye had a chance to reveal his perfidy," Laird MacKenzie added.

"Then maybe he'll have no problem with me staying here."

"We can hope," said Angus, but he sounded doubtful.

"Hope, Angus? What are ye worried about?"

"Noth—"

"Don't ye dare say *nothing*. I can tell it isn't nothing."

Elizabeth had watched the exchange silently. Lady Wynda's concern worried her.

"I didn't want to bother ye with this, Wynda, but I fear I can't stop ye worrying. If Laird Macrae wanted the secret kept badly enough, he isn't likely to leave the one person who knows the truth here under my control. If we don't send her back, I believe he will send someone for her—and if we hand her over, I am not certain she would reach Castle Macrae alive."

"Oh, Angus, we can't let that happen."

"I don't intend to let it happen. For now I don't think we have anything to worry about. As long as ye're pregnant, he's not likely to do anything. He'll believe Elsie is afraid enough to keep his secret. But just in case, Elizabeth, I don't want ye ever to leave the village without an escort. I hear ye're in the habit of taking a walk by the loch occasionally. Ye mustn't do that anymore. At least not alone. Ye must have a guard with ye. Do ye understand?"

Elizabeth could scarcely believe her ears. After following Laird Macrae's orders he'd kill her to ensure his secret was safe? "Aye, Laird, if ye think I'm in danger, I won't leave the village alone."

"One last thing, Angus. I understand this caused quite a spectacle at the festivities last night. Ye will make certain the clan understands it was all a mistake."

"Aye, Wynda, I'll fix things. I'll also speak with that minstrel. Since Cade and the other men confirmed that Elsie didn't leave by her own choice, Robin believes that too now. But he mustn't ever let Laird Macrae know or his life is in as much danger as Elsie's is."

Chapter 23

That night at the evening meal, Laird MacKenzie announced that there had been a mistake and that Elsie was exactly who was needed to attend Lady Wynda. He apologized to Elsie and those assembled seemed satisfied. It heartened Elizabeth when it became clear that most of the MacKenzies hadn't believed the accusations anyway.

When the meal was over, Elizabeth realized how extremely tired she was. She wished she could simply be transported to her bed. *Scotty beam me up.* She put her head in her hands for a moment and only realized she'd dozed off when Deirdre tugged at her elbow.

"Elsie, ye're exhausted. Go on to bed now. I've just lit the brazier in yer chamber and put a warming pan between the sheets."

Elizabeth smiled. Deirdre's thoughtfulness was even better than being *beamed up.* She stood up and hugged her friend. "Thank ye, Deirdre. That is exactly what I need right now. And thank ye too for staying with me last night. I've never had a better friend."

Deirdre blushed but looked very pleased. "Ye're welcome. I'm glad ye think of me as a friend. Good night, Elsie."

"Good night. I'll see ye in the morning." With that she walked towards the stairs. She sighed when she saw Cade rise from the head table and walk towards her. Perhaps if she hurried she could avoid this, but he reached the stairs just as she did.

~ * ~

Cade reckoned the last couple days had been among the worst in his life. He had suffered through the previous evening watching the woman he adored from a distance because she'd asked him to. They were from two different worlds.

Then the unthinkable happened. A minstrel called her out for being a fake and his father believed the man. Initially, Cade didn't know what to think. Even though Elsie seemed to be as skilled as she had claimed, she'd clearly lied to them. Or at least she allowed them to accept Laird Macrae's lies. She didn't deny it.

He should have been as angry as his father was—but he couldn't bear the thought of her being locked in the dungeon. He had tried to prevent it, but his father had him restrained. The only thing he could do, while trying to get his father to release her, was to ensure she was made as comfortable as possible.

The rest of the night had been spent arguing with his father, but in the end Elsie was still in the dungeon and his father still believed that she had deceived them. Perhaps worst of all, his own faith in her had begun to waver. He didn't know what to think and couldn't help but feel a little ashamed that he had believed her so thoroughly.

It had been midafternoon when his father, after speaking with Wynda, finally escorted Elsie from the dungeon, but he strode through the great hall and up the stairs with her, offering no explanation. Elsie had glanced towards Cade once. She seemed so young and guileless, but he'd allowed himself to be fooled by that before. He had looked away.

Then everything turned upside down again. When his father returned to the hall, he'd announced that Elsie had not dealt falsely with them. She was the skilled midwife and healer they'd believed her to be. Cade had been relieved, but confused. She'd admitted that Laird Macrae had lied to them.

Then too, he believed Elsie had lied to him about something else. While she hadn't actually said it, she'd led him to believe she didn't have a suitor among the Macraes when all the while there was a young minstrel who cared enough about her to follow her. Cade tried again to speak to his father—to learn what had happened. He felt compelled to understand why the minstrel had said what he had—that he knew for a fact Elsie wasn't a midwife. And more importantly, he wanted to know what had changed his father's mind? But Angus had refused to explain.

The lass herself had been surrounded by people the rest of the day. It was clear the MacKenzies loved her and were pleased that she was back in the laird's good graces. She'd said no more than she had the previous night. The story she told was that Laird Macrae didn't intend to send his best midwife, but he didn't know how skilled Elsie actually was.

It was exactly the conclusion Cade had drawn when he first met Elsie. And it was believable enough that the clan had accepted it.

But Cade no longer did. He was certain there was something more.

He'd watched her throughout the evening meal, intending to speak with her privately. Now he finally had his opportunity. She appeared to be going up to her chamber alone. He reached the entrance to the tower stairs just as she did.

"Elsie, ye've had quite a day." His tone was sharper than he'd intended.

She frowned. "Aye, I have. I can never thank ye enough for sending Deirdre to me. I don't know how I would have made it through the night without her. Even so, I didn't sleep much and I'm exhausted. Thank ye again. I'll see ye in the morning. Please excuse me." She started up the stairs.

"Nay."

She stopped and turned slowly to face him. "What did ye say?"

"Ye heard me. I did not excuse ye."

Her back stiffened and an angry flush rose in her cheeks.

Even as irritated as he was, he had to suppress a smile. He had enjoyed needling her from the day he met her. Ah, the day he met her—that's what he was irritated about now.

"Well, if ye have something to say to me, please say it. I need some rest."

"Ye lied to me. I told ye if ye and yer laird tried to fool us, ye'd both be sorry."

"And I told ye there was no one better able to assist Lady MacKenzie than I. It was true then and it's true now."

"Ye knew yer laird was trying to fool us, and ye looked me in the eye and lied. But ye also said ye had no one special in yer life and evidently that wasn't true either." If Cade was being honest with himself, this was the thing that bothered him the most. She had a man in her life who loved her enough to risk his life trying to ensure she was safe and she had led Cade to believe otherwise.

She frowned. "I'm sure I never said that."

"Ye implied it on the ride here, and clearly it wasn't true. Ye certainly haven't behaved as if ye had someone ye loved at home."

"Because I didn't. I had only just met the lad Robin was talking about. I didn't know he loved me. Sir Cade, I didn't lie to ye about anything. It is true that Laird Macrae intended to pass me off as my aunt. But as repugnant as this is to admit, when Laird Macrae said if anyone could help Lady MacKenzie it was I, he wasn't lying either. He didn't believe that anyone—including Aunt Dolina—could help her. But he was wrong and I knew it. I knew I could help."

"Ye can dance around the issue with words if ye wish, but the bottom line is that Laird Macrae was attempting to deceive us, ye knew it and ye went along with it."

"Aside from the fact that he might have beaten me to death had I done anything else, what do ye think I should have done? If I'd said, 'Nay, Laird Macrae ye're wrong, not only can Lady MacKenzie be helped, but I know more about how to do it than my Aunt Dolina,' what do ye think would have happened? Do ye think he would have let me come then?"

Cade clenched his teeth. He knew she was right but he was angry and frustrated. Nothing was making sense. "Ye can't possibly be more skilled than yer aunt. Why are my father and Wynda so willing to believe that?"

"Because they are and right now, it really doesn't matter to me whether ye believe me or not. I'm too tired to keep trying to convince ye of the truth. If ye don't believe me, ye don't believe me. This conversation is over." She turned and started up the stairs again.

Anger flared within him. No clan member could be allowed to show that level of disrespect. He followed her, grabbing her by the arm. "Don't take another step. Ye forget yer place. Yer impudence knows no bounds, and I did not give ye leave to go."

"Frankly, I couldn't possibly care less." She yanked her arm from his grasp and ran up the stairs.

Her defiance stunned him for a moment, but he recovered quickly and followed her. She was surprisingly fast; he caught her just outside her door. "How dare ye?" He spun her around, but his next chastisement died on his lips.

Her eyes blazed with fury, and yet she trembled and appeared to be fighting tears. "If ye have an issue with me, take it up with yer father, but please, just let me go to bed now."

He released her arm and took a step back. She was hiding something—he was certain of it—but he didn't like seeing her so distressed. And it absolutely gutted him to know he had been the cause of it. "Aye, lass. Forgive me. I know ye've had a hard day and I'm sorry to have upset ye so. I guess I...well, I'm sorry. Sleep well and I'll see ye on the morrow."

She looked slightly surprised that he had given in. Her voice was little more than a whisper when she said, "Thank ye. Good night," and entered her chamber.

~ * ~

Cade was not prepared to let the subject drop completely and he did raise it with his father again the next morning. "Why won't ye tell me what happened yesterday?"

"With what, son?"

"By the Almighty, Da, with Elsie."

"We discussed this yesterday and I told ye I'd made a mistake."

"At the feast ye were so fully convinced she deceived us that ye threw her in the dungeon."

"And ye argued with me for hours over that. Why are ye upset now that I've let her out?"

"Because *ye* argued with *me* for hours and convinced me that along with her laird, she'd lied to us."

"I was wrong and I know now that she didn't lie."

"What gives ye such confidence? I'm dead certain she's hiding something."

"That's because she is and she has a very good reason to keep it to herself."

"But ye know what it is?"

"I do now and I'm convinced she's a...*unique* lass."

"But she only chose to reveal this secret after her lies were exposed?"

"Nay, as it turns out, Wynda has known the complete truth from the start. Morag has known for quite a while as well."

"So what is the complete truth?"

"It isn't for me to tell ye. But suffice to say, when Elsie said there was no one in Scotland better able to attend Wynda, it was the absolute truth."

"And so we'll just send her back after Wynda delivers and accept that the Macrae lied to us?"

"That's her home."

"That's not an answer. Do ye intend to send her back knowing what ye do about what the Macrae did?"

"If she wishes to stay, I will allow it."

"She belongs to the Macrae. Can ye just keep her?" Although as he said it, Cade hoped fervently that she could stay.

"We'll cross that bridge when we come to it, son."

"Ye're convinced she didn't lie to us and if we believe the minstrel, we know the Macrae lied to his clan about why she left. Why would he have done that?"

"I'm not sure we know the complete truth about anything surrounding Laird Macrae. Maybe the story Robin tells is a lie. He could have made up the whole thing because of some grudge he has against Elsie."

"I suppose that could explain things, if ye believe Elsie is a skilled midwife. But even she maintains the Macrae intended to deceive ye. What do ye make of that?"

"I don't know and I expect it will all be sorted out eventually. But I am certain Elsie is the midwife we needed."

"Because of whatever her secret is?"

"Aye, son. Can ye let this drop now?"

Cade nodded. "I suppose. But if the lass chooses to tell me herself?"

"That's up to her."

He'd let it drop, but not forever. He believed Elsie was unique, and he couldn't help wonder what she had revealed to convince his father of that. Still, this completely changed things. If there was a way she could stay, perhaps there was also a way he could have her as a wife. Aye, this could work, but it required patience.

Elsie had requested distance and he'd agreed to give it to her. However if chance brought them together, he couldn't be blamed. If she felt as strongly about him as he did about her—and he believed she did—she would soon grow as frustrated as he was.

Chapter 24

Cade began implementing his plan to win Elsie the next day. He knew he could not pursue her overtly, as he had initially. He had to keep her off balance—keep stirring her attraction to him. In essence, he intended to subtly do exactly what she had asked him not to do. Over the next week he took every opportunity to interact with her. Sometimes intentionally, others by pure, blessed chance.

The very first morning he'd learned that running into her on the tower stairs was pure gold. He had met her on his way up the stairs as she was coming down for the morning meal.

"Good morning, Elsie." His eyes roved down her body and back up, taking a moment to appreciate every inch of her lovely form. "Ye're looking well this morning." Pleased to see a slow blush creep across her cheeks, he leaned casually against one wall of the stairwell while putting a hand on the other wall—completely blocking her descent.

"Th-thank ye."

"And how is Lady Wynda?"

"Lying flat is trying, but she's faring well."

"Excellent. What do ye have planned for today?"

She frowned at him. "Well, I thought I'd start by breaking my fast, but ye're blocking my way."

There it was, the cheekiness he adored. "How churlish of me. I beg yer pardon." He stepped aside to let her pass, but as she did he noticed her blush had only grown deeper. He had flustered her. Perfect. After that brief encounter, he made certain it happened again. Frequently.

Lady Wynda's confinement proved helpful in his pursuit. Ever since he had learned Wynda would have to spend months in bed, Cade tried to stop in to see her for a few minutes every day. He could only imagine how hard a confinement like that would. While he had never thought of her as a mother—he'd been away training when his father married her—she made his da happy and Cade liked and respected her. He wanted to do what he could to help break up the monotony of her days. As it happened, Elsie spent a lot of time with Wynda too. It was a very simple thing, to make certain his visits occurred when she was there.

But occasionally, an opportunity presented itself, which was so perfect he could only believe it was heaven-sent. One afternoon he rode into the village with a hunting party. She stood in front of a cottage, holding the bag of supplies she had begun to carry with her when she visited a patient. She looked wistfully towards the loch.

He called to her, "Good afternoon, Elsie. Are ye visiting Alma? Is she ill?"

"I'm just leaving. She has a touch of catarrh but I think she'll be fine."

"Ye look as if something's bothering ye."

"Nay, not really. It's just a lovely day and a walk would be nice."

"Ah, but ye need a guardsman to go with ye."

"Aye."

"Eric, would ye escort Elsie on a walk to the loch?"

She shook her head. "Nay, I hate to ask," but the look of longing in her eyes was unmistakable.

"Nonsense, Eric wouldn't mind, would ye, coz?"

Eric chuckled. "Not at all. However, I haven't seen ye riding in ages, Elsie. Maybe ye'd rather ride than walk?"

Elsie's eyes lit with pleasure. If Cade wasn't much mistaken, the last time she'd been for a ride was weeks ago when he'd ordered her to go with him and she'd asked for distance.

"I'd love to, Sir Eric. Thank ye."

"Then we will. But it's a shame to go all the way back

up to the stable for Edda. Affric, yer gelding is a fine calm mount isn't he?"

"Aye, he is Eric. Elsie, I'd be happy to loan him to ye." It was a mark of how well Elsie was respected that he was already off the horse and leading it towards her before he'd finished speaking.

She looked hesitant. "I don't really have much experience. Edda is the only horse I've ever ridden."

Eric smiled at her. "'Twill be good for ye to sit a different horse then. Ye really should learn how to read and adjust to other mounts."

"I guess—if ye're sure it will be all right."

"I won't let anything happen to ye," Eric assured her.

Cade watched, trying to appear disinterested.

Once Affric had helped Elsie onto his horse and adjusted the stirrups to fit her, Eric said, "Shall we go, lass?" He clicked to his mount and turned to head out of the village.

Elsie too urged Affric's gelding into a walk, following Eric.

This was the moment. "Lads, now that I think on it," Cade said. "I'd like a ride to the loch too. I'll go with them."

He couldn't see the expression on her face, but her back had gone stiff. He grinned for a moment, before schooling his features and riding up next to her. "Elsie, have ye forgotten everything? Don't sit so stiff in the saddle, lass," he scolded.

He was rewarded with a scowl from Elsie and a low chuckle from Eric.

They rode for about an hour. Elsie eventually dropped her guard and enjoyed the ride.

As they were riding back towards Carraigile, Eric fell back to a discreet distance. Cade knew he owed his cousin a huge debt for his role in orchestrating this.

"I've missed this, Elsie."

She sighed wistfully. "I have too."

He knew better than to push it more. That she'd admitted it was a start.

After that, Cade continued to find ways to coax Elsie into letting her guard down. It required finesse and would not happen overnight. He could afford to be patient. At least he thought he could, until things changed a few days later.

A messenger from Laird Macrae arrived during the midday meal. His father took the missive, his face grim as he read.

Cade scanned the trestle tables for Elsie. He realized the messenger too had spotted her and stared her direction.

~ * ~

The thing Elizabeth had been dreading had finally happened. A Macrae messenger had just delivered a message to Laird MacKenzie and was now glaring at her. She didn't know what to do. She wanted to run from the hall, but she knew that would be foolish. She could only wait to see what the message contained.

Laird MacKenzie frowned as he read it, giving nothing away. When he had finished reading, he looked up at the messenger.

"Will there be a reply, Laird?"

"Eventually. For the time being, find a seat and have some refreshment." He motioned for servants to bring the man food and ale.

Without another word to the messenger, Laird MacKenzie rose from the table. Cade too stood but the laird shook his head slightly, indicating that Cade should stay. Cade frowned but sat back down.

The laird walked to the tower stairs, motioning for Elizabeth to follow him.

She hurried out of the hall and up the stairs. When she reached the top, Laird MacKenzie waited there for her.

"Eliz—er—Elsie, come with me to my solar. We need to discuss this message from Laird Macrae."

She nodded, following silently in his wake.

When they reached the solar, he bade her sit in one of the chairs, taking the one opposite for himself. "Well, lass, I suppose ye can guess what's in Laird Macrae's message."

"He wants ye to send me back?"

"Not in so many words, but, aye, that's the gist. He says he was pleased to be able to assist me, but surely if anything could be done to help Lady MacKenzie, it's been done. He says ye're needed at home as soon as ye can return. If all is well, I'm to send ye back with this messenger."

Panic rose. "Laird, I can't go back."

"Don't worry so, lass, I don't intend to send ye. I'm going to tell him Lady Wynda still needs ye. I just want my message back to him to be accurate, in case he questions a midwife about my response."

Elizabeth relaxed a little. "Well, she's only five months along. Granted that's longer than she carried the last bairn, but it is way too soon to make any judgment. The next three months are the most critical to ensure that both Lady Wynda and the babe are well. But since it's commonly believed nothing can be done, he may not believe ye anyway."

"Then it should buy us a bit of additional time. I had hoped to have several more months before we had to face this, but ultimately, I will have to confront Macrae. He might be convinced to let ye stay if he realizes he'll have a feud on his hands if he doesn't."

Elizabeth was aghast. "A feud? Ye can't start a feud over me."

"It isn't just over ye. The Macrae sought an alliance through deception. That's more than sufficient grounds for a feud. Even though we want to keep ye, nothing changes his intent."

That didn't give Elizabeth a lot of comfort. She looked down.

He leaned forward in his chair and raised her chin until she met his gaze. "This will all be worked out, Elizabeth, I promise. But now that things have heated up, I don't want ye leaving the castle walls without an escort. I'll inform my men."

"But there are people who need me."

"Aye, but a guardsman will always be with ye. 'Tis for yer safety, lass. Promise me ye'll abide by this."

"Aye, Laird, I promise." The fact that Laird MacKenzie was so worried about her safety unsettled Elizabeth.

"Now, I am going to prepare a message to send back to Macrae. I want ye to stay out of the hall until that messenger leaves. I saw him glare at ye. I don't want him to be anywhere near ye."

"Aye, Laird. I'll go sit with Lady Wynda for a while."

He smiled warmly. "She always loves the hours ye spend with her. She says time speeds by in yer company."

Elizabeth nodded, but was too worried to summon a smile. "I'm glad I'm able to distract her." She rose to leave, but before she reached the door, she asked, "Laird, can I tell her about the messenger?"

He sighed heavily. "I would rather keep this unpleasantness from her, but that upsets her even more. Aye, tell her if ye wish."

When Elizabeth reached Wynda's chamber, as ever Wynda was delighted to see her and chivvied Alice out of the room so they could be alone.

Wynda was not pleased by Laird Macrae's request, but neither was she worried. "We'll work this out, Elizabeth. I promise ye we will."

"I know. I just hope it doesn't spark a feud."

"I doubt that it will, but don't worry about it for now."

"I'll try, my lady."

"Good. Now ye need to settle my worry."

"What are ye worried about?"

Lady Wynda tilted her head sideways. "Ye don't know?"

"Nay, my lady, I'm sorry."

"Well that goes quite a way towards making me feel better."

"Lady Wynda, I don't understand."

"Do ye know what tomorrow is?"

Elizabeth frowned, "Nay, I'm sorry, I don't."

Wynda gave her a huge warm smile and tears filled her eyes. "Tomorrow is day sixty. Ye and Elsie have only one day left to switch places if ye wish to."

Elizabeth smiled. "I committed to staying weeks ago and then again ten days ago. I've thought no more about it. Unless Elsie changes her mind within the next twenty four hours, and based on my discussion with Gertrude, that seems unlikely, I'm here to stay."

~ * ~

Cade kept an unobtrusive eye on the Macrae messenger. The man tried several times to engage MacKenzie clansmen in conversation. Cade had to smile when, each time the messenger attempted to steer the conversation to Elsie, the MacKenzies refused to be drawn in.

When his father returned to the great hall, he carried a sealed letter. "Here is the return message for yer laird."

The man took the parchment but frowning said, "Laird Macrae said I was to escort Elsie home."

"Not today. I've explained it all in the letter. If ye leave now ye should be able to reach the Matheson holding not long after dark."

"Aye, Laird." The man nodded and took the letter. He looked irritated at being rushed away. Normally, unless a message was extremely urgent, a messenger could expect a bed for the night allowing him to rest and leave the next morning, refreshed.

When the messenger had left, Cade asked his father, "What was in the missive?"

"Ye heard the man, Macrae wanted me to send Elsie back."

"But Wynda hasn't had the baby yet."

"That's what I told him in the letter. I informed him that Elsie needs to stay until Wynda delivers."

"Do ye think he'll accept that?"

"Only time will tell. But I am concerned about what he might do. I've told Elsie she's not to leave the walls without an escort. Now that I think more about it, make sure the men know that a single guard is only sufficient if she is going to the village. If she wishes to venture beyond that, I want at least two or three men with her."

Cade cocked his head and looked at his father for a moment. "Ye're guarding her as ye would a noblewoman—as ye do Wynda."

"Aye, I am."

Cade grinned. "Ye don't ever intend to return her, do ye?"

His father looked him squarely in the eyes. "Nay, I do not. Laird Macrae intended to deceive us, and therefore, I am under no obligation to return her."

"Da, I don't understand how ye can have it both ways. Macrae either lied about her abilities or he didn't."

His father actually laughed. "It's a puzzle, isn't it? But the truth is exactly what Elsie has maintained from the start. Macrae intended to pass an inexperienced apprentice off as an expert midwife, but he was unaware of the skills she actually possessed."

"And so ye're just keeping her. Is this what she wants?"

"Aye, but even if she it wasn't I'm not sure I could let her return. I believe she's in real danger from Laird

Macrae. Ye're well aware that the story Robin revealed—the one Macrae has reportedly told his clan—is untrue. I suspect Macrae doesn't want her returning with the real version of events."

"God's breath, that hadn't occurred to me. Aye, she needs guarded well. So she's under our protection now? Forever?" This thrilled him, but he wasn't ready to reveal that to his father yet.

"Aye, she is. And trust me, son, we are the victors in this. I assure ye, she'll be an asset to this clan, which will have far-reaching benefits."

There was the secret again.

Chapter 25

Macrae sent another messenger just before Pentecost in May. The message was still polite, but worded more strongly. Laird Macrae was pleased to hear that Lady MacKenzie was doing well. Surely Elsie had done what she could and was now needed by her own clan.

Angus's reply was equally politely worded. He simply clarified that when he asked for the assistance of the Macrae's *most experienced midwife*, the intention was always for her to attend Lady MacKenzie during delivery. With three months to go yet, he was certain that as a father of three healthy children, Laird Macrae would understand the need for Elsie to stay until after the bairn was safely delivered.

Angus intended to continue to politely refuse any request Alban sent. However, he could no longer ignore the fact that he needed to find a way to keep Elsie permanently. The evening after he sent the messenger back to Macrae, he asked Hamish, Sully, Eric and Cade to join him in his study.

When they had gathered, Angus didn't mince words. "Ye're all aware that Macrae has asked again for me to return Elsie and I do not intend to. I had initially hoped that as he intended to deceive me, he wouldn't push terribly hard for her return, but it appears he is doing just that. As ye're also aware, I fear for her safety. Given that he has lied to his clan about her, it is possible he intends to ensure she neither reveals his secret nor returns home."

"Angus, if he pushes for her return and ye refuse, it could start a feud," his brother observed.

"Aye, it might, but he set that course when he decided to deceive us in the first place."

Hamish nodded. "Fair enough."

"Do ye want to try to solve this diplomatically at all, or are ye ready to simply declare that ye intend to keep her and deal with the consequences?" asked Sully.

"I would like to avoid a feud if we can. If he demands her return, I will disclose what we've learned about his original intention. He has to know it would do him immeasurable damage if other clan leaders become aware of his treachery. Perhaps our silence is the only price we'll have to pay to keep her."

"That could work as long as he doesn't find out how talented she truly is," agreed Sully. "But if word reaches him of her abilities, then we have nothing with which to bargain, because he'll say he did not deal falsely with us."

"Aye, the truth of the matter is, he actually did us a great service. We have no proof that he didn't know it at the time," said Eric. At Cade's affronted look he added, "I'm not questioning Elsie's word. I'm just pointing out what he might say in his own defense. If others believe him, then it is the MacKenzies who will be judged harshly."

Angus nodded. He had considered all of these scenarios.

"There is one way to ensure she remains here regardless of what happens between ye and Alban," said Hamish.

"Aye, that's what I'm thinking too," agreed Angus.

"Care to share it with the rest of us?" asked Cade.

"Marriage?" asked Sully.

"Aye, marriage," said Angus.

The expression on his son's face was unreadable.

"But to whom?" asked Hamish.

"Da, ye can't just force her to marry."

"Of course I can, but I hope force won't be required. She's a smart lass, and she wants to stay. She'll see the wisdom of it."

"Well, Uncle Angus, if ye think she's smart and will see the wisdom of it, perhaps ye should ask her if there is a MacKenzie she's…attracted to. Someone she might wish to marry."

Angus recognized the mischievous twinkle in his nephew's eye. "Do ye have yer eye on her, lad?"

"If I did, would ye allow it?"

Hamish frowned at his son, but Angus considered the idea. "It's important enough…aye, I might consider it."

"Laird, the feast of Pentecost is upon us. Ye could watch and see who courts her and whose attention she seems to enjoy," offered Sully. "Then it may only take a few careful suggestions to the right man and the problem will work itself out."

~ * ~

Cade had been blindsided by his father's discussion of marriage for Elsie. This didn't figure into his plans at all. But Eric's apparent interest in her infuriated him. As soon as they were away from the others, Cade rounded on him. "What the hell was that about?"

"Well, the short version is, yer da wants to keep Elsie and figures marrying her to a MacKenzie is the most expedient way to do that."

"That's not what I meant and ye know it. Since when have ye been interested in her?"

"I'm not."

"Then why did ye let my father think ye were?"

"Tell me, Cade, if ye could, would ye marry her?"

"Aye, of course I would."

"But ye know as well as I do, if ye just came out and told yer da that, he wouldn't allow it. He has other plans for ye."

"Aye, I know that. Get to the point."

"The laird has other plans for me as well, but we just learned this is important enough to him that he would consider letting me marry her."

"How does that help me at all?"

"Once he becomes used to the idea of her marrying me, the idea of her marrying ye might not be so outrageous."

Cade frowned at him. "God's teeth, Eric—that might work."

Eric shrugged. "I doubt it, but this way ye at least have a chance. If ye'd just declared yer undying love for her, as I feared ye were preparing to do, his immediate reaction would've been to refuse ye."

~ * ~

Even though Angus was not allowed to *engage in marital relations* with Wynda, from the start, he'd refused to sleep in another chamber. He adored his wife, and if holding her in his arms while they slept was the only intimacy they were allowed, so be it.

The morning after the Pentecost feast he stayed abed later than usual. He stretched and groaned. His throbbing head reminded him that he had imbibed more freely than usual at the feast.

"Angus, my love, is something wrong?" Wynda's teasing tone told him she knew exactly what was wrong.

"Aye, I overindulged a bit last night, but I expect ye knew that."

She lay on her side and caressed his cheek. "I'm sorry. Perhaps Elizabeth will have something to ease yer headache."

"Aye, she might." But the mention of her real name reminded Angus of his other most pressing problem. Sully had suggested he watch her during the dancing to see if she had a growing affection for any of his men. The problem was, he knew how men behaved when they were attracted to a woman, and damn near every man in his garrison seemed interested in the young midwife. But he wasn't sure how to tell if the lass felt anything in return.

Wynda frowned. "Angus, what troubles ye? And don't dare tell me 'nothing'."

Angus sighed. He had tried to keep the issue with Laird Macrae from her as much as possible. He didn't want her to worry. But Wynda spent as much, if not more time with Elizabeth than anyone else. She might know the lass's preferences.

"My love, I promised ye I would do whatever it takes to keep Elizabeth with us."

Wynda's eyes narrowed. "Has something happened?"

"Laird Macrae sent another messenger. He arrived several days ago."

A look of horror marred his lovely wife's features. "Oh, Angus. She can't go back."

"Now, Wynda, if ye want me to tell ye what's happening, ye mustn't allow yerself to get so upset. I have no intention of ever sending Elizabeth back. Ye know that."

Wynda nodded. "I know. But what are ye going to do?"

"So far, the messages have been cordial requests and I have responded with polite refusals. I have said each time that ye still need her. I expect that the next message he sends will be more insistent. I've considered several options to deal with Macrae, but both Hamish and Sully agree, the best way to ensure that she stays here is to see her married."

"Married? To whom?"

"That's my problem. Sully suggested I watch her during last night's celebration to see which of my men seemed interested in her."

Wynda gave a most unladylike snort. "And that narrowed the field did it?"

"Clearly, by yer reaction, ye know it didn't."

"Aye, I wouldn't have expected it to. I suspect most of the unmarried men were falling over themselves to gain her attention."

"I'd hoped that she might show some sign of growing affection for someone, but she didn't seem particularly attracted to any of them."

"Did she not? Did she dance with Cade?"

"Cade? Nay, I don't think so. She danced with Eric, but not Cade."

"Well then, that's why ye didn't see any attraction."

"She's after *my son*?"

Wynda frowned. "First of all, if she was, ye have no room to be affronted."

Angus opened his mouth to argue, but she put up a hand to stop him.

"Nay Angus, let me finish. If she really were Elsie, and had been raised to understand our class structure, aye, I can see how ye might think she was simply trying to improve her station. But she comes from a place where a person's position in society is largely driven by education and hard work. In her mind, she is exactly where she wants to be. Marrying Cade would have no impact on that. And secondly, Cade is the one who has fallen hard for Elizabeth."

"Ye're not serious"

Wynda laughed. It was probably Angus's most favorite sound on earth. "I'm very serious."

"How do ye know?"

"He stops by to visit for a few minutes more days than not."

"Does he?"

"That surprises ye?"

"A little. I never thought the two of ye were particularly close."

"We aren't, but Angus, yer son is a kind man. I think he realizes how hard it is to be stuck in bed for so long and it's just his attempt to distract me a little."

Angus smiled, pleasantly surprised by Cade's

thoughtfulness. "And he told ye he's fond of Elizabeth?"

Wynda laughed again. "Nay, of course not. But ever since Easter, almost all of his visits have occurred when she was here too. And the charming rogue leaves her flustered and off-balance every time."

Angus chuckled. That didn't surprise him at all. "It sounds more like she's the one who's fallen for him."

"Well, I suspect she has, but ye're missing the point. Cade doesn't have to work to gain a lassie's attention, and yet he obviously puts a concerted effort into turning Elizabeth's head. I've never seen him do that."

Angus frowned. "Aye, I haven't either. But I cannot throw away the opportunity to make an alliance with a strong clan by allowing my son to marry a common-born lass."

"I understand that, my love. However ye want to marry her to someone to ensure she can stay here. So if ye see her as an asset to the clan and ye want to make yer son happy too, ye'll consider it."

Angus leaned forward and kissed his wife. He didn't want to tell her there wasn't the slightest chance he'd allow Cade to marry a midwife, but he didn't want to hurt her feelings by simply dismissing her idea. He settled on, "I won't rule it out."

~ * ~

Angus received Laird Macrae's third message just before the feast of St. John the Baptist. The polite veneer was growing very thin.

> *Laird MacKenzie,*
> *I am distressed that ye*
> *would keep my young*
> *clanswoman away from*
> *her loved ones for so*
> *long. Out of courtesy*
> *and respect, perhaps she*

*hasn't told ye this, but
she is to be married
shortly after St. John's
Eve. I apologize for the
misunderstanding, but
clearly, because of her
pending wedding, it was
never my intention for
Elsie to attend Lady
Wynda through her
entire pregnancy.*

*The Macraes are
prepared to be strong
allies to the MacKenzies,
but there is a limit to my
generosity. I'm certain
ye will want to
demonstrate yer
commitment to our
burgeoning alliance by
allowing Elsie to return
home immediately. Not
only are her skills
needed here, her
intended grows
impatient for her return.
– Alban Macrae*

Alban's subtle threat was plain and he had blatantly lied about Elsie's pending wedding. The minstrel for whom she might have had a budding affection had gone missing and was presumed dead. Thinking on it now, if Laird Macrae had known the young man's plans, he could easily have had the lad killed. Macrae certainly wouldn't want a minstrel—a man whose very livelihood was based on carrying news and telling stories—to know what had really happened. Nay, Alban clearly believed that Elsie continued to keep his secret. Angus did not wish to disabuse him of that, so he sent a carefully worded message containing his own veiled threat.

Laird Macrae,
I do appreciate yer
generosity and certainly
would not wish yer clan
to be without the skills of
a midwife. However, it is
my understanding that
whilst Elsie is yer very
best, her aunt has many
years of experience and
is an extremely skilled
midwife in her own right.

Out of concern for my
wife's delicate condition,
as ye suspected, Elsie
had not informed me of
her pending nuptials.
However, she agrees
that delaying her
wedding by a few weeks
is not an unbearable
hardship. I assure ye, the
burgeoning alliance
between our clans will
not be served at all by
forcing Elsie to return
home before Lady
MacKenzie delivers the
bairn. – Angus
MacKenzie

Angus had no doubt that all pretense of civility would

be dropped in the next message. In other circumstances, he would have simply called Alban out on his initial deception. But that could very well have resulted in Macrae riding on Carraigile with his full garrison.

Wynda was well into her seventh month. It was the longest she had carried any child before. He could not afford to allow her or the babe to be endangered in the slightest way. Therefore, he intended to put off Laird Macrae with diplomacy as long as possible.

Chapter 26

Cade was becoming impatient.

Once his father had decided that Elsie needed to marry, he became an insufferable matchmaker. To Cade's endless irritation, the men his father encouraged were beyond eager to try to win Elsie's affection. Perhaps his subtle assault on her was working, however, because she didn't seem interested in any of them. She didn't blush, become flustered or make a single cheeky comment to any of the men his father encouraged.

But Angus redoubled his efforts after the third messenger from Laird Macrae arrived. Cade could wait no longer. He had to launch the final attack and show no mercy.

As the bonfires were lit outside the village at sunset on St. John's Eve, Cade scanned the merry-makers until he found her. As usual she was in the company of some of the serving maids and they were surrounded by young men— including Eric—who sought dancing partners. Cade made his way through the crowd towards them.

Shauna spied him, extricated herself from her companions, stepped in front of him and slid her arms around his neck. "Sir Cade, it's a lovely evening for dancing, wouldn't ye say?"

"Aye, that it is, lass. Daniel, Shauna is anxious to join the dancing. Ye won't make such a fine lassie wait any longer, will ye?"

The man grinned. "I wouldn't dream of it, Cade." He put a hand at Shauna's waist and pulled her towards the dancers."

"Cade, it's good ye could join us, coz. After Easter and Pentecost, I feared ye'd sworn off dancing for good."

"Nay, never that, Eric." Catching Elsie off-guard, he pulled her into his arms, leaned close to her ear and whispered, "My toes needed a brief reprieve." To his utter delight she blushed and sputtered, but before she could manage an intelligible comeback, he drew her towards the dancing.

"Sir Cade, I—"

"—can't talk and dance at the same time if my poor toes have a hope of surviving the night."

She shook her head and laughed. "Sadly that's true."

She let him guide her through the steps of one dance. As the dance ended, he said, "Ye've gotten much better."

She flashed him her cute lopsided smile. "I sincerely doubt that."

He grinned. "Fine, a little better."

~ * ~

From the moment Elizabeth had let Cade pull her into the first dance, he had completely overwhelmed her senses. In fact, he'd been doing it for the last few weeks and tonight she simply gave into it. During the next couple of hours, he let her venture no farther from him than his fingertips. His nearness was intoxicating—his touch invigorating. She didn't want the evening to end, but it was well after midnight, and she was so tired she could barely walk without stumbling, much less dance.

"It's late, I'm tired and I really should find my bed."

"Don't go. The celebration will continue until dawn."

With only about six hours between sunset and sunrise, dawn was only few hours away, but even so, she would never last that long. "I can't dance another step. I'm terrible to start with. Mix that with weariness, and no one's toes are safe."

He pulled her close, nuzzled her ear and whispered, "No one's toes have been safe all night, but there isn't a lass I'd rather dance with."

His voice, rich and husky, was like molten butterscotch. She smiled. "Calling it dancing at all is quite a compliment."

He chuckled, sending shivers down her spine. "We don't have to dance, but I'm not ready to let ye go. Walk with me." He took her hand, leading her away from the dancing, outside the ring of light cast by the bonfires.

She knew she shouldn't go with him, but God help her, she couldn't resist. They walked in silence around the edge of the loch until they came to the cluster of boulders she had been sitting on the day she told Gertrude she wanted to stay. He walked to them and sat on one, pulling her down beside him, continuing to hold her hand.

He looked at her for a moment, his brow furrowed. "Elsie, I'm sorry, but I can't grant yer request."

"My request? What are ye talking about? I've asked nothing of ye."

"Aye, ye have. Ye asked me to give ye distance, but I can't."

Elizabeth sighed. "Sir Cade—"

He put his hand up. "Don't. I don't ever want ye to call me that again."

"But—"

"Nay, Elsie. I adore ye. In fact, I love ye. Trying to keep my distance was excruciating."

She chuckled. "Not to mention the fact that ye weren't very good at it."

"Obvious, was I? That's because I want ye in my life, at my side, forever."

She shook her head. "We've been through this."

"Nay Elsie, ye misunderstand me. I want ye to be my wife."

Elizabeth smiled sadly at him. "Ye know yer father will not allow that—bird and fish, remember?"

"Putting that aside for a moment, do ye wish to marry me?"

"Of course I do. I have never met someone who can infuriate me one minute and make me weak in the knees the next."

He grinned. "I make ye weak in the knees?"

"Ye know ye do. When I asked ye for distance, it wasn't because I didn't love ye."

He kissed the back of the hand he held. "So ye agree, we love each other and should be together forever."

"Aye but yer da—"

"My da wants ye married. It is the only sure way to keep ye here."

"Are ye serious?"

"Absolutely. He hadn't raised the issue with ye, because he thought there was time and he'd hoped ye would develop an interest in someone. I prayed to God ye wouldn't."

"Cade, ye know he won't let ye marry me."

"What I know, Elsie, is that I cannot live without ye. Aye, if I ask him for permission, he'll say no. But, if I simply marry ye, he'll bluster a bit and then be relieved that the problem of how to keep ye here is solved."

"What if that isn't his response? What's the worst thing that can happen?"

"He could disown me and banish us both."

"What does that mean?"

Cade gave her a questioning look. "Ye don't know what banishment means? It means I would no longer be his heir, we would no longer belong to the clan, and we would have to find a place to live away from Carraigile."

"Ye'd marry me, knowing this could happen?"

"Aye, I would. I don't think it'll come to that, but I'd accept it in order to spend the rest of my days with ye."

"Ye're certain?"

He chuckled, pulled her close and kissed her with a passion and intensity she had never experienced. Every conscious thought, every reason why she shouldn't give in, fled. Nothing existed outside of them. When he broke the kiss, his eyes twinkled. "Aye, I'm certain."

"Certain of what?"

He laughed. "Ye asked if I was certain I'd accept banishment for ye, and I am, Elsie."

Elsie.

She couldn't accept his proposal and marry him without telling him who she really was.

"Then there is one more thing ye need to know and accept before I'll agree to marry ye."

"Yer secret?"

"Ye knew?"

"I knew ye had a secret. I don't know what it is. After everything happened at Easter, I was certain there was something ye weren't telling me. There are things about this whole situation that don't seem logical. I was sure Macrae was lying when he said ye were his most skilled midwife. But I also firmly believed ye were telling the truth when ye said there was no one better able to assist Wynda. I never fully understood how yer stories matched but he could be lying while ye were telling the truth. I had to be missing a vital piece of information."

"Ye're right. I'll tell ye my secret, but I warn ye, it's hard to believe. Yer da, Lady Wynda, and Morag are the only people who know it."

"And they believe ye." It was a statement, not a question."

"Aye, they believe me. So please promise to hear the whole story before ye draw a conclusion."

He kissed the back of her hand. "I promise."

She proceeded to tell him the story of the pocket watch and all that had happened from the moment she met Gertrude, right through to when Gertrude came to see her in the dungeon.

When she had finished, he looked astonished. "Ye stayed? Ye had the chance to leave. Twice. Why did ye stay?"

"The first time was because I had fallen in love." He grinned and she laughed. "Don't be so sure of yerself. I fell in love with this clan. I'd never really felt so much a part of a community before, and I liked it. I also liked being able to make a difference in the lives of these people who had become dear to me."

"And the second time?"

"Well, to start with, I couldn't let Elsie return to the mess I'd made."

"Ye didn't make the mess, Elizabeth. Laird Macrae did."

"Still, I couldn't let her face the consequences of my decisions."

"All of that was sorted out before the last day. Ye could have gone back and Elsie would have been safe here."

"Aye, but she'd found happiness in my time. I didn't want to take that from her."

"So the only reasons ye stayed were because ye loved my people and ye wanted Elsie to be happy?"

Elizabeth laughed. "Those might not be the *only* reasons." She gave him a cheeky grin. "But I can't seem to think of any others at the moment."

"Can't ye? How about this?" He kissed her lightly. "Or this?" He kissed her again, his lips more demanding this time. "Or maybe this?" He pulled her onto his lap, and cradling her head in one hand, gave her a passionate, toe-curling kiss.

When he released her, she could barely think. She rested her head against his chest. "Aye, it might have been one of those. So, ye believe me, Cade MacKenzie?"

"Aye, I do. And, ye'll be my wife and take me as yer husband, Elizabeth Quinn?"

"Aye. I will."

"Well let's go make our vows."

"What do ye mean?"

"Ye've said ye'll be my wife. There's no time like the present to make things official."

"Cade, it's the wee hours of the morning. Father Henry has likely been asleep for hours."

"It's better if he's a little groggy. Then he'll have an excuse for having not talked us out of it when my father blusters at him in the morning." Cade stood, pulling her up too. "Marry me, Elizabeth. Marry me now."

Could she do this? Could she simply marry him without gaining anyone's permission? She had always played by the rules and done exactly what was expected of her and this was likely to infuriate Laird MacKenzie. David's words came to her: *I want you to discover what makes you happy—not what you think other people want from you. And once you find your destiny, I want you to embrace it.*

Cade made her happy and along with this clan whom she loved, he was her destiny.

"Aye, Cade. I'll marry ye now."

Chapter 27

As they walked back towards the bonfires, Elsie could scarcely believe she was doing this. If she had fallen in love with a man in her own time and eloped—even if he were perfect husband material in her family's eyes—there would have been hell to pay. She suspected there would be this time too, but her emerging rebellious streak delighted in it.

Before they reached the merry-makers, Cade turned to her. "Stay here for a moment. I am going to get Eric; we need a witness. Better yet, just make yer way through the crowd and wait for me at the edge of the village. Eric and I will meet ye there."

"Aye, that's a good idea."

He gave her a quick kiss. "See ye in a moment."

She smiled. "Hurry."

He strode towards the crowd. Elizabeth decided going around the merry-makers would be easier than weaving through them. She circled to the right, staying just beyond the people and the light cast from the fire. Lost in her happy thoughts, she didn't notice the two men, who also skirted the crowd deeper in the darkness, until it was too late.

A huge hand clamped over her mouth and before she realized what was happening, her captor stuffed a gag in her mouth while the other man tied her hands behind her back. Then the bigger of the two men threw her over his shoulder and ran towards the tree-line, his companion guarding from behind.

Elsie tried to kick, but the man had a vice-like grip on her legs. The fabric was stuffed in her mouth far enough to tickle her gag reflex. Add to that the pounding her stomach took from his shoulder as he ran through the trees and it was all she could do to keep herself from vomiting.

After what must have been about ten minutes, they stopped. Another man waited there with horses. They mounted up, threw Elsie face down across her captor's lap and rode hard away from Carraigile.

~ * ~

It took Cade a few moments to locate Eric in the crowd. He finally discovered him sitting on a plaid spread on the ground, nibbling the ear of the giggling crofter's daughter, in his lap.

"I'm sorry to interrupt ye, coz—"

"—then don't," he said between nibbles.

"Ah, sadly, I must. It's urgent."

"Nothing could be so urgent as to make me abandon this bonny lass."

"I fear it is. The future of Clan MacKenzie rests on it." Well it was true. Cade couldn't begin working on an heir until he married Elizabeth.

"Ye can't be serious."

"I'm very serious."

"Well, lass, I fear clan duty calls." The lass pouted prettily as Eric slid her off his lap. He stood and pulled her to her feet. "Don't sulk, sweetling, I'll be back as soon as I've secured the future of the clan. He planted a quick kiss on her lips.

Picking up his plaid, he turned to Cade, "This had better be important."

"Aye it is, let's go." Cade headed towards the village.

Eric followed. "Are ye going to let me in on what this urgent mission is?"

"I need a witness."

"For what?"

"For my marriage."

Eric stopped and stared. "Yer what?"

"My marriage."

"Tell me ye don't intend to marry Elsie behind yer da's back."

"I can't do that, coz, because it's exactly what I intend to do."

"Have ye lost yer mind? Yer da will be furious."

"I'll deal with it."

"Ye aren't the only one he'll be furious with."

"He'll get over it. He wants Elsie married. It's in the clan's best interest if she stays and I am happy to oblige."

Eric shook his head and laughed, "Ye know coz, if he banishes ye and Wynda gives birth to a wee lass, I'll be laird someday. Do ye really think that's in the best interests of the clan?"

Cade grew serious. "Ye'd be a good laird, Eric." Then his face split into a wide grin, "But I don't think I'll be banished."

Eric fell in step beside him again. "Aye probably not. If he banished ye, he'd lose Elsie too. I guess if ye can stand his wrath, so can I."

When they reached the edge of the village where Elsie was supposed to meet them, she wasn't there. Cade frowned. "She must have gotten waylaid. She'll be here soon."

Cade became uneasy after they had waited a few minutes. She should have gotten here before them. "Stay here. I'm going to see if she was pulled into the crowd. If she shows up have her wait."

Cade searched the crowd for several minutes but didn't find her. No one he asked had seen her. He went back to Eric, hoping to find her waiting there, but Eric was alone.

"Maybe she misunderstood ye. Maybe she waits for ye at the church."

"That could be it." Cade practically ran to the village church with Eric on his heels, but she wasn't there.

"Eric, something's wrong."

Eric frowned, "Aye, I fear there is."

"Go to the keep, just to make sure she didn't return there. I'll go back to the bonfires and check one more time. If she isn't at the keep, bring men and horses. We need to find her."

Cade tamped down his panic as he ran back to the bonfires. She had to be there. It took a moment, but he silenced the crowd. "Has anyone seen the midwife, Elsie?"

People looked around, shaking their heads.

Someone called, "Not since she left with ye, Sir."

"Is something wrong with Wynda?" called his Uncle Hamish.

"Nay, Uncle, she's fine. But Elsie is missing."

His uncle frowned. "Maybe she's just gone back to the keep."

"Eric has gone there to check."

"Who was guarding her?"

"Guarding her? I-I was."

"And who else? Yer da said she was to have two or three guards if she were outside the village."

By all that's holy, Cade had forgotten that. "We were here, surrounded by most of the clan, I didn't think about her needing additional guards."

"But, lad, ye left with her."

His Uncle Hamish's voice had been gentle and held no accusation, but the realization of how Cade had endangered his beloved came crashing down on him. "And I let her walk to the edge of the village alone. I thought she was safe in the crowd. She must have walked around it. What have I done?"

Hamish put a hand on his shoulder, "Don't borrow trouble. She may be at the keep. But until we know for sure we'll begin searching." To the crowd he said, "Men, grab a torch and search the area for some sign of what happened."

Several minutes later, Cade's heart fell when his father and Eric rode out of the village with a contingent of mounted men. Eric led Cade's mount.

Angus looked furious. "How did ye lose her?"

"Da, I'm sorry. I thought she was safe in the crowd."

His father shook his head. "We don't even know which direction to search."

"We were here, on this side of the gathering when I saw her last."

"That might mean they took her northward, but they could have just circled the lake on the north side before turning southward."

Just then a shout went up from the edge of the forest to the north. "The underbrush is disturbed here. It looks like someone came through here recently."

"Then we search to the north. But Sully, take more men and ride south, just in case."

Cade mounted his horse and rode into the woods. He was heartsick. Macrae had Elizabeth and it was his fault.

Before long it became abundantly clear that they were going in the right direction. It appeared the man or men who abducted Elizabeth had met up with riders and it was much easier to follow the trail left by several horses.

~ * ~

Alban Macrae stood on the deck of his ship, at anchor in the deep inlet that was MacKenzie's northern boundary. He was ready to be done with this whole mess. When Laird MacKenzie had grasped at straws to help his wife, Alban knew there was nothing to be done, so Drummond's suggestion to send an apprentice for a few weeks seemed reasonable. Lady MacKenzie would lose the baby and they would send the lass home.

She had only been gone a few hours when he realized the position he had put himself in. He had to explain why Elsie had gone, and every member of his clan knew she wasn't a midwife. If he had told them he sent her under false pretenses, he couldn't be sure the truth wouldn't make it back to MacKenzie. It was a minstrel, of all people, who first pushed for answers. If Alban had told the lad the truth, songs lamenting the Macrae's deceit might be sung for decades.

So he told a slightly different version of the story. Elsie was the one who lied and ran away with the MacKenzies. But several people didn't believe that. Dolina and the damned minstrel being chief among them. Still it surely wouldn't be long before Elsie returned. He could threaten her into silence and everything would be fine.

When two months had passed and Elsie hadn't returned, things got worse. Dolina was still extremely upset, and he learned his own wife, Una, was expecting. With Dolina upset, his wife was upset and she started pushing Alban to ask the MacKenzies to send Elsie home. He sent a polite message requesting her return.

Angus declined.

He sent a second messenger just before Pentecost, this time accompanied by several men-at-arms. If Angus refused, their instructions were to simply take Elsie. He had hoped they might gain easy access to her during the Pentecost celebrations. Angus didn't budge nor were his men able to gain access to her and steal the lass away. Apparently she was always in the company of a guardsman. They had finally returned empty handed. Based on the content of Laird MacKenzie's messages, the only blessing Alban could discern was; Elsie had evidently kept her mouth shut.

Still this couldn't go on. Again he sent several men with the third message, but he needed to have another plan. He gave his messenger enough time to deliver the message, then he sailed with a contingent of men. If Laird MacKenzie refused him again, he wanted to be in position to act. His timing of the third message was as intentional as the second. If Angus refused the request, the revelry of St. John's Eve might afford his men the opportunity to snatch her.

He prayed fervently they would be successful tonight. If they weren't he would have to negotiate with MacKenzie to get her back, and if that didn't work, he didn't know what he would do. Elsie had been with the MacKenzies for over four months but only his most loyal men, those he brought with him, knew the real story. If most of his clan believed Elsie went with the MacKenzies by her choice, he couldn't very well threaten to go to war for her return. Nor could he risk leaving her with the MacKenzies. She knew exactly what he had done.

~ * ~

When the men who had captured Elizabeth finally stopped their horses, they were on the shore of a large body of water. Someone lifted her off the horse and stood her on the ground. There were many more men waiting here and in the predawn twilight, she could see a small ship anchored off shore. It must be a bay or inlet from the sea.

Several men rowed a tender to shore. She recognized two of the men in the boat as Laird Macrae and Drummond, the man who had been dragging her through the village when she and Elsie had exchanged souls.

When the boat landed, the man over whose lap she had been thrown took her by the elbow, pulling her towards Laird Macrae.

The laird looked her up and down once before asking, "Why is she bound and gagged?"

"She fought us, Laird," said one of the two men who had captured her.

"Did ye tell her ye were rescuing her? Taking her home?"

"Nay, Laird."

"Eejits," he muttered. "Go, see to yer mounts. When they are rested and watered, ye need to hie yerselves home. The rest of us will return by ship."

The men did as their laird bid them, leaving her alone

with Laird Macrae and Drummond, Laird Macrae pulled the gag from her mouth but left her hands tied behind her back.

"Did ye keep my secret, Elsie?"

"Did I tell them I was an apprentice? Nay, I didn't."

"Very good. So that's why MacKenzie didn't want to let ye go? He still believes ye're my best midwife?"

"He believes I have the skills needed to care for Lady MacKenzie."

"Well now, we are in a bit of a spot."

"Why? I did what ye asked."

"Aye, but ye see, I couldn't very well let the whole clan know our secret. It wouldn't stay a secret long that way. So, I told them ye ran away with the MacKenzies."

"Then let me stay."

"I can't do that either. Yer aunt's worried about ye, and wants ye to come home. Besides, if I leave ye here, I have no way to ensure that ye'll hold yer tongue forever."

"Ye needn't worry."

"Now, ye see, I don't believe that."

She huffed. "Then what makes ye think I'll keep yer secret when ye take me home?"

Pain exploded in her cheek as he struck her hard across the face. "Ye've grown impertinent living with the MacKenzies. I will not tolerate that. Do ye understand me?"

In almost a reflex reaction that she couldn't have stopped if she'd wanted to, Elizabeth bowed her head. "Aye, Laird. I'm sorry, Laird."

He gave her a smug smile. "Good. And ye'll keep the secret because I'll give ye an incentive."

"An incentive?" She didn't like the quaver she heard in her voice.

"Aye. An incentive. Drummond here has taken a liking to ye, and I think ye'd make him a fine wife. If ye're a good lass, keep yer mouth shut and do as ye're told, he'll be a good husband. If ye cause any problems…well, he'll make sure ye won't."

Elizabeth considered herself a strong, capable woman. She believed she could deal with anything. Anything but being forced to marry the beast of a man who stood before her. Panic stirred in her gut. It took every ounce of fortitude she possessed to maintain control.

Laird Macrae lifted her chin with a finger and peered at her. "But ye'll be a good lass. I'm sure ye will."

She was terrified and one look in Laird Macrae's eyes told her he know that. "Aye, Laird." Again her response was reflexive and clearly Elsie's memory at work. That was probably a good thing, because her face throbbed. If she had said "No damn way," as she longed to he certainly would have struck her again, or worse.

Evidently satisfied by her fear and humility, Laird Macrae smiled. "Untie her, Drummond. She understands now."

The huge guardsman slipped his knife from the sheath on his leg, stepped behind her and sliced through her bonds.

Another automatic response, "Thank ye, sir," spilled out of her mouth as she rubbed her chafed wrists.

"Now, let's get her onboard the ship. Men, to the tenders."

Chapter 28

Dread gripped Cade's heart when he realized the men they followed were heading to the inlet. If they had a ship anchored there, they could be sailing away before he reached Elizabeth. As the MacKenzies neared the shore, they spread out, slowed their mounts and moved through the forest as quietly as possible. On Angus's signal they thundered out of the forest, weapons drawn.

The Macraes were climbing into tenders.

Elizabeth sat in the bow of one boat, next to a large Macrae guardsman.

Caught unawares, the Macraes scrambled for their weapons as the MacKenzies surrounded them.

"Hold and we won't kill ye," commanded Angus.

Laird Macrae made a subtle motion with his hand and the men near the tender holding Elizabeth moved to launch it.

"I'll run yer laird through if ye move another muscle."

They stopped.

"Alban, ye and I need to talk."

"She's my clanswoman, Angus, and I'm taking her home."

"Nay, ye aren't. She stays with us."

"Ye have no right. I didn't say ye could keep her until Lady MacKenzie delivers. I need her now. My own wife is with child."

"Now, I'm glad ye brought that up, because the way I understand it, Elsie's aunt is a highly respected midwife with years of experience."

"Aye, she is, but Elsie—"

"—is only an apprentice?"

Macrae cast a furious glare in Elizabeth's direction.

"That is the truth, is it not?"

"Is that what the lying wench told ye?"

"Nay, Alban, she didn't tell me. Some minstrels who had been at Castle Macrae did. She has maintained, from the moment she arrived, that she was the midwife we needed. So the way I see it, ye lied to me. Ye played on my fears for my wife, sent me an unskilled apprentice and expected my undying gratitude for yer deceit."

"Well, it seems to me yer wife is unharmed—in fact she's still pregnant which is both a miracle and a blessing. But clearly, the talentless lass I sent ye has had no impact." His tone dripped with sarcasm. "Therefore, she doesn't need to stay until yer wife delivers."

"Ye aren't taking her. She'll stay with the MacKenzies forever."

"Ye can't keep her."

"The hell I can't."

"She's my clanswoman."

"Who, at yer own admission, ye lied about in order to gain an alliance. What do ye think yer other allies will make of that? Do ye suppose they'll wonder what ye've lied to them about?"

"Ye *borrowed* her. What will yer allies say when ye don't return what ye borrowed?"

"I asked to borrow a skilled midwife. Ye lied and sent an apprentice."

"Perhaps not. Perhaps I didn't lie. It seems to me yer wife is doing very well under Elsie's care. Maybe she isn't without knowledge."

"Ye're a fool. Ye wanted an alliance with me, Macrae. But in lying to me to get it, ye've created a powerful enemy. I will signal the battle this instant if ye don't hand her over."

In the blink of an eye, the guardsman in the tender with Elizabeth had a dirk to her throat.

"Hold!" roared Angus.

"Ye can attack if ye wish, but she'll be dead before ye can take two steps if ye do," warned Laird Macrae.

Horrified, Cade could do nothing. A single wrong move and he could lose her forever. The pink light of dawn illumined her face, revealing how very frightened she was.

"She's yer clanswoman." His father's tone was incredulous. "If ye are willing to kill her, why not just leave her with us. Ye can be on yer way."

"If ye don't need her as a midwife, why do ye insist on keeping her?"

Laird MacKenzie's eyes narrowed and in a deadly calm voice he said, "Because I know what ye did. I know that ye threatened her. Killing her won't silence the truth." In a slightly gentler voice Angus said, "I understand ye believed no one could help Wynda, so ye didn't think it mattered who ye sent. I know that ye lied to yer clan about how and why she left. Only a fool would believe she's in no danger if she returns with ye, so I can't allow that to happen. I also suspect not only do ye not want yer clan to know what ye've done, ye don't want yer allies to know either. But I assure ye, if ye continue to push for her return, everyone in the Highlands will know. I will make certain of it."

"If ye're going to spread those lies through the Highlands, I have a few stories of my own to tell. Ye borrowed my best midwife and refused to return her."

"Ye've just admitted that she isn't yer best midwife."

"I told ye I wasn't so sure about that. The way I see it, yer wife, who has lost four pregnancies, is well along with this bairn. That's quite remarkable. I have also heard tell the lass brought Laird MacLennan's heir through a serious fever. It seems she's rather skilled after all. I reckon plenty of people will believe that's reason enough for ye to want to steal her from me and then lie about it. Besides, I have the lass herself who will swear I'm telling the truth."

"If ye take her Macrae, it's war. My forces exceed yers

by four-fold. Furthermore, Carrs, MacLennans, MacDonnells and Mathesons are all allies of mine, and they all border yer holding. Yer own wife is expecting. Do ye really want to go down this path?"

"Nay, I don't. But Elsie belongs to *me*, and if I have her, I can control her. She's to be married to one of my guardsmen."

The man holding his knife to Elizabeth's throat grinned. Cade knew instantly he was the guardsman Macrae intended Elsie to marry. Cade had to stop this. He said the first thing that came to his mind, "She's not free to marry. She belongs to me."

Macrae's mouth fell open in astonishment. "Ye let yer son marry a midwife, MacKenzie? I don't believe that."

"We handfasted. My father didn't know until after it was done."

His father did not react to this announcement, but only nodded. "Aye, Macrae, I was livid when I learned of it." The tick in his father's jaw suggested that he *was* livid. "But as ye well know, a handfasting is as binding as a betrothal."

"A betrothal can be set aside in some circumstances. Elsie is my clanswoman and didn't have my permission to marry. That's reason enough."

"But a handfasting can't be set aside if it has been consummated," said Cade.

Macrae fairly trembled with rage. He glared at Elizabeth. "I didn't send ye here to whore for the MacKenzie pup."

His father looked every bit as angry as Laird Macrae. "Be that as it may, Macrae, what's done is done and we've reached an impasse. I will not allow ye to leave with her, and if ye kill her, ye'll all die on this shore today. We had no formal relationship before, but neither were there hostilities between us. Ye were willing to lie to have an alliance with me and that's reason enough for a clan war, but it can be avoided."

Alban looked at him cautiously. "What are ye saying?"

"I'm saying our alliance went to hell when ye lied about who she was. She is now my son's wife. If ye release her, we will part ways. I'll accept that ye believed no one could help Wynda so ye didn't act out of malice. I'll say no more about it. No alliance. No hostilities." Alban seemed to be considering the proposal. Angus added, "Leaving her with us is a small price to pay, to ensure yer reputation isn't ruined."

Alban clenched his teeth. "And the little whore will keep her mouth shut too?"

"Mind yer tongue. Ye're speaking about my good daughter, and I am losing patience. I have assured ye, word of this will go no farther."

"Elsie's aunt is heartbroken. Allow her to go with us for a while and then she can return after her aunt is assured of her safety."

"Nay, Alban. Ye can reassure her aunt that Elsie is both safe and happy. I am offering to not only to forgive the wrongs ye've done me, but also to stay silent about them. The cost of my goodwill is Elsie. She stays with us. Her aunt is welcome to visit at any time. Or, after my child is born, I will have Elsie escorted to either Laird Matheson or Laird MacLennan. Her aunt can visit with her there. Elsie will never return to Macrae land unless I allow it."

Laird Macrae was cornered and he knew it. Finally, through clenched teeth, he ordered, "Release her."

"But, Laird—"

"—*I said release her!*"

"Aye, Laird," growled the guardsman holding her, but he let her go.

Cade dismounted as Elizabeth clambered out of the tender and ran to his arms. He gathered her close, simply holding her for a moment. "I'm so sorry, my love. I should never have left ye alone," he whispered.

"It isn't yer fault."

"Aye, it is, but we have ye back now. Are ye ready to go home?"

"Aye." Her voice was tremulous, as if she fought back tears.

Taking her face in his hands, he gave her a quick, tender kiss before lifting her onto his horse and mounting behind her.

His father said, "Thank ye, Laird Macrae. As ye can see, she has become very dear to my son. Be sure her aunt knows that. Now, ye and yer men are free to return to the ship. Several of my guardsmen will escort yer horsemen to our border."

Chapter 29

The sun was fully up by the time Laird Macrae's ship had set sail and his horsemen were on their way under MacKenzie guard. Only then did the rest of the MacKenzies turn towards home. Elizabeth could barely process all that had happened over the last few hours, but the lies Cade had told about them being married worried her the most. It didn't take long for Laird MacKenzie to begin asking questions.

"So, Elsie, when did my son marry ye?"

"I…we…aren't married."

"Da, I told ye, we handfasted *de praesenti*."

"Then why did Elsie say ye aren't married?"

"Because she doesn't completely understand what handfasting means." He gave his father a pointed look. "And our vows haven't been solemnized."

Angus frowned. "Elsie did ye agree to take Cade as yer husband?"

She had agreed when Cade had said: *And, ye'll be my wife and take me as yer husband, Elizabeth Quinn?* "Aye, I did."

"And he agreed to take ye as his wife?"

"Aye, but—"

Cade put a finger on her lips. "There are no 'buts', Elsie, we handfasted."

"And when did this handfasting take place?" Cade opened his mouth to answer but his father put up his hand. "I want Elsie to answer."

"Last night. Just before I was taken by the Macraes."

"Then how could it have been consummated?" Angus demanded.

"It wasn't," answered Cade.

"But ye told Macrae it was."

"Nay Da, I didn't. I said a handfasting couldn't be set aside if it had been consummated. I never said ours was."

His father laughed. "Nay ye didn't. It looks like ye beat him at his own game of words."

Elizabeth frowned. "I don't understand. There was no priest. We didn't make vows. How can we be married?"

"Do ye not understand what a handfasting *de praesenti*, is, lass?" Asked Hamish.

"A betrothal?" But wasn't a betrothal just an engagement? Engagements fell apart all of the time.

Hamish nodded. "Aye. It's a binding agreement to marry and once entered into, it can only be broken in certain, extreme, circumstances. When a couple handfasts *de praesenti*, it means they consider themselves married at that moment. Is that what happened? Do ye consider yerself married?"

Marry me, Elizabeth. Marry me now.

Aye, Cade. I'll marry ye now.

She felt Cade tense at her hesitation and she smiled. "Aye, I do. We were going to see Father Henry and I thought that was required to seal the marriage."

Cade relaxed and gave her a little squeeze with the arm that encircled her.

"Aye, well it is. Not to make it binding, but ye must say vows before a priest too," Angus informed her. "Of course, strictly speaking, a couple should not consummate their marriage until *after* it has been solemnized by the Church."

"Da, we'll be riding right past the church. I'm sure Father Henry would be happy to oblige."

Angus nodded. "Aye, we'd best take care of it right away."

"This morning? Like this?" Elizabeth was appalled. "I was bound, gagged, and then thrown across a horse and hauled away. I'm tired and dirty...and...and...tired. I am not getting married like this. I want a bath and a nap first."

Hamish frowned. "Lass, I simply cannot fathom how ye became so bold living under the rule of that devil. Angus is a good man, but if he tells ye to marry, ye'll marry."

Cade chuckled and whispered, "I told ye that wee sharp tongue would get ye in trouble."

She felt her face warm as she blushed. "I'm sorry, Laird. I'm…I'm…"

"Tired. I know." He gave her a stern look before his face relaxed into a smile. "Cade, I think yer vows can wait until Elsie has had a bath and a rest."

Although the sun had been up for nearly two hours, it was still very early in the morning when they reached Carraigile. Cade helped her off the horse, gave the beast to a stable hand to tend and walked with her into the keep. With most of the clan having only found their beds at sunrise, nearly everyone was still sleeping.

She stopped just inside the doors. She wanted to bathe first, while everything was quiet. But as tired as she was, she didn't want to climb the stairs to her chamber to get clean clothes.

"What's the matter?" Asked Cade.

"Nothing. I'm just very tired and at the moment, climbing the stairs to get my things is more than a little daunting."

"Then don't. Go on to the bathing room. Someone will bring yer things to ye."

"Nay, everyone's still asleep."

"Not everyone. Go have yer bath."

She sighed. "I'm too tired to argue. Thank ye." As she had hoped, the bathing room was empty. She built the fire in the hearth, hung pots of water over it to heat and partially filled the tub with cold water. In the four months she had lived at Carraigile, readying a medieval bath had become second nature. In the twenty-first century she would have been in and out of the shower in less time than it took to draw enough water from the well for a bath. She smiled to herself when she remembered what Gertrude had said about the *powers that be* stepping in to slow her down. *Well it worked.*

She added the hot water to the tub, put two pitchers of warm water for rinsing her hair within reach, took off her clothes and eased herself into the water. *Paradise.* She washed quickly, then closed her eyes to relax for a moment. Maybe she'd just take a little nap in the luxurious warmth of the bath. She was just nodding off when someone entered. Opening one eye, she expected to see Deirdre or one of the other maids, but it was Cade who stood just inside the door, a bundle in his hand, devouring her with his gaze.

She smiled to herself and closed her eye again. She was a twenty-first century woman and he was the man she loved. She wasn't about to play the shy maid. "As I understand it, *a couple should not consummate their marriage until after it has been solemnized by the Church.*"

She heard his low throaty chuckle. "Aye, I've heard the same thing. But as I went to get yer things I imagined ye down here taking yer clothes off. Then I imagined ye in yer naked glory sinking into the warm water and that was a sight I simply had to see."

She heard him put the bundle down before moving behind her.

"And then I remembered how very tired ye are, so I thought ye might need some help bathing." His voice was low and sensual. He touched her shoulders, massaging them lightly.

She groaned with pleasure as he slid his hands down her arms and back up, kneading her shoulders again.

"Cade…" she whispered, relaxing into his touch.

He leaned over her, capturing her lips in a tender, upside down kiss. Then he kissed the edge of her lips, moving to her jaw line and down the column of her throat.

She arched her head back, granting him greater access. He planted kisses along her collarbone, and back up her neck, nuzzling behind her cheek.

"Do ye?" he whispered, his breath tickling her ear.

"Do I what?" Her voice sounded breathy.

He chuckled again. It was a sound she thought she would never tire of hearing.

"Do ye need help bathing?"

She smiled dreamily. "Do I?"

"Elizabeth, ye're practically asleep."

"Because a very handsome man has enchanted me with his kisses and his touch."

"And I'd kiss ye more, but I fear when ye told my da ye were tired it was a gross understatement. Let me help ye finish yer bath so ye can go to bed."

"I just need to wash my hair."

He took her thick braid in his hand, removed the strip of leather tied at the end and pulled his fingers through her hair until it hung loose. "I've wanted to do that since the night we arrived at Carraigile and ye sat by the hearth drying it after yer bath. Yer tresses are beautiful."

"I'm glad ye think so." She leaned forward, wetting her hair in the tub. Then scooping up some soapwort, she worked it into a lather. When his hands joined hers, she thought she had died and gone to heaven.

After her hair was thoroughly washed, Cade picked up one of the pitchers of warm water. "Close yer eyes."

She did and he poured first one and then the other pitcher over her head, rinsing out the soap. Then he wrapped a linen towel around her and helped her out of the tub.

He befuddled her with kisses as he ran his hands over her whole body, drying her.

Before she knew it, he had pulled a clean léine over her head and draped a plaid around her shoulders. He gave her one more kiss. "Now, go to bed." As he said it, he pulled off his own léine.

"What are ye doing?" she asked, bemused.

He laughed. "There's a tub of warm water and rumor has it, I'm to be married this afternoon. I figure I ought to take a bath."

She grinned. "Shall I help ye?"

"As delightful as that would be, I fear ye're practically asleep standing up. Go rest and I promise ye can see me in my naked glory later."

She blushed but smiled coyly. "I'll hold ye to that."

She left him in the bathing room and returned to the keep. People were beginning to stir. Slowly. Most of them hadn't slept for more than four hours. A few had headaches from imbibing too freely in stronger drinks.

As she made her way to the stairs, several people called, "Elsie, lass, could ye make me some of yer willow bark infusion?"

She laughed. "It sounds as if an entire cauldron is needed."

"Ye're a wicked lass to laugh at our pain," teased Affric.

"Nay, a wicked lass would brew ye a purgative instead of a pain reliever." Her quip was met with both chuckles and groans.

Affric put his hand over his heart. "Ah, lass, ye wouldn't torture us so."

Lady Lilliana stepped in. "Ignore them Elsie. Go on and get some rest. I'll tend to the sore heads this morning."

"Thank ye, my lady."

Elsie barely remembered climbing the stairs and was asleep as soon as she snuggled into bed.

Chapter 30

The persistent rapping at her door finally drew Elizabeth from her deep sleep. She tried to get out of bed but couldn't quite manage, so she called "Come in," groggily and curled back up.

Deirdre came in radiating sunshine and energy, her arms piled high with what appeared to be garments. "Elsie, I mean, *my lady*, ye need to wake up now."

Elizabeth groaned. "My lady? What's that about?"

"Didn't ye handfast with Sir Cade last night?"

"Aye."

"And ye're exchanging vows this afternoon?"

"Aye."

"Well…"

"Well what?"

Deirdre gave an exasperated sigh. "Ye married Sir Cade. Ye're a *lady* now. Ye're Lady Elsie MacKenzie."

Oh. Dear. God. Elizabeth hadn't thought of that. She had no idea how to be a noblewoman and knew nothing about the workings of a clan or how to run a castle.

Her distress must have been written on her face because Deirdre frowned. "What's the matter? Aren't ye happy? Did ye not want to marry him?"

"Nay Deirdre, I'm thrilled to be married to Cade. I just hadn't thought the rest of it through."

"Ye mean about being a lady now?"

"Aye, that, and everything that goes with it."

"Don't worry. Lady MacKenzie and Lady Lilliana will help ye. In fact, they asked me to wake ye and help ye dress. And they sent these lovely things for ye to wear. After ye're dressed ye're to go to Lady Wynda's chamber."

Deirdre spent nearly the next hour helping Elizabeth

don the finery, before working her hair into a series of intricate braids. When Deirdre was finished, she held up a looking glass for Elizabeth. "See what a beautiful bride ye are?"

It still always surprised her a little to see Elsie's reflection looking back. Dressed in a cream colored silk léine, under an embroidered blue linen surcoat with a sheer veil over the delicate braids, she did feel beautiful.

"Thank ye, Deirdre, ye're a good friend."

"Ye're welcome, my lady."

"Don't call me that. I'm just Elsie."

"I have to call ye that. It would be rude if I didn't."

"Well, at least when we're alone, please just call me Elsie."

Deirdre smiled. "All right, Elsie."

"Another thing, is it customary to have someone stand with ye when ye marry?"

"Aye. I expect Sir Eric will stand with Sir Cade."

"Would ye stand with me?"

"I don't know if it would be proper."

"Please, Deirdre. Ye're my dearest friend. I don't have a father, or any family member to give me away. Please stand with me."

She smiled shyly. "Aye, I will."

Elizabeth hugged her. "Thank ye."

Deirdre blushed but looked very pleased. "Ye're welcome. Now, ye need to go see Lady Wynda."

"Aye, I'll go straight there."

When she reached Wynda's chamber, Lady Lilliana greeted her at the door. "Elsie, ye're a radiant bride."

"Thank ye, my lady. And thank ye both for the lovely garments. I've never worn anything like them."

Wynda smiled from the bed. "I suppose not. Ye do look stunning, dear."

"Thank ye, my lady."

"I think we can dispense with the 'my lady's' now. As

Cade's wife, ye bear that title too."

"Ah, well, I'm glad ye brought that up. Ye see…" she glanced at Lilliana, "I suppose I…uh…have some questions."

Wynda nodded. "I thought ye might. I wonder if ye would mind if Lilliana stayed. I expect there are a number of things ye'll need to learn and it will help if she knows."

"Ye mean…ye think I should uh…"

"Aye, lass, if ye're comfortable with that."

Lilliana looked a bit confused. "I can give ye privacy if ye like."

Elizabeth shook her head. "Nay, I think ye should stay. There's something I need to tell ye." Elizabeth launched into the tale.

Lilliana seemed to consider things for a few moments after Elizabeth finished. "That's a very difficult tale to believe."

"I know it is."

"If ye had told me this when ye arrived, I think I would have doubted ye. But with Wynda doing so well, and all the other things ye've done, not to mention Gertrude's involvement, I can only believe ye're telling the truth."

"Lilliana, the reason I wanted Elizabeth to tell ye her story is because I suspect she'll need help learning what to do—as a noblewoman. Of course Cade and Angus know, but with me here in bed for six more weeks, I wanted her to have a woman to turn to who wouldn't be shocked by her questions."

"Of course, Wynda, I'd be happy to."

For the next few minutes Elizabeth answered Lilliana's questions about time travel and the future. But soon Alice arrived.

"My ladies, the Laird sent me up. He says it's time for the wedding."

"Well, Elsie, I would dearly love to be there, but ye'll have to accept my apologies. However, I will ask ye one boon."

"Aye, anything."

"Come here tomorrow morning and allow me to tie yer kertch on ye."

The kertch was a triangular white head covering that all the married women in the Highlands wore. Elizabeth had learned it was a symbol of the Holy Trinity and as important a symbol of marriage to Highlanders as a wedding ring. A bride's mother was usually the one to present her with her kertch.

Tears welled in Elizabeth's eyes. "I'd be honored. Thank ye." She leaned down and kissed Wynda's cheek.

"My darling lass, go now and receive God's blessing on this union."

"Aye, thank ye again, for everything."

Elizabeth left with Lilliana. "I hope it's all right, I asked Deirdre to stand with me."

Lilliana smiled. "I assumed ye would."

When they reached the hall, only Hamish and Deirdre were there. "Where is everyone?"

"They've all gone on to the church, lass," explained Hamish. "I was waiting to escort my lovely wife there."

Lilliana smiled at his complement. "The Laird, Cade and Eric will be waiting on the steps of the church. Hamish and I will go ahead of ye. The rest of the clan are outside and will fall in behind ye as ye pass."

Hamish frowned. "Is that not the way the Macraes do it?"

"I'm just making certain," said Lilliana. "We should go now, Hamish."

As soon as they had left, Deirdre handed her a bouquet of what appeared to be herbs. "Oh my, what is this?"

"It's yer bouquet. It contains lavender for devotion, myrtle for everlasting love and...uh... marital bliss." Deirdre blushed profusely, causing Elizabeth to stifle a smile. "There's also sage for long life, rosemary for remembrance, parsley for happiness, and mint. I can't remember what it's for, but it smells nice."

"Thank ye. It's lovely."

"I'm glad ye like it. Are ye ready?"

"I was ready weeks ago."

Deirdre laughed. "Well, we'll hurry then."

Just as Lilliana said, the bailey and the entire route to the church was lined with people who fell in behind Elizabeth as she and Deirdre passed. As they approached the church, Father Henry, Cade and Eric waited in front with the Laird, Hamish and Lilliana nearby.

When she and Deirdre reached them, Elizabeth was surprised that they all stayed outside.

Before he started the ceremony Father Henry asked, "My child, is yer given name Elsie or is it a diminutive for Elizabeth?"

She smiled broadly, thrilled to be able to use her own name. "It's a diminutive for Elizabeth."

He nodded. "Very well. Does anyone know of any reason why Cade and Elizabeth cannot be married?" The question was met with silence, so he continued. "Cade MacKenzie, will ye have this woman to thy wedded wife, will ye love her, and honor her, keep her and guard her, in health and in sickness, as a husband should a wife, and forsaking all others on account of her, keep ye only unto her, so long as ye both shall live?"

Cade answered, "I will."

"Elizabeth, will ye have this man to thy wedded husband, will ye obey him and serve him, love, honor, and keep him in sickness and in health; and, forsaking all other on account of him, keep ye only unto him, so long as ye both shall live?"

Obey and serve? Is he serious?

Cade looked amused, as if he knew the part of the vow she struggled with. "Elizabeth?"

She leaned towards him and whispered, "I'm not sure

I'll be very good at obeying."

He winked. "Don't worry, I'll help ye."

She rolled her eyes. Ah well, she chose the thirteenth century, she'd have to make it work. "I will," she answered.

"Is there a ring?" asked Father Henry

"Aye, Father." Eric handed him the ring. The priest blessed it and gave it to Cade, who placed it on the third finger of Elizabeth's left hand. "With this ring, I thee wed, in the name of the Father and the Son and the Holy Spirit."

Father blessed them and led them into the chapel, followed by Deirdre, Eric, Laird MacKenzie, Hamish, Lillian and the rest of the clansmen and women present.

As Father Henry said the nuptial Mass, Elizabeth thought back to her first day here when she had been so moved by the sense of community. She quickly grown to love them with everything in her. As Ruth said to Naomi: *whither thou goest, I will go; and where thou lodgest, I will lodge, thy people shall be my people, and thy God my God.*

When the Mass was over, Father Henry gave the couple a final blessing, announcing loudly, "Sir Cade, ye may kiss yer bride."

Cade needed no urging. With a hand behind her neck and one at her waist he kissed her soundly. A deafening cheer went up. As ever, she was momentarily lost in his kiss.

~ * ~

Cade could scarcely believe the lass he adored was finally his. The story she had told him the previous evening, the secret which made her unique, was too astonishing to believe—except he did believe it. It explained every inconsistency that had puzzled him for weeks and, at the same time, was too fantastical for her to have made it up. And this inimitable woman, from the distant future, had just become his wife.

They turned to face his cheering clan. He leaned down,

kissed her one more time and whispered, "We have a wee feast to get through and then, my love, my virtue is yers."

She laughed and he let the beauty of it simply wash over him.

As it turned out, the "wee feast" wasn't so very "wee." It was, after all, the Feast of St. John the Baptist and thus had been planned for days. Finally, late in the evening, Cade pulled her to the stairs. He called, "My wife and I bid ye all a good night." Then he scooped her into his arms and carried her up the stairs.

When they reached the second floor, he said, "I had Father Henry bless the bed earlier today."

"Which bed?

"What do ye mean, which bed?"

She flashed him her lopsided smile. "Did he bless my bed or yers?"

"Well ye were in yers most of the day."

"An exaggeration."

He chuckled. "Aye. But I had him bless my bed. Ours now. It is much more comfortable."

He carried her to his chamber, entered and with her still in his arms began kissing her. Her fingers threaded through his hair and tightened, holding him to her. He broke the kiss, resting his forehead against hers. "Ye're mine."

"And ye're mine."

"Aye, I am. Now, I want to see the lovely vision ye treated me to earlier." He stood her on the floor, and divested her of her léine and surcoat, leaving her standing in only her shift.

She cocked her head. "I think ye've done this before."

He put his hands on her hips, pulling her intimately against him and devouring her lips in another passionate kiss. Then he whispered, "Once or twice, but never have I cherished the prize as I do ye. I love ye, Elizabeth."

"And I love ye." She smiled and pulled at his clothes.

"Ye promised me yer naked glory earlier today and I have been counting the moments. Don't keep me waiting longer."

He helped her remove his clothes, then lifted the delicate silk shift over her head. He took a step back and simply gazed at her beautiful form. He frowned. "Turn around."

"Why?"

"Ye promised to obey remember?" He winked at her.

She rolled her eyes and turned around. "Is this just an attempt to see my soft round backside?"

"Well that is a benefit, but nay." He stepped close, removed the ribbons securing her elaborate braids and pulled his fingers through them, releasing her hair until it formed a soft cloud around her shoulders. When he was done, he turned her back around, holding her at arm's length. His eyes roved lazily over her body. "Perfection."

She surveyed him boldly and with a coy smile said, "Ye're nearly perfect yerself."

He chuckled, "Nearly?"

"Aye. Ye'd be absolutely perfect if ye weren't so far away."

"That's easily fixed." He closed the distance between them, molding her soft body to his. His hands roamed freely over her silky skin before cupping her bottom.

She too explored his body with her hands, her feather light touch inflaming him. She snaked her arms around his neck, entwining her fingers in his hair and drawing his lips down to hers.

He groaned, if possible pulling her even tighter to him. The feel of her against his hardness was almost more than he could take. He moved her gently backwards, towards the bed, lowering her onto it, never breaking contact with her lips. His hands wandered over her body. He caressed first one soft breast, then the other, rubbing his thumb lightly over their firm peaks. Her lips became more demanding as he stroked her silky skin.

~ * ~

Elizabeth had never felt such intense desire. It was as if Cade's kisses, his touch, were oxygen and she had been holding her breath for far too long. She simply couldn't get enough. She held on fiercely, writhing under him, entangling her tongue with his. When his hand slid down to stroke her heat, she was transported to a world of pure bliss. And for the first time, Elizabeth, always in control and three steps ahead, let go. She trusted him to guide her to ecstasy and he did. While she was still soaring in oblivion, he pressed his length into her, filling her. She was vaguely aware of a momentary flash of pain, but it did nothing to quench her longing. She arched against him, lost in sensation, held completely in thrall. She shattered beneath him, existing only with him. As the muscles at her core contracted around his hardness, he too found his release.

Cade dropped his head to hers, panting, and whispered, "Elizabeth." He slowly withdrew from her and moved to lie beside her. Pulling her into the curve of his body, he trailed tender kisses from her lips to her shoulder.

"Did I hurt ye overmuch?"

"Nay, I was too lost in your touch to notice."

He sighed, appearing relieved. "I was worried."

"About hurting me?"

"Aye. I've heard it can be painful but I'd never…"

She grinned. "Despoiled a virgin?"

He grinned, shaking his head. "Ye're too bold by half, lass. But, aye, ye were my first."

"And yer last."

He laughed. "Aye. My last." He kissed her temple. "Good night my love."

She smiled, turned her head and kissed his lips. "Good night." Then she relaxed into his embrace, savoring the warm cocoon of his love. Thinking only of this man she adored and the bliss she shared with him, she drifted to sleep.

~ * ~

Cade woke just after sunrise and could not resist making love to his beautiful, responsive, wife once more before rising for the day. She was every bit as open and enthusiastic as she had been the night before. She delighted him. Afterward, as she lay in his arms relaxed and satisfied, he gave in to a moment of awe, as he realized the series of miracles that had brought her to him.

Finally she said, "I don't suppose we can stay in bed longer? All morning? All day? Forever?"

He chuckled. "That would be heaven, but alas, we can't."

He rose from the bed and began to dress.

She sighed and rose too. She took a few moments to wash but when she had finished, she frowned. "I'm going to have to do the walk of shame."

"The what?"

She laughed. "The only clothes I have were the ones I was wearing last night." At his confused look, she continued, "In my time, when a lass spends the night where she ought not, and has to put on the same clothes she wore the previous evening to go home, it's called *the walk of shame*."

He smiled. "Ah, I understand. But ye do belong here and ye're already home." He opened his wardrobe cabinet to reveal her clothing hanging in it. "Deirdre moved yer things for ye."

"Of course she did. I should have known. She's a good friend."

He frowned when he realized how very few garments she had. "I'll speak with Aunt Lilliana to make sure ye have a few more choices."

Elizabeth smiled in the lopsided way he found so adorable. "I won't lie, I'd quite like that."

He laughed.

After she had dressed he asked, "Shall we face the clan?"

"I promised I would stop by Wynda's chamber first, but then, aye."

Before opening the chamber door, he took her hand, leaned down and gave her a tender kiss, grinning as he pulled away. "Oh, lass, there was something I meant to tell ye last night."

"What's that?"

"Ye were wrong."

"About what?"

"Ye were wrong when ye said ye could restrain yerself. Turns out, ye're not very good at that at all."

She slapped at his chest. "And it's glad ye are."

He grinned. "Aye, it's glad I am."

Chapter 31

Elizabeth was perfectly happy and very much in love. Gertrude had been right, until she landed in the thirteenth century, her life had been a series of calculated chess moves, always three steps ahead. David had been right too; nearly every step she had taken in her life had been based more on what was expected of her than what she most desired. This time and place had forced her to slow down and live life each day, and she grew to love the pattern of those days. Serving the clan as a healer and midwife was more fulfilling than she could have imagined. She was even becoming accustomed to being *Lady Elsie*, although it still made her a bit uncomfortable.

She loved her life, she loved the clan, but more than anything else, she loved Cade. He had captured her imagination and overwhelmed her senses from the day she met him. It was hard to imagine that a modern woman and a medieval man were destined for each other but as each day passed, Elizabeth was more and more confident they had been. Perhaps that was the purpose of the pocket watch, to repair displaced destiny.

Wynda continued to do well, but by the middle of July, her cervix had begun to efface.

"The baby is growing nicely, which is wonderful. But as I told ye early on, it is pressure from the baby that causes the opening of yer womb to soften."

"But it's still too early." Wynda could not hide her fear.

"Aye it's a little early, but there's no reason to worry. Ye haven't started labor. We are just going to continue to reduce the pressure by elevating the foot of yer bed. I fear it will be more uncomfortable than simply lying flat, but the longer we can delay labor, the better."

"I don't care. I said I'd hang from my heels if I had to and I will.

So Elizabeth had blocks put under the foot of the bed.

Angus, in a move that caused Elizabeth's respect for him to grow tenfold, continued to sleep beside his wife. "If she has to put up with it all of the time for the next month, I can suffer through the nights beside her."

When Elizabeth mentioned this to Cade, he smiled. "Aye, my da adores Wynda."

"And did he feel the same about yer mother?"

"My mother was a MacInnes and their betrothal had been arranged when they were both young. I think my mother was nine, making da three and ten. My father was Laird MacInnes' squire and apparently the old laird thought highly of him, so he sought the betrothal."

"I suppose it was nice that they had the chance to know each other."

"Perhaps, but have ye ever heard the saying: 'familiarity breeds contempt'?"

"They didn't like each other?"

"Not exactly that. I don't remember, of course. From what I've heard, their marriage was congenial. It's just that there was no strong affection between them—no passion." Cade cast a sideways glance at her. "He kept a mistress, apparently at my mother's urging."

"Ye're not serious."

"Aye, I am. I've told ye before, 'tis a common enough thing. They were young. Da was but yer age when I was born and my mother was ten and seven. She died giving birth three years later."

"He didn't remarry for nine years?"

Cade nodded. "And his mistress is probably the reason. He was very fond of Bradana. I do remember her. She was a good woman."

"But he didn't marry her?"

"Nay, Elizabeth, bird and fish. She was a common lass, the brewer's daughter."

"What happened to her?"

"The year I went away to train—I was ten—a sickness swept the village. Most everyone fell ill and a good few died. Bradana had some knowledge of healing herbs and helped care for the sick, but eventually she too succumbed and it took her life."

"Yer poor father."

"Aye, he mourned her as one would a spouse."

"I expect he did. It had to have been a terrible loss."

"It was. I really don't think he intended to marry again."

"What changed his mind?"

Cade chuckled. "Wynda. She was a MacLean. Uncle Hamish had trained with Laird MacLean and he and Da attended her older brother's wedding. Apparently Da fell hard and fast. At two and twenty Wynda was a little older than most brides. She had been betrothed before, but her groom kept postponing the wedding and then got himself killed in a raid on a neighboring clan. Once Da met her, he would have moved heaven and earth to marry her. That's what brought him around about us."

"What do ye mean?"

"When he upbraided me the morning he learned we handfasted—"

"He yelled at ye?"

"Well, aye. Elizabeth, I know ye see things differently, but marrying without the laird's permission is a very disrespectful thing to do."

"When did he do it and why didn't he yell at me?"

"He did it while ye slept and if ye hadn't been from the future, ye'd have gotten the same lecture. He figured ye didn't know just how unacceptable it was."

She smiled at him. "I didn't. But I don't think it would have changed my mind if I had."

Cade laughed. "Ye're a wicked lass and I quite like that about ye. As it was, he had barely started his rant when I asked him what he would have done if Wynda had been a midwife instead of a laird's daughter."

"And that stopped him?"

"Aye. He agreed that some people are simply meant to be together."

"Well, I'm shocked. Yer da has a romantic streak."

"A little one at least."

"Thanks for telling me all of that. It explains a lot. But, Cade, just one thing."

"What's that, my love?"

"It may be *a common enough thing*, but if ye ever take a mistress, I'll slice off yer cods."

He laughed and gave her a quick kiss. "I'm certain ye would, but ye needn't worry. Ye're quite enough to handle—I don't need two women."

At her indignant frown, he kissed her again. "Elizabeth, ye are the heart of my heart. I want only ye in my arms."

~ * ~

Near the end of July, life's realities came crashing in with force. One afternoon, she and Morag had just finished visiting the clan's pregnant women. They sat down in Morag's cottage for a chat over an herbal tisane.

"I think I'm getting old, Elizabeth."

"Why do ye say that?"

"I have more trouble getting around and I've been awfully tired the last week or so."

"Perhaps ye should take a rest in the afternoons."

She grimaced. "I may just do that."

"Is something wrong, Morag?"

"This tisane isn't sitting well. I feel queasy. A little unsettled-like. I've felt much the same off and on for days."

Elizabeth frowned and reached for the old woman's

wrist to feel her pulse. "And ye're just telling me about it?" Her pulse felt a little fast.

"It's not terribly distressing. I reckoned it would go away."

"Has anything else been bothering ye?"

"Oh, I have a bit of dropsy from time to time. It may be a little worse."

"Dropsy?"

"Aye, dropsy." Morag lifted the hem of her skirt to show Elizabeth her ankles.

Dropsy was obviously the word for edema and Morag had pitting edema up to her knees.

Dread began to form in Elizabeth's heart. "Can I listen to yer breathing?"

"Aye, of course ye can."

"Let's take off yer outer garment so I can hear better."

With that accomplished, Elizabeth opened the back of Morag's léine, and placed her ear directly on the old woman's back. It wasn't as effective as a stethoscope, but it didn't matter. There was enough fluid in Morag's lungs that amplification wasn't required to hear it.

Damn-it. She's in congestive heart failure—probably having a heart attack and there is nothing I can do.

"Morag, come lie down and put yer feet up. I'm going to make ye a willow bark infusion."

"I'm uncomfortable lying flat, pet, and I'm not really having much pain."

"We can prop yer head up if ye wish, but I'd like for ye to rest."

When she had Morag situated, and had the willow bark steeping, she stepped out of the cottage. She called to the first person she saw, Kirstie's little brother. "Cam, lad, I need ye to do something for me."

"Aye, my lady."

"Please run to the keep. Tell Sir Cade and Lady Lilliana that Morag is ill and I am staying with her."

"Aye, my lady."

Then she closed the door and sat beside Morag's bed.

The old midwife frowned at her. "What has ye so worried, Elizabeth?"

"The symptoms ye're having suggest that there's something wrong with yer heart. I can't explain it all to ye, but it is very serious. I'm going to give ye the willow bark infusion not so much for pain, but because it might help a little."

"Serious is it?"

"Aye."

"And there's nothing ye can do for it?"

"I'm sorry, Morag, there isn't. If we were in my time, there are a lot of things that could be done, but not here."

"Am I dying, lass?"

"I don't know."

"But ye're worried?"

"Aye, I'm worried."

She grimaced again. "Well then, there's something I need to tell ye."

"Nay, try to rest."

"Not if I might be dying. Ye need to know this."

"All right, I'll listen."

"I'm the reason ye're here."

Elizabeth frowned. "I don't understand."

"Years ago we had several midwives. All fine skilled women." She smiled, "I trained most of them. And all were younger than me. I thought I had taken care to ensure my clanswomen would be looked after if something happened to me. But, as ye know, life here can be hard. Through the years, they have all passed away. The last, and youngest died over a year ago, sadly while giving birth to her own child." A tear slipped down her cheek.

"I'm sorry, Morag."

"I am too, lass." She closed her eyes and was still for a moment, appearing to offer a silent prayer for the women.

"Well, sometime around the end of the harvest season last year, Gertrude passed this way. I shared my fears with her. I didn't really have a new apprentice to train and I worried the clan would be left without a midwife altogether. I thought maybe in her travels, she might know of someone."

Elizabeth smiled. "And what did Gertrude say?"

"She said I wasn't to worry. The universe unfolds as it should. Whatever that means."

"It means things that are meant to happen will happen."

"Well, I guess they do, but evidently it takes a little meddling from an old crone from time to time."

Elizabeth laughed. "Evidently. Is that why ye were so willing to give me a chance?"

"Aye. And why I believed ye about the pocket watch. I've felt guilty about it for months."

"Why on earth would ye feel guilty?"

"This isn't yer time. Ye left yer family and everything ye knew because the MacKenzies needed ye."

"I left my family and everything I knew because *I* needed *the MacKenzies*. This was my destiny. It was my choice to stay Morag, and I don't regret anything. I'm happy."

"Ye're sure?"

She took the old woman's hand. "Aye. I'm sure."

Morag grimaced again. "Well, be sure ye train up a good few apprentices. We don't want to have to call on Gertrude twice for the same problem."

"I'll do that. Now I want ye to drink some willow bark tea."

"Whatever ye say, lass."

"Is there anyone I should send for?"

"Nay. 'Tis yer hand I wish to hold."

Elizabeth's heart lurched and she blinked back tears. "I won't leave ye then."

Lady Lilliana arrived a few minutes later. Together she

and Elizabeth tried to make Morag comfortable through the evening. But with little else to be done, Elizabeth sat and held Morag's hand.

Just after sunset, Morag started having severe pain in her arm and shoulder.

Lilliana sent for Father Henry.

Morag was growing more short of breath. It was clear she had very little time left, and she knew it. "Lady Lilliana, please tell Lady Wynda, I'm sorry. After everything she's been through, I wanted to share this joy with her but I fear I can't."

"I'll tell her, Morag," Lilliana assured her.

The old woman closed her eyes, grimacing with pain. After a few minutes she opened them again. "Elizabeth, ye're a blessing. I'm so very proud of ye. Take good care of our clan."

"I will, Morag." Tears slipped silently down Elizabeth's cheeks.

Morag closed her eyes again.

When Father Henry arrived to administer the Last Rites, Cade and Hamish were with him.

After Morag received the sacrament, Elizabeth never left her side. The old woman was mostly still but grimaced occasionally over the next hour or so. Shortly after midnight, she breathed her last.

Elizabeth couldn't contain her tears. Cade wrapped his arms around her and held her as she cried, just as Hamish comforted Lilliana.

Gertrude's words came to Elizabeth once more:

There was a time when doctors, healers and midwives experienced exactly what ye say ye want. They knew their patients and spent time with them. When they brought a new babe into the world they could rejoice with the family. When a life was tragically lost, they could mourn. They experienced the full spectrum of human emotion and existence, and helped their neighbors through it.

~ * ~

Elizabeth missed Morag more that she thought possible. For the next few weeks, many was the moment when she thought, *I'll just go ask Morag,* only to have the pain of loss take her breath away.

But even that loss couldn't dim the joy of the pending birth of Wynda's baby. After the first week of August, Elizabeth breathed a sigh of relief. By her calculation, Wynda had reached thirty eight weeks and the baby should be fine. On the morning of the third Wednesday in August, Wynda went into labor. By the middle of the afternoon, Elizabeth placed a perfect baby girl, with a lusty voice, in Wynda's arms. The other women helping with the birth laughed and cried and rejoiced with Lady MacKenzie.

Wynda beamed and whispered, "My lovely wee lassie, I've waited a long time for ye."

When the chamber had been set to rights and Wynda was at last sitting in a freshly made bed, with her daughter in her arms, Angus and Cade came to see the new arrival.

When Angus held his daughter for the first time, he looked ready to burst with joy.

Elizabeth had to bite her cheeks to keep from laughing when Cade first held his baby sister. Babies have an amazing ability to turn the biggest, toughest men on the earth into blithering ninnies.

When the baby was tucked snuggly back into her mama's arms, Angus turned to Elizabeth. "Elizabeth, I will never be able to adequately express my gratitude. I know yer life was turned upside down when ye accepted that...*pocket watch*...from Gertrude. But I will be eternally grateful that ye did, and further, that ye chose to stay here."

"It is as much a blessing to me, I assure ye," Elizabeth answered.

"I'll be honest, I was irritated with Cade when I found out he'd married ye without my leave. Still, it didn't take long for me to realize ye were more of an asset to this clan than the best alliance I could have forged. And, what's more, ye love each other. That's a rare gift, but it will never match the gift of hope ye've given us. So, good daughter, Wynda and I have decided to name our wee lass Hope Elizabeth—if that's all right with ye."

Elizabeth was overwhelmed. "I'm honored, Laird. Thank ye."

~ * ~

The birth of baby Hope was cause for great celebration and Elizabeth was the hero of the day. Tankard after tankard was raised in her honor. It was rather late when Cade was finally able to extricate his wife from his adoring clan.

He was no sooner through the door of their chamber than he pulled her close, put a hand behind her neck and kissed her until she melted against him.

"Shall we start a bairn of our own?"

She sighed dreamily. "Too late."

"Nay, lass, ye can sleep a little longer in the morning."

She chuckled. "That's not what I meant."

"Then what did ye mean?"

"It's too late to start a baby, because one is already started."

"Ye're carrying?"

"Aye."

"Ye're sure?"

She arched a brow at him. "Pretty sure. I do know a bit about it. My courses haven't come since we were married. I expect we'll be parents by the middle of March."

"Sweetling, that's wonderful." He picked her up and swung her around, then planted kisses over her face and neck.

"Cade, there's something I have to tell ye."

The seriousness of her tone gave him pause. "What is

it?"

"Do ye recall what I said to yer da the night I arrived?"

He thought back and groaned when he remembered. "Ye said he and Wynda couldn't have marital relations."

"Aye I did." She paused looking very serious before her face split into a wide, lopsided grin. "But we can."

"Ye're a wicked, wicked, lass for scaring me like that."

He scooped her in his arms and carried her, laughing, to the bed.

Epilogue

Twenty-four years later

Elizabeth rubbed Nora's back as the contraction began to ease.

Tears ran down the lass's flushed cheeks. "Mama, I don't think I can do this. I'm so tired."

Elizabeth gathered her daughter in her arms. She had been laboring all day, and now night had fallen. "Of course ye're tired, sweetling, but ye can do this. Come sit with me and rest." Elizabeth sat on the bed, with her back against the carved headboard and helped Nora sit in front of her, between her legs. She wrapped her arms around her daughter, pulling her gently until Nora's back rested against her chest. Then she hummed a lullaby as she had when Nora was a baby.

Wynda sat next to the bed, holding Nora's hand. Her daughter, Hope, sat at the foot of the bed. Jessie, one of the women Elizabeth had trained to be a midwife, stood nearby.

Elizabeth gently stroked her daughter's hair as she hummed. This scene had played out over and over again in the twenty-four years she'd lived here. She had brought a lot of wee souls into the world. Sadly, she had lost some as well. Each time she suffered a private heartache because she knew many of them would have lived with the help of modern science. Still, Elizabeth was confident that she was able to provide the best care possible, under the circumstances.

But now the pregnant woman in her arms was her own child. Her mother-in-law sat beside them. Her lovely young sister-in-law and namesake sat at the end of the bed, and

Ceci Giltenan

the first terrified young mother who she had tended here was the calm midwife standing to one side. They would come through this night together.

And they did.

Several hours later, Elizabeth brought her first grandchild into the world. "Nora, my love, ye have daughter."

When Elizabeth finally found her bed several hours later, she lay in the strong comfort of Cade's arms.

"I don't know how ye did that, Elizabeth."

"Delivered the baby? I've a wee bit of experience."

"Delivered *Nora's* baby. Hearing her cries was almost as bad as hearing yers."

"Ye know, I've told ye before, in my time men stay with their wives."

"That may be, but I bet there aren't many that stay with their daughters."

Elizabeth chuckled. "Perhaps not, but mothers have helped their daughters bring bairns into the world since the beginning of time."

"So it was just like any other bairn?"

"Are ye jesting? She's my daughter. I was terrified, just like every other mother who helps her daughter deliver a baby."

It was his turn to chuckle. "Well, I'm sure someone told my da once that there's no one in Scotland better able to tend her than ye."

She smiled. "Did Cadha get over her pique at not being allowed in the room?"

"Probably not, but she will. Why didn't ye let her? She's attended other births with ye."

"Aye she has, but this was her sister. I knew it was going to be hard enough for me. I'll talk to her in the morning."

"We should have just had boys."

Elizabeth snorted. "I don't know how ye can say that

when ye have the barbaric custom of sending them away when they are just lads."

"Well we didn't send them away when they were *just lads*, did we? Ewan was ten and four and he only went to the Davidson's, less than a half day away. He's been back for three years now and Daniel's three and ten and hasn't gone yet."

"They grow so fast."

"Aye they do." He kissed the top of her head. "Have ye ever regretted yer choice?"

"Never. Ye've never asked that before. Why tonight?"

"What ye said about mothers helping their daughters. I wonder if at times like this, ye miss yer mother."

"I loved my parents, but frankly I can't picture my mother holding Nora's hand through labor as Wynda did. When I arrived here, it felt as if I had come home. I think this is where I was always meant to be."

"I knew the minute I saw ye that this is where ye were meant to be."

"Ye did not. Ye were too consumed with my soft round backside to think beyond that."

"Aye, well, I still am," he said, snuggling against it. "But it didn't take long for me to notice the rest of ye too. Still, it wasn't just yer assets that attracted me. From the moment ye arrived, ye opened yerself and poured out yer love freely to my clan and family. That made ye irresistible." He kissed her behind the ear. "But now that ye've called my attention to yer other assets…"

About The Author

Ceci started her career as an oncology nurse at a leading research hospital, and eventually became a successful medical writer. In 1991 she married a young Irish carpenter who she met when his brother married her dear friend. They raised their family in central New Jersey but now live with their dogs and birds in paradise, also known as southwest Florida. After a rewarding career in the pharmaceutical industry, she is thrilled to put her feet up and write "happily ever afters."

Her bestselling, Duncurra series, Highland Solution, Highland Courage, and Highland Intrigue are available as e-books, audiobooks, and paperbacks. There are also inspirational versions of each of these which close the bedroom door. Ceci will be continuing this series in the near future.

The Fated Hearts series begins with Ceci's novella Highland Revenge (originally appearing in Highland Winds, The Scrolls of Cridhe – Volume 1) and continues with Highland Echoes and Highland Angels.

The Pocket Watch Chronicles were actually born in the early eighties, when Ceci was in college when she first wrote *The Pocket Watch*. The next one, *Once Found*, is to be released as an e-book in May, 2016.

The Pocket Watch Chronicles

If you enjoyed The Midwife,
read Elsie's side of the story in:

Once Found: The Pocket Watch Chronicles

Elsie thought she had found love.

The handsome young minstrel awoke her desire and his music fed her soul. But just as love was blossoming, the inconceivable happened—Elsie awoke more than seven hundred years in the future, in someone else's body.

Gabriel Soldani thought he had found love several times, only to have it slip from his grasp. In medical school he had fallen hard for Elizabeth Quinn but their careers led them in different directions. When their paths cross again, he hopes they've been given another chance.

There's only one problem...the woman he's never forgotten doesn't remember him.

Once love is found...and then lost...can it be found again?

You also might enjoy the novella that started the story:

The Pocket Watch:
The Pocket Watch Chronicles

When Maggie Mitchell, is transported to the thirteenth century Highlands will Laird Logan Carr help mend her broken heart or put it in more danger than before?

Generous, kind, and loving, Maggie nearly always puts the needs of others first. So when a mysterious elderly woman gives her an extraordinary pocket watch, telling her it's a conduit to the past, Maggie agrees to give the watch a try, if only to disprove the woman's delusion.

But it works.

Maggie finds herself in the thirteenth century Scottish Highlands, with a handsome warrior who clearly despises her. Her tender soul is caught between her own desire and the disaster she could cause for others. Will she find a way to resolve the trouble and return home within the allotted sixty days? Or will someone worthy earn her heart forever?

The Pocket Watch is available as an e-book, audiobook and paperback.

More from Ceci Giltenan

The Fated Hearts Series

Highland Revenge

Does he hate her clan enough to visit his vengeance on her? Or will he listen to her secret and his own heart's yearning?

Hatred lives and breathes between medieval clans who often don't remember why feuds began in the shadowed past.

But Eoin MacKay remembers.

He will never forget how he was treated by Bhaltair MacNicol—the acting head of Clan MacNicol. He was lucky to escape alive, and vows to have revenge.

Years later, as laird of Clan MacKay, he gets his chance when he captures Lady Fiona MacNicol. His desire for revenge is strong but he is beguiled by his captive.

Can he forget his stubborn hatred long enough to listen to the secret she has kept for so long? And once he knows the truth, can he show her she is not alone and forsaken? In the end, is he strong enough to fight the combined hostilities and age-old grudges that demand he give her up?

Highland Echoes

Love echoes.

Grace Breive is strong and independent because she has to be. She has a wee daughter to care for and, having lost her parents and husband, has no one else on whom she can rely. Driven from the only home she has ever known, she travels to Castle Sutherland to find a grandmother she never knew she had.

As Laird Sutherland's heir, Bram Sutherland understands his obligation to enter into a political marriage for the good of the clan, but he is captivated by the beautiful and resilient young mother.

Will Bram and Grace follow the dictates of their hearts, or will echoes from the past force them apart?

Highland Angels

Anna MacKay fears the MacLeods. Andrew MacLeod fears love.

Anna, angry with her brother, took a walk to cool her temper. She had no intention of venturing so close to MacLeod territory—until she saw a wee lad fall through the ice.

Andrew becomes enraged when it appears the MacKay lass has abducted his son, his last precious connection to the wife he lost—until he learns the truth. Anna, risked her life to save his beloved child.

Now there is a chance to end the generations old hate and fear between their clans.

Fate connects them. The desire for peace binds them. Will a rival tear them apart?

Highland Solution

Laird Niall MacIan needs Lady Katherine Ruthven's dowry to relieve his clan's crushing debt but he has no intention of giving her his heart in the bargain.

Niall MacIan, a Highland laird, desperately needs funds to save his impoverished clan. Lady Katherine Ruthven, a lowland heiress, is rumored to be "unmarriageable" and her uncle hopes to be granted her title and lands when the king sends her to a convent.

King David II anxious to strengthen his alliances sees a solution that will give Ruthven the title he wants, and MacIan the money he needs. Laird MacIan will receive Lady Katherine's hand along with her substantial dowry and her uncle will receive her lands and title.

Lady Katherine must forfeit everything in exchange for a husband who does not want to be married and believes all women to be self-centered and deceitful.

Can the lovely and gentle Katherine mend his heart and build a life with him or will he allow the treachery of others to destroy them?

Highland Courage

Her parents want a betrothal, but Mairead MacKenzie can't get married without revealing her secret and no man will wed her once he knows.

Plain in comparison to her siblings and extremely reserved, Mairead has been called "MacKenzie's Mouse" since she was a child. No one knows the reason for her timidity and she would just as soon keep it that way. When her parents arrange a betrothal to Laird Tadhg Matheson she is horrified. She only sees one way to prevent an old secret from becoming a new scandal.

Tadhg Matheson admires and respects the MacKenzies. While an alliance with them through marriage to Mairead would be in his clan's best interest, he knows Laird MacKenzie seeks a closer alliance with another clan. When Tadhg learns of her terrible shyness and her youngest brother's fears about her, Tadhg offers for her anyway.

Secrets always have a way of revealing themselves. With Tadhg's unconditional love, can Mairead find the strength and courage she needs to handle the consequences when they do?

Highland Intrigue

Lady Gillian MacLennan's clan needs a leader, but the last person on earth she wants as their laird is Fingal MacIan.

She can neither forgive nor forget that his mother killed her father, and, by doing so, created Clan MacLennan's current desperate circumstances.

King David knows a weak clan, without a laird, can change quickly from a simple annoyance to a dangerous liability, and he cannot ignore the turmoil. The MacIan's owe him a great debt, so when he makes Fingal MacIan laird of clan MacLennan and requires that he marry Lady Gillian, Fingal is in no position to refuse.

In spite of the challenge, Fingal is confident he can rebuild her clan, ease her heartache and win her affection. However, just as love awakens, the power struggle takes a deadly turn. Can he protect her from the unknown long enough to uncover the plot against them? Or will all be lost, destroying the happiness they seek in each other's arms?

Other Titles from Duncurra

New York Times Bestselling Author
Kathryn Lynn Davis

Highland Awakening

Can the transforming power of magic help two people on a perilous journey create a miracle—even when one of them doesn't believe?

Since she lost her brother and nearly her father, Esmé Rose fears the world beyond her family and her garden. But one year when winter clings overlong, a dream begins to haunt her, forcing her to take a journey and face a challenge more difficult than she could ever imagine.

Magnus MacLeod is a skilled healer, always curious to know more. He, too, is called by a dream he doesn't quite believe in, despite its physical effects on him. He and Esmé travel a treacherous road that takes them to a magical place. There they must put aside their feelings for one another— and their difference in beliefs—long enough to make a miracle.

Sing to Me of Dreams

One woman's journey of discovery...through all the mysteries of the human heart.

As a child, Saylah held the magic and wisdom of her Salish Indian people. But when tragedy ravages the Salish, she must leave them for the world of the Ivys – an English/Scottish family whose traditions are as strange to her as her spirit world is to them. The Ivys have come to fertile British Columbia in search of paradise, but the secrets and mysteries surrounding them are overwhelming – until Saylah comes to help them understand the darkness holding them back.

Frustrated Julian Ivy, in whom sophistication and fury entwine, is drawn to Saylah's healing strength and disquieting beauty. Through sorrow and elation, the two discover the fullness of love...but no one can resolve for her the contradictions of her birthright. Following the songs of her heritage, she will finally make the most wrenching choice of all...

Internationally bestselling author:
Lily Baldwin

Jack: A Scottish Outlaw

Freedom is not won…it is stolen

Jack MacVie and his brother are thieves, robbing English nobles on the road north into Scotland. They're about to attack the Redesdale carriage when another band of villains, after more than Lady Redesdale's coin, sweeps down and steals their prize. Despite his hatred for the English, Jack's conscience forces him to kidnap the lady to save her life.

In the aftermath of the Berwick massacre, Lady Isabella Redesdale's world is shattered. Her mother is dead, her father lost to grief, and she's risking it all, journeying north into war-torn Scotland to be with her sister.

Although they come from different worlds, Jack and Isabella are more alike than they first realize. They both crave freedom from war and despair, but in a world where kings reign and birth dictates one's station, freedom is not won, it is stolen.

Ceci Giltenan

Quinn: A Scottish Outlaw

He is an outlaw...And the only man she can trust.

Quinn MacVie is in pursuit of a prize, but it is unlike any plunder he has stolen before. He seeks neither gold nor jewels, but something infinitely more valuable—Lady Catarina Ravensworth. Sent by the lady's sister, who fears Catarina is in danger, Quinn's mission is to steal the lady away from Ravensworth castle. But nothing there is as Quinn expected.

Lady Catarina has been accused of a horrific crime and is forced to run or face a fate worse than death.

But she is not alone.

Thief and Scottish rebel, Quinn MacVie, is at her side. With a price on her head, they must disappear into the wilds of the Scottish Highlands where the only thing greater than the danger following at their heels is the desire burning in their hearts.

Stephanie Joyce Cole

Compass North

Can you ever run away from your own life?

Reeling from the shock of a suddenly shattered marriage, Meredith flees as far from her home in Florida as she can get without a passport: to Alaska.

After a freak accident leaves her presumed dead, she stumbles into a new identity and a new life in a quirky small town. Her friendship with a fiery and temperamental artist and her growing worry for her elderly, cranky landlady pull at the fabric of her carefully guarded secret. When a romance with a local fisherman unexpectedly blossoms, Meredith struggles to find a way to meld her past and present so that she can move into the future she craves. But someone is looking for her, someone who will threaten Meredith's dream of a reinvented life.

MJ Platt

Somewhere Montana

Can Callum "Mac" Maclain make Sage Burnett believe in his love for her and save her from her stalker?

Escaping from a stalker, Sage Burnett crashes her plane on a mountain, part of the ranch owned by the man who rejected her eight years ago. She still loves him and prays he isn't around because she dreads facing him to only have him reject her again.

Callum "Mac" MacLain, the ranch owner, a Marine home on medical leave rescues her from the mountain. He persuades her to stay until she heals. He realizes he is still in love with her. Can he save her from her stalker and convince her his love is real?

Look for exciting new titles from Duncurra in 2016!

www.ingramcontent.com/pod-product-compliance
Lightning Source LLC
Chambersburg PA
CBHW032153190626
46814CB00005BA/1971